Praise for Gish Jen's

TYPICAL AMERICAN

"A terrific novel. . . . Full of winning ironies."
—*People*

"Heartbreaking. . . . Sidesplitting. . . . A rich addition to the ever-growing body of immigrant literature, lovingly imagined, thoroughly satisfying."
—*The Washington Post Book World*

"Bittersweet, absorbingly told, deeply moving and funny. . . . The emotional impact is stunning."
—*Newsday*

"Brilliant and hilarious. . . . Jen's novel lives up to its name. . . . Illumines both the unique and the familiar. . . . A story of disillusionment and discovery, of romance and betrayal. Jen's saga reads like a John Cheever story, but with a sparkling humor uniquely her own."
—*San Francisco Chronicle*

Gish Jen

TYPICAL AMERICAN

Gish Jen is the author of three novels and a book of stories. Her honors include the Lannan Award for Fiction and the Strauss Living Award from the American Academy of Arts and Letters. She lives with her husband and two children in Cambridge, Massachusetts.

ALSO BY GISH JEN

The Love Wife

Who's Irish?: Stories

Mona in the Promised Land

For Charlotte

TYPICAL AMERICAN

A Novel

GISH JEN

With every good wish,

Gish Jen

VINTAGE CONTEMPORARIES
Vintage Books
A Division of Random House, Inc.
New York

FIRST VINTAGE CONTEMPORARIES EDITION, JANUARY 2008

The Cataloging-in-Publication Data is on file at the Library of Congress.

Vintage ISBN: 978-0-307-38922-0

www.vintagebooks.com

Printed in the United States of America
20 19 18 17 16 15 14 13 12

I would like to thank the Bunting Institute, the Copernicus Society, the Massachusetts Artists' Foundation, the MacDowell Colony, and the National Endowment for the Arts for the generous support that made this book possible. Heartfelt thanks also to my many kind and persnickety readers — Dave, Eileen, Jeanne, Neal, Louise, Jayne Anne, Suzanne, Maxine, Camille, Jayne, Ruth, Sam, and Mom.

Please note that, as there is no standard transliteration for Shanghainese, all Chinese phrases in this novel are given in Mandarin. *Pinyin* is used except for surnames, which are romanized as they would have been at the time.

To D.O., giver of life

PART I

Sweet Rebellion

A BOY
WITH HIS HANDS
OVER HIS EARS

IT'S AN American story: Before he was a thinker, or a doer, or an engineer, much less an imagineer like his self-made-millionaire friend Grover Ding, Ralph Chang was just a small boy in China, struggling to grow up his father's son. We meet him at age six. He doesn't know where or what America is, but he does know, already, that he's got round ears that stick out like the sideview mirrors of the only car in town — his father's. Often he wakes up to find himself tied by his ears to a bedpost, or else he finds loops of string around them, to which are attached dead bugs. *"Earrings!"* his cousins laugh. His mother tells him something like, It's only a phase. (This is in Shanghainese.) After a while the other boys will grow up, she says, he should ignore them. Until they grow up? he thinks, and instead — more sensibly — walks around covering his ears with his hands. He presses them back, hoping to train them to bring him less pain. Silly boy! Everyone teases him except his mother, who pleads patiently.

"*That's not the way.*" She frowns. "*Are you listening?*"

He nods, hands over his ears.

"How can you listen with your hands over your ears?"

He shrugs. *"I'm listening."*

Back and forth. Until finally, irked, she says what his tutor always says, *"You listen but don't hear!"* — distinguishing, the way the Chinese will, between effort and result. Verbs in English are simple. One listens. After all, why should a listening person not hear? What's taken for granted in English, though, is spelled out in Chinese; there's even a verb construction for this purpose. *Ting de jian* in Mandarin means, one listens and hears. *Ting bu jian* means, one listens but fails to hear. People hear what they can, see what they can, do what they can; that's the understanding. It's an old culture talking. Everywhere there are limits.

As Ralph, who back then was not Ralph yet, but still Yifeng — Intent on the Peak — already knew. His mother wheedles, patient again. *"No hands on your ears during lessons, okay? As it is, you have trouble enough."* If he stops, she promises, she'll give him preserved plums, mooncakes, money. If he doesn't, *"Do you realize your father will beat me too?"*

"Lazy," says his father. *"Stupid. What do you do besides eat and sleep all day?"* The upright scholar, the ex–government official, calls him a *fan tong* — a rice barrel. He has an assignment for his son: Yifeng will please study his Older Sister. He will please observe everything she does, and simply copy her.

His Older Sister (Yifeng calls her *Bai Xiao*, Know-It-All) blushes.

Hands over his ears, Yifeng presses, presses, presses.

It's 1947; Yifeng's more or less grown up. The Anti-Japanese War has been over for two years. Now there's wreckage, and inflation, and moral collapse. Or so it seems to his father as, on a fan-cooled veranda, he entertains apocalyptic thoughts of marching armies, a new dynasty, the end of society as they know it.

"Might there be something nicer to talk about?" suggests his mother.

But his father will talk destruction and gloom if he wants to. *Degeneracy!* he says. *Stupidity! Corruption!* These have been his lifelong enemies; thanks to them he no longer holds office.

"*Too much rice wine,*" muses Ralph's mother.

This is in a small town in Jiangsu province, outside Shanghai, a place of dusty shops and rutted roads, of timber and clay — a place where every noise has a known source. Somewhere in the city, the girl who will become Helen hums Western love songs to herself; on a convent school diamond, Know-It-All (that is, Theresa) fields grounders from her coach. Ralph, though — Yifeng — is on his way home from his job at the Transportation Department. His mother knows this. As his father prepares to write an article — he has an inkstone out, and a wolf's hair *maobi* — his mother prepares to speak up.

His father announces that he's going to write about *Degeneracy! Stupidity! Corruption!*

"*America,*" his mother says then.

His father goes on grinding his ink. Yifeng simply cannot be going abroad.

"*But it seems, perhaps, that he is.*"

Silence. His father's hand hovers over the inkstone, circling. He presses just so hard, no harder. He holds his ink stick upright.

A fellowship from the government! Field training! His son, an advanced engineer! No one knows what's possible like a father. His ink blackens; and in the end he can't be kept from making a few discreet inquiries, among friends. This is how he discovers that things are indeed more involved than they at first appeared. Though Yifeng has scored seventeenth on the department exam, he is one of the ten picked to go.

"*No door like a back door,*" says his father.

"*Your only son,*" pleads his mother.

His father looks away. "*Opposites begin in one another,*" he says. And, "*Yi dai qing qing, qi dai huai*" — one generation pure, the next good for nothing.

Of course, in the end, Yifeng did come to the United States

anyway, his stomach burbling with fool hope. But it was privately, not through the government, and not for advanced field training, but for graduate study. A much greater opportunity, as everyone agreed. He could bring back a degree!

"*A degree,*" he echoed dully.

His mother arranged a send-off banquet, packed him a black trunk full of Western-style clothes.

"*Your father would like to give you this,*" she told him at the dock. As his father stared off into the Shanghai harbor — at the true ships in the distance, the ragtag boats by the shore — she slid a wristwatch into Yifeng's hand.

Yifeng nodded. "*I'll remember him always.*"

It was hot.

On the way to America, Yifeng studied. He reviewed his math, his physics, his English, struggling for long hours with his broken-backed books, and as the boat rocked and pitched he set out two main goals for himself. He was going to be first in his class, and he was not going home until he had his doctorate rolled up to hand his father. He also wrote down a list of subsidiary aims.

1. I will cultivate virtue. (A true scholar being a good scholar; as the saying went, there was no carving rotten wood.)
2. I will bring honor to the family.

What else?

3. I will do five minutes of calisthenics daily.
4. I will eat only what I like, instead of eating everything.
5. I will on no account keep eating after everyone else has stopped.
6. I will on no account have anything to do with girls.

On 7 through 10, he was stuck until he realized that number 6 about the girls was so important it counted for at least four more than itself. For girls, he knew, were what happened to even the cleverest, most diligent, most upright of scholars; the scholars kissed, got syphilis, and died without getting their degrees.

He studied in the sun, in the rain, by every shape moon. The ocean sang and spit; it threw itself on the deck. Still he studied. He studied as the horizon developed, finally, a bit of skin — land! He studied as that skin thickened, and deformed, and resolved, shaping itself as inevitably as a fetus growing eyes, growing ears. Even when islands began to heave their brown, bristled backs up through the sea (a morning sea so shiny it seemed to have turned into light and light and light), he watched only between pages. For this was what he'd vowed as a corollary of his main aim — to study until he could see the pylons of the Golden Gate Bridge.

That splendor! That radiance! True, it wasn't the Statue of Liberty, but still in his mind its span glowed bright, an image of freedom, and hope, and relief for the seasick. The day his boat happened into harbor, though, he couldn't make out the bridge until he was almost under it, what with the fog; and all there was to hear were foghorns. These honked high, low, high, low, over and over, like a demented musician playing his favorite two notes.

How was anyone supposed to be able to read?

Years later, when he told this story, he'd claim that the only sightseeing he did was to make a trip back to the bridge, in better weather, to have his picture taken. Unfortunately, he forgot his camera. As for the train ride to New York — famous mountains lumbered by, famous rivers, plains, canyons, the whole holy American spectacle, without his looking up once.

"So how'd you know what you were *passing*, then," his younger daughter would ask. (This was Mona, who was just like that, a mosquito.)

"I hear what other people talk," he'd say — at least usually. Once, though, he blushed. "I *almost* never take a look at." He shrugged, sheepish. "Interesting."

New York. He admitted that maybe he had taken a look around there too. And what of it? The idea *city* still gleamed then, after all, plus this was the city of cities, a place that promised to be recalled as an era. Ralph toured the century to date — its subway, its many mighty bridges, its highways. He was awed by the Empire State Building. Those pilings! He wondered at roller coasters, Ferris wheels. At cafeterias — eating factories, these seemed to him, most advanced and efficient, especially the Automats with their machines lit bright as a stage. The mundane details of life impressed him too — the neatly made milk cartons, the spring-loaded window shades, the electric iceboxes everywhere. Only he even saw these things, it seemed; only he considered how they had been made, the gears turning, the levers tilting. Even haircuts done by machine here! The very air smelled of oil. Nothing was made of bamboo.

He did notice.

By and large, though, he really did study. He studied as he walked, as he ate. The first week. The second week.

The third week, however, what could happen even to the cleverest, most diligent, most upright of scholars (and he was at least diligent, he allowed) happened to him.

"She was some — what you call? — tart," he said.

A BOY
WITH HIS HAT
OVER HIS CROTCH

PICTURE HIM. Young, orotund. Longish hair managed with grease. A new, light gray, too dressy, double-breasted suit made him look even shorter than his five feet three and three-quarter inches. Otherwise he was himself — large-faced, dimpled, with eyebrows that rode nervously up and up, away from his flat, wide, placid nose. He had small teeth set in vast expanses of gum; those round ears; and delicate, almost maidenly skin that tended to flush and pale with the waxing and waning of his digestive problems. Everywhere he went, he carried a Panama hat with him, though he never put it on, and it was always in his way; he seemed to have picked up an idea about gentlemen, or hats — something — that was proving hard to let go.

In sum, he was a doll, and the Foreign Student Affairs secretary, though she loathed her job, loathed her boss, loathed *working,* liked him.

"Name?" he repeated, or rather "nem," which he knew to be wrong. He turned red, thinking of his trouble with long a's, th's, l's, consonants at the ends of words. Was it beneath a scholar to hate the alphabet? Anyway, he did.

"Naaame," she said, writing it down. She'd seen this before, foreign students who could read and write and speak a little, but who just couldn't get the conversation. N-A-M-E.

"Name Y. F. Chang." (His surname as he pronounced it then sounded like the beginning of *angst*; it would be years before he was used to hearing Chang rhyme with *twang*.)

"Eng-lish-name," said Cammy. E-N-G-L-I-S-H-N-A-M-E.

"I Chin-ese," he said, and was about to explain that Y. F. were his initials when she laughed.

"Eng-lish-name," she said again.

"What you laughing?"

Later he realized this to be a very daring thing to ask, that he never would have asked a Chinese girl why she was laughing. But then, a Chinese girl never would have been laughing, not like that. Not a nice Chinese girl, anyway. What a country he was in!

"I'm laughing at you." Her voice rang, playful yet deeper than he would have expected. She smelled of perfume. He could not begin to guess her age. "At *you!*"

"Me?" With mock offense, he drew his chin back.

"You," she said again. "Me?" "You." "Me?" They were joking! In English! *Shuo de chu* — he spoke, and the words came out! *Ting de dong* — he listened and understood!

"English name," she said again, finally. She showed him her typewriter, the form she had to fill out.

"No English name." How to say initials? He was sorry to disappoint her. Then he brightened. "You give me."

"*I*-give-you-a-name?"

"Sure. You give." There was something about speaking English that carried him away.

"I'll-hang-onto-this-form-overnight," she tried to tell him. "That-way-you-find-a-name-you-like-better-you-can-tell-me-tomorrow."

Too much, he didn't get it. Anyway, he waited, staring — exercising the outsider's privilege, to be rude. How colorful she was! Orange hair, pink face, blue eyes. Red nails. Green dress. And under the dress, breasts large and solid as earthworks. He thought of the burial mounds that dotted the Chinese countryside — the small mounds for nobodies, the big mounds for big shots. This woman put him in mind of the biggest mound he had ever seen: in Shandong, that was, Confucius's grave.

Meanwhile, she ran through her ex-beaux. Robert? Eugene? Norman? She toyed with a stray curl. Fred? John? Steve? Ken? "Ralph," she said finally. She wrote it down. R-A-L-P-H. "Do you like it?"

"Sure!" He beamed.

Walking home, though, *Ralph* was less sanguine. Had he been too hasty? He did this, he knew; he dispensed with things, trying to be like other people — decisive, practical — only to discover he'd overdone it. His stomach puckered with anxiety. And sure enough, when he asked around later he found that the other Chinese students (there were five of them in the master's degree program) had all stuck with their initials, or picked names for themselves, carefully, or else had wise people help them.

"Ralph," said smooth-faced Old Chao (Old Something-or-another being what younger classmates called older classmates, who in turn called them Little Something-or-another). He looked it up in a book he had. *"Means* wolf," he said, then looked that up in a dictionary. *"A kind of dog,"* he translated.

A kind of dog, thought Ralph.

For himself, Old Chao had Henry, which turned out to be the name of at least eight kings. *"My father picked it for me,"* he said.

It would have been better if Ralph sounded a bit more like Yifeng; in the art of picking English names (which everyone seemed to know except him), that was considered desirable. But so what? And who cared what it meant? Ralph decided that what was on the form didn't matter. He was a man with a mission; what mattered was that he register for the right courses, that he attend the right classes, that he buy the right books. All of this proved more difficult than he'd anticipated. He discovered, for instance, that he wasn't on the class list for two of his courses, and that for one of them, enrollment was already closed. To address these problems, he did what he did when his tuition didn't arrive, and when his other two classes turned out to meet at the same time: he found his way to the Foreign Student Affairs Office, where gaily colored Cammy would help him.

Ralph had noticed by then that she was pretty, or figured she must be, as about half the men with affairs to discuss with her didn't seem to be foreign students. ("Fan club," explained Old Chao, idiom book in hand.) With her big barbarian frame and long nose and hairy forearms, though, she just wasn't Ralph's type (the hair bothered him especially — like a monkey's, he thought); and anyway, he was too exhausted to be thinking about such things — having come, he belatedly realized, to the complete other side of the world. Mile after mile, he'd travelled, *li* after *li*, by boat and by train, only to have to get himself going. His degree, his degree!

And so to Cammy he was grateful, nothing more.

"Tank you," he said. "Tank you." One day he helped fix her pencil sharpener, and when she said "Tank *you*," he answered, "Sure!" And after that, whenever he said "Tank you," she answered "Sure!" too. This came with a wink, and a kind of sideways look that made Ralph's pants bulge — lucky thing he was still carrying that hat around.

Did he confuse this phenomenon with love? Not yet. He stacked paper for Cammy. He taught her to say thank you in Chinese. "Shay shay!" she said now, whenever she saw him, whether she had reason to thank him or not. "Shay shay shay shay!" Ralph tried to get her to speak more correctly. "Sh-yeh," he told her. "Sh-yeh, sh-yeh." He concentrated on getting his own pronunciation right, not wanting to pass on to her his Shanghainese hiss. So little of what he knew counted here; he offered what he could on a kind of tray. "Isn't that what I said?" she asked. "Shay shay?" And before he'd had a chance to say yes or no, she was back to "Shay shay shay shay!" again, with such exuberance, Ralph didn't have the heart to do anything but nod. "Good!"

"You know, one of these days I'm going to study Chinese," said Cammy. "Chinese or French. Or else ballet, I've always loved ballet."

"Ah," said Ralph (this being the sort of thing he was beginning to understand he should say instead of "Wha?" when there was something he couldn't catch).

More favors, innocent enough — packages to the mailbox, expeditious disposal of a bumblebee. And, of course, help with her boss, Mr. Fitt.

Now Mr. Fitt was a grim man, an enforcer, with a small, sneering mouth; in another life he might have been a carnivorous fish. In this life, he carried a rolled-up newspaper in his thick hand like a bat he meant to use on someone. When Ralph wandered onto the scene, Mr. Fitt was tapping that bat on his thigh; his other hand was all five hairy fingers on Cammy's neat desk.

"But I w-was here. At one on th-the b-b-button." The sound of Cammy choked up made Ralph's throat catch. "Wasn't I, Ralph? Wasn't I?"

Ralph gave solemn testimony. Mr. Fitt straightened up, glaring. Cammy was all shay shays. "Tell me how to say it again," she said. "I know I don't say it right. I don't do anything right."

"No, no, you pronounce very good."

"No I don't. You say it again, the right way."

Ralph hesitated. "Shay shay."

"Shay shay." She lit up. "Shay shay! You mean, I *am* saying it right? Shay shay?"

Ralph nodded, beamed, situated his hat.

More and more now, he was beginning to know what was what. He was lonely still, but it was only a mist, a weather front that passed through him when he was alone, a feeling of having turned too permeable. When he was working, he was fine. And having launched into his work, he did not go to the Foreign Student Affairs Office anymore, but rather to the stone-stepped library, where he studied and studied at the endless oak tables; or else to the kitchen at the end of the hall in his rooming house on 123rd Street. There, on the blackboard by the stove, he puzzled out problems with his classmates. Between equations, they marvelled that their tests would be scored to the whole point, instead of to five decimal places. Was it fair? Who knew? This was America. They forged on, mostly speaking Mandarin, saving their English for impersonations of certain professors.

The kitchen was where Ralph spent his free time too, learning to cook. He could make three dishes now — boiled rice, egg rice, and fried eggs. Having thrown several successful *shui jiao*–making parties, his classmates were organizing a cooperative cooking program, and Ralph was practicing up, to be sure he'd be able to participate. Other developments: he'd discovered supper for a dollar at General Lee's, and also banana splits with extra nuts and marshmallow sauce (the specialty of the luncheonette down the street). Also, he'd bought a lamp for his room, from the secondhand store next to the grocery he used to go to. Already he had a history in America. Now he went to a new, cheaper grocery, even though the first grocer was friendlier than the second, and had been so nice as to count his change out slowly, one coin at a time.

From his doorway, the first grocer scowled at him.

The problem sets got harder.

His lamp turned out to have a short in it.

His problem sets started to come back red.

More red.

Who had ever thought the rice barrel could become an engineer?

New York lost its gleam. He drifted through its streets as if through an exhausted, dusty land, no detail of which had changed in a thousand years.

Then he remembered a form he was supposed to have handed in (some form, he had always been bad at that sort of thing) and, stopping into the Foreign Student Affairs Office, discovered Cammy arguing once again with Mr. Fitt. What a bully that man was! His whole long belly overhung Cammy's desk; he had his arms spread and bent, his fingers on her blotter. Cammy was holding her hands over her ears.

Ralph's heart rumbled like a Peking Opera drum; it was the crescendo before — *crash of the cymbals!* — a hero appeared.

LOVE

OLD CHAO summed thing up. *"If cats have mice to eat, they don't chase flies,"* he said. Meaning, You wouldn't be in love, Little Chang, if your schoolwork were going better.

This, during problem review. As Old Chao popped an aspirin, Ralph snuck a look at Old Chao's homework sheet. Not a single red X.

"You've gotten completely hutu" — muddle-headed — Old Chao went on. (A large man, he was usually careful to be delicate; only his concern was blunt.) *"You should know better."*

But *ting bu jian* — rebels would know what they wanted to know. That Cammy was like the stars and sky, for instance. Sometimes Ralph thought of her as Yang Guifei incarnate — that's a Tang Dynasty courtesan for whom an emperor went to ruin. More often, though, he stuck dreamily to, "She is like a star. Like a star in the sky." Or else, "She is like a bird. Like a bird in the sky." No longer did she seem big and barbarian to him. Her features had shrunk, her nose especially; and the hair on her arms had vanished, his eyes having laid in a supply of their own loving depilatory.

"Think of your parents," urged Old Chao. His shirt pocket stretched with its load of mechanical pencils. *"Think of your father. If he hears what you're doing, it will kill him."*
Ralph mooned harder, with oedipal glee.

Now he had had some experience pitching woo before. For instance, during the War, after the pipelines were blown up, he and his classmates had ferried water up to the girls' dorm, each leaving his bucket at the door of a particular resident. The particular residents had fluttered gratifyingly in response. But this was America he was in now, which meant who-knew-what. Research: as his classmates grappled on with Finite Element Analysis of Structures, Ralph began watching Americans and, his English having improved, even talking to Americans — who, he was surprised to discover, actually liked to sit back, and scratch their sandy chins, and tell him what they thought a young Chinaman should know. This was how he learned that the ceilings in the White House were ready to fall down, as well as other things. That he ought never put a bumper sticker on a new car. That when dames had dandruff, it was often just flakes from their hairspray.
The last of these wisdoms came from an old man in the luncheonette.
"Dames?" chewed Ralph.
"Holy Jesus," said the man, going on to explain not only what a dame was, but other basics. What was wrong with politics (dames); what was wrong with the Yankees (dames); and what was wrong with America.
"Dames?" said Ralph.
"Dough," said the man. He gripped his sandwich so hard, its contents bulged. "That's all anyone understands in this country. Dough, dough, dough."
"Dames too?"
"Dames got it the worst. You know what dames understand?"
"Dough."

"Diamonds. Pearls. Big fat fur coats."

"Presents?"

"You got it." He nodded so emphatically, his sandwich laid a pickle chip. "Big fat presents."

On the way home, Ralph bought a scarf. The next week it was a jar of cold cream. Presents paved roads in China too; this was a type of construction he knew. Pins, belts, booties. A hat, a pot holder, a can opener. She would understand; that was how he felt in the stores.

In person, though, he was just so much ardor next door, a boy whispering his heart through a solid garden wall. "Oo-oo-ooo," Cammy crooned, upon being presented with a box. "Shay shay!" But then she never wore any of the pins or anything else. Sometimes he wondered if she returned all of his presents for cash, the way she had with a radio she'd been given at a school picnic. He tried making little pen marks here and there on things he gave her, as tracers, but then couldn't bring himself to check for them in the stores. Instead he stood in front of her empty desk in the evening, after everyone had gone home, and touched her things — her typewriter, her scissors, her pencil cup, her blotter — as if trying to coax them into yielding up what somewhere in their atoms they had to know. Did she love him?

That year was the year of the big blizzard, twenty-eight inches. The sidewalks turned to tunnels; cars were lost for the season. It seemed the drifts would never melt.

But magically, one day, they had; and there then were Ralph and Cammy, going out for coffee every so often. The atmosphere had indeed warmed. If Ralph had not yet won her, at least he'd won her confidence. Now, over doughnuts, she told him how she'd leave her job, except that she'd sworn to Mr. Fitt's boss that she'd stay.

"The dean," she sighed. "He's put me down for another raise. I don't know." She batted her lashes as though bothered by something in the air. "Do you think that's wrong?"

Reassurance. It was all she'd ever wanted, though they did

talk too about houses and cars, and about how she'd always dreamed of going to Paris for her honeymoon.

"Hmm," mulled Ralph. "That's far."

Then one afternoon in the spring, they were out, by chance, at dusk. They went to the same luncheonette they always had, but this time its front glowed gold; and when they emerged a little later, it turned out that they'd been talking longer than they'd realized, so that it was — who would have thought it? — already night. The clamorous street had turned private, a blue path such as should rightly lead to a hidden knoll, and so on. They headed for the park by the river, hushing their voices. The tree leaves rustled obligingly.

"Of course you will happy," he told her.

"I'm not happy."

"You know . . ." He hesitated, but courage fought its way to him. "You know, you are like star in sky." He gestured awkwardly, hat in hand.

"I'm not a star."

"You are like bird," he went on.

"Bird?"

"Bird. You know . . . in sky."

She looked at him as though she'd never heard of a thing higher than ceilings.

"You know," he said. "Up."

"Those are clichés." She started to sniffle.

"Cree?"

"You're just like the other guys. You are." Now she was crying. "You think you're different, but you're exactly the same! A peapod! You are! No one listens! No one cares a-a-bout m-m-me-eee . . ."

What had happened? He didn't even know.

Still she was crying.

"Cold?" he asked finally; and when she didn't answer, he stretched his free arm around her, gingerly. Was this how women cried, their whole bodies trembling? He folded her toward him carefully, half expecting her to object. She dropped her wet face to his shoulder. Her breasts against his chest were nothing like earthworks at all.

America!

Crushing his hat between his knees, he gently kissed the top of her sweet-smelling head.

With morning, though, came day.

"Second form from the right," said Cammy, her face closed. "By Tuesday." It was as if she'd filed herself away. "If you have a question, Mr. Fitt would be happy to answer you."

He went back to buying her presents. Things would change, he thought, they had to. But they didn't; so that when Cammy left suddenly, in June, Ralph was stuck with a veritable stockpile to bury away in the darkness of his black trunk. Her last day, Cammy softened enough to tell him how Mr. Fitt had fired her in open defiance of the dean.

"Our plans," she lamented.

Plans?

Honeymoon. Paris. Snails. The dean had a house and car, and had had a wife, until the papers finally came through. With nobody except Mr. Fitt suspecting anything. . . . What a hard time he had given her! Over what — a few long lunches.

Ralph picked a pencil out of her pencil cup. He pressed it to her desktop. The lead broke off neatly, leaving a kind of headless cone, a wooden volcano. He did another.

Cammy went back to ignoring him. Until Mr. Fitt strode out of his office; and then, though she didn't actually say anything, she did give Ralph a crooked smile, which Ralph took to mean she might have cared for him. He ought to have bought her diamonds, he thought later. Not that he had the money to buy her diamonds, but still he thought it anyway. He ought to have bought her a fat fur coat. He ought to have bought her a car.

"Forget her," said his friends. *"If you have to give her a car, she doesn't love you."*

This made a certain amount of sense, even to Ralph. Yet he moped and moped — not eating, not talking, indulging his misery as though it were a child. His was a low-key style, the sort certain people can sustain indefinitely.

And so, no doubt, he would have, had not the Communists liberated Manchuria in the fall.

THESE
THINGS HAPPEN

KINGDOMS rise up, kingdoms collapse. Whatever China went
through in 1948 — whether she sadly fell or was gladly liberated — she did it, for an old lady, fast. It was an onstage costume
change. Out of an acre of worn silk emerged a red, red comrade.
A whole different person! Or so it seemed. Isn't this the story
of every transformation, though, that the past lies about its feet,
in folds, so that when it should dance, well . . .

But that's to skip ahead. At the time no one even knew for
certain that the footlights ought to be up; all there was then was
Manchuria, the shock that in a way was no shock. Everyone
knew that its ports had been served up to the Russians at Yalta;
also that the Russians, retreating, had surrendered their guns,
not to Nationalist troops, but to Communist. So what did it
mean, that the Communists now occupied the region? They
hadn't so much taken it, people said, as been given it. An un-
fortunate development.

Then, in the winter, the Huai River Basin. Now that was no
development; that shock was a shock. With more shock to follow
as the Communists moved south, and south again. The old silk

was dropping — *whoosh* — but still: the Communists would not, could not, cross the Yangzi River. That much remained clear.

Until the spring, improbable as ever, brought among its pretty new fashions, the greatest shock yet.

Come home! In the last letter Ralph was ever to receive from his parents, his father had written, *Your mother asks that you please listen this one time.* But Ralph could not obey. He wrote back, *The U.S. won't let us leave; they're afraid we'll use our training to help the Communists. People are being taken off the boats in Hawaii . . .*

It was a letter many students were writing, in outrage. The Americans, with their law and order, with their traffic lights everywhere — how could the Americans of all people do this? Later the students would guess that the Nationalists had put them up to it. At the time, though, they did not guess, they railed. It was illegal, completely illegal! Not to say wrong. Ralph was as mad as anyone, if only because the anger drew him together; his doubts, on the other hand, dispersed him. Would he have gone back if he could have? He wished he knew that he would have risked his life for his family and country — that he loved them the right way. Instead, he only hoped. He hoped that the Communists would prove unable to hold the country. How could they, when the United States wouldn't so much as recognize them?

He refused to be made an American citizen. He thumbed his nose at the relief act meant to help him, as though to claim his home was China was to make China indeed his home. And wasn't it still? Even if his place in it was fading like a picture hung too long in a barbershop — even if he didn't know where his family was anymore? Or was it exactly because he didn't know where his family was? For certainly he felt more attached to them for their having turned abstract — missing them more than he had liked them, the missing being simpler. Though not that simple, not when a family disappeared the way his had, vanishing as if into a crowd, or into a clutch of wilderness, or into some kidnapper's hidden cove. Suddenly no more letters. Who knew why, who knew what had happened? Their story was an open manhole he could do nothing to close.

Yet he dreamed about saving them anyway — of a simple ending, the missing lid found. The filial son, smashing apart the rock mountain prison. The filial son, talking things out with Mao. (Sure, Mao said, he understood, after all he had parents too.) The filial son, offering his wife Cammy in sacrifice, whispering *I'm sorry* as men drew their muddy fingers down her skirt.

Cammy, he dreamed. Still, after all these months, Cammy.

This, when he could sleep. Other times he thrashed all night, thinking nothing, his body cramping, dry, racked, beside itself. He banged his ankles on the bed frame, his elbows and wrists against the wall; until, at daybreak, battered and exhausted, he could finally reflect on the whole sobering state of things — appreciating as if from a book how colossal his China was, how fragile his family's house, their garden, their little systems for keeping food from spoiling, for presenting his sisters to company in the very best light. Memories filled him — New Years' feasts, fireworks, chestnuts. His two sisters, a pair of not-boys. Know-It-All kept an all-white kitten; he itched just to think about it. His too large mother, his even larger father. He remembered second aunt with her cactus collection, fifth uncle with his beard, eighth uncle with that opium addict, socialite wife. His grandfather with all those spots on his face. The cousins with their bugs — those bugs — and that funny wooden bridge over the neck of the pond, collapsing once under their collective weight. A single warning creak; then there they all were, waist deep in mud and carp, laughing, their shoes unglued.

Of course, there were other sorts of times too. His first day of middle school, in front of everybody, he mixed up the strokes of his own name. Then he was coming home; then he was in the far back courtyard, with the servants, breaking a rooster's neck. He was lopping off its head with a cleaver — *ruining the meat!* the servants yelled. So much talk! The kitchen help chattering, chattering, chattering . . .

But here was a thing to be happy about. Now the servants chattering have become a choir in a silent movie, a line of O mouths — or a school of fish, blub blub. And his father striding up — underwater, he has turned boneless, a ballet dancer. His black gown clings, his shoes have been ruined.

Ralph, in New York, kicked one of his hard leather wing tips across the room.

His downstairs neighbor knocked his immediate protest with a broom handle. High-strung, this neighbor was. When Ralph tossed and turned, he did too, he said. He wanted Ralph to buy a rug. A rug! Ralph sent his other wing tip to join the first, and toed one of his slippers besides, imagining his father being tortured. Not that he hoped his parents were tortured. He hoped they weren't so much as touched, he hoped nothing happened, nothing. He saw a hairy Communist swagger into his father's study, belch, spit on the floor, pick up a scroll . . . and already Ralph was outraged. Fingerprints! The scoundrel's left fingerprints!

Ralph could also envision a different scene, though. The man swaggers in, belches, spits. Ralph's father goes on grinding his ink. Now the glint — a cleaver. Ralph's father quotes from the classics. The Communist is breaking Ralph's father's neck.

But that wasn't what has happened, that couldn't be.

This is what Ralph would have liked to think about instead: a chicken cooked and cooling. The servants stalking mosquitoes at twilight, crafty, pouncing on the window screens. As a result of their efforts, the screens bulge toward the courtyard. Ralph's father is always telling them not to hit so hard, all they need to do is press a bit. He demonstrates, elegant. Mosquitoes prove indeed delicate, easily overcome. Still the servants swat gustily. *Thwack!* Another down! It's as much power as they'll ever enjoy.

Outside, the cicadas whirr. Summer. The paddy fields have turned a feathery yellow. The lotus pads lift themselves huge out of the lake, plates for the gods.

What Ralph did think, though — that was many other things. And especially, strangely, this: he shouldn't have taken that watch from his mother when he boarded the boat in Shanghai. *Your father would like to give . . .*

Or did he steal it? He remembered that he didn't, but still wondered, somehow, just as he sometimes wondered if there weren't something inside it, if that ticking weren't some secret life she was passing him, some essential heartbeat, without which the rest of the family was wasting away, bloodless. He's stopped wearing the watch, thinking of them. They are ancient paper lanterns, translucent, unlit, strung across the courtyard, too fragile to move — though when he sees Ralph, his father, still a brave man, tries to speak.

We are alive. His voice is faraway, a sound heard through a wall; yet the corners of his mouth crease and tear with effort. Pained, he blinks. His eyelids crackle like candy wrappers. *We are dead.*

Ralph launched his slipper across the room.

More knocking, knocking.

Knocking. And the next thing Ralph knew, he was having visa trouble.

"Forgot?" said his friends. "*Forgot the immigration office? Forgot to renew your visa?*" They shook their heads, mystified.

How to explain it? Something about not wearing a watch, he ventured. And he hadn't been sleeping right.

But the only one who accepted his answer was Little Lou, who was like that, an absorber. As for the spouters, if they had a chief, it was Old Chao. "*You should go to bed the same time every night.*" He knit his smooth brow. "*Get up the same time the next day.*"

Sound advice for a formless time. Ralph, though, hung in his own time, in the many times he'd wanted more than anything to destroy his father's world. What son doesn't? But he wasn't supposed to succeed, that was the thing.

As mysteriously as he'd let his visa lapse, he found he could do nothing about it.

"Better go see the foreign student advisor," said Old Chao. *"Better bring Fitt some candy."*

As if a friend of Cammy's could risk going to Mr. Fitt with an expired visa! Rumor had it that Mr. Fitt had tipped someone off about Cammy's raises, and that as a result the dean had been forced to take a leave of absence. The chair of the Engineering Department was taking his place for now, some said. Others said he was taking it forever. Ralph imagined Mr. Fitt on the phone again. He imagined the deportation team arriving instantly, with snarling dogs, and ropes.

Xiang banfa. An essential Chinese idea — he had to *think of a way.* In a world full of obstacles, a person needed to know how to go around. What *banfa* did he have, though? All he could think of was how many stories he knew about people smarter than he was. The advisor in *Three Kingdoms,* for instance, who, needing arrows, floated barges of hay down an enemy-held river. It's night; the enemy shoots and shoots; downstream at dawn, he plucks from the hay arrows to last weeks. Now there was a Chinese man! Another story: the emperor despairs of finding a horse able to run a thousand *li.* Until his advisor tells him, just wait — and the next day returns with a dead horse he's bought. *A dead horse?* says the emperor. *For five hundred pieces of gold?* Replies the advisor, *Ah, but when people hear what you've paid for a dead horse, they'll know what you'll pay for a live one.* And sure enough, the emperor soon has so many to choose from that he easily finds the one he needs.

If only Ralph had an advisor like that! But he had to be his own advisor; and though he tried to think, tried to think, he could not find any *banfa.* Endlessly, the weeks stretched out, like mile upon mile of ocean. What to do, what to do. What about just lying low, he thought finally, feebly. Having finished with his coursework that spring, he was only scheduled for thesis hours in the fall anyway. If he stayed out of the lobby, out of the halls, weren't chances good that people would forget about him? Except for the professor working with him on his master's thesis. But Pinkus, luckily, liked him.

Or at least used to.

"You mean you want me to lie?" Pinkus said now, stroking his scraggly gray beard. "When they ask, you want me to say I don't know where you are?" This was in Pinkus's narrow, paper-stuffed office.

"Probably that question no one ask it," said Ralph.

"But in case they do, you want me to lie."

It was the sort of afternoon when every car in the city seemed to be having trouble with its horn. The window was open only a crack, but still the din resounded. *Eeeeep. Eeeeeep.*

"Not that I don't wish you good luck," Pinkus said. "Good luck. But excuse me, I don't like to lie. Let me tell you, even if you don't lie, there are people who'll call you a sneak. On the other hand, if you lie, and they call you a sneak, it's worse." He paused. "I'm just telling you what I know."

Ralph bit his lip. "If I send home, Communists catch me," he said.

That at least made Pinkus stroke his beard again. His features bunched low on his face, as though shrinking with awe from his shiny domed forehead. Ralph explained how he could be put in prison, maybe even killed.

"Maybe they'll kill you, or definitely they will?"

Ralph hesitated. "Maybe."

Pinkus sighed. "Please excuse me for pointing this out," he said. "If you don't go to school, you won't get caught."

Ralph stood up.

"I'm sorry." Pinkus sounded tired. "But one thing I need to explain to you. Some men have to watch out for their reputations. You understand me?"

"No," said Ralph.

"Even in their own countries, some men are not at home."

"Not home?"

"You read the newspaper?"

"Chinese paper. Once a while."

"Look. Maybe I'm paranoid. But the way things are going, pretty soon everyone's going to be a spy or a Commie or both. Do you know what I'm talking about?"

Ralph shook his head.

"You should read the newspaper. We all have to be a little careful." Pinkus explained how when times got ugly, things got uglier for some people than for other people.

"People don't like you?"

"It's a matter of religion."

"People don't like you because of your religious?"

"Where've you been, Antarctica?" said Pinkus. "The Germans, for example. The Germans don't like us. 'Because of our religious.' "

"Ah," said Ralph. "I get. You Jewish guy."

Pinkus worked his paper clip into a pretzel. "You should read the newspaper," he said again. "That's good advice, take it, you're going to need it, I can see." He tossed the paper clip onto his desk blotter; now he stroked his beard some more. "All right, all right," he went on, as if to himself. "If they ask, they ask. But for you, such an innocent . . ." He stood up from his chair, paced around, shut the window.

The month of September, Ralph held his breath. October. November. Then the snow came, burying everything. Even the pile of debris outside Ralph's rooming house window turned picturesque, its jagged rustiness tempered into drifts, swoops, and in one corner, a series of pretty balls, like a snowman laid down for a nap. Ralph drew back his window curtain, moved his desk so that the sun kept his tea warm. He had thought he would miss the library, and was glad he still cooked with everyone else; at least he saw people in the evening. But to his surprise, he found that he liked working alone during the day, that in solitude he'd found a jet of concentration he'd never felt behind him before. His "Stress Analysis of Gears by Photoelastic Analysis" went better than he could have believed possible; and soon he found that despite the horror stories he'd heard about impossible research topics, and advisors who kept their students ten, twenty years, he actually looked forward to working on his doctorate. His doctorate! Just thinking about it made him feel like a man in possession of something. Every day he thought how lucky he was. Every day he thought how proud his family would have been to see him like this. What was the matter with his life all these years, that it had stood in anxious whitecaps? For once in his life, he thought, he was actually doing things the right way.

With the March mud, though, came notes. Would Ralph come see Mr. Fitt — that was the first. Immediately, added the second. And the third, signed by Mr. Fitt personally, in a curdling black hand — would Ralph please come or face the consequences.

Heavyhearted, Ralph pushed his desk back against the wall, shut the curtain, clipped together his equations and charts.

"Fitt never liked you," observed Old Chao, huffing loudly, as he set down a box of books. He killed a roach and showed it to Ralph.

And surely Ralph's new building was not like his old one. Now that he was moving he realized how fond he'd grown of the square brick apartment house, with its layers of windows and fire escapes, its hidden stack of predictable halls — how fond he'd grown of its schedules. The every so often it was mopped, the every so often sprayed. Order: not only were all its door numbers of the same font, a family, but the ones on the mailboxes were the door markers in miniature — kin. Even the tenants were a more or less matched set.

His new building, on the other hand, had at one point been turned into offices, and was now still mostly offices on the first floor, but with rooms and storerooms on the second floor, and rooms and more offices on the third. Everyone seemed to be missing something. There was a family with no mother, a couple with no furniture, a man with no legs. The businesses seemed to have no business. What the various tenants did have, though, was visitors, lots of them, so that (as some of the doors were marked with numbers, some with letters, and some not at all) a day in residence was a succession of strange heads popping in, sometimes with bodies attached. At least until Ralph fixed his lock; and then it was the sound of his knob being tried, communication attempted. "Bruce? Bruce? You in there?" Bang, bang. Or, "Wouldja openitup, Jane, comeon, knockitoff."

Ralph, though, was in no position to be picky. Mr. Fitt, apparently, had mobilized. Now Ralph was receiving letters from the Department of Immigration. "It has come to our attention . . . ." And what about that strange man hanging around his Chinese friends lately? *"Tall man,"* said Old Chao, *"with a dog."*

Ralph moved again, this time to a building with fleas. Then he moved once more, to a former hotel, after a tall man started walking a dog on his block; and yet again, after a dream about Mr. Fitt poisoning his water with lead. And now what about these phone calls? He had of course stopped using the phone, as his Chinese friends all knew; his landladies too he'd instructed never to admit they'd ever heard of him, much less that they knew where he lived, or how he could be reached. Yet someone had called twice, asking for him by name.

"So I sez go blow." This was Mrs. Ritter, his current landlady. "I sez, I don't rent to no Chinks. So far's I'm concerned they bring bugs."

Ralph moved. Ten days later, the calls started again.

"Listen," said Mrs. Bellini. "I don't care what kinda trouble you in, no funny business in my house, or I kill you."

IN
THE BASEMENT

BY AUGUST he'd moved nine times, in a spiral away from his Chinese friends. They and the university still formed some center to his universe, but only as a point of origin; he hardly ever saw anyone anymore. Not that he lived so far. Henry Chao, and Freddy Wang, and Milt Chen, and George Lee had all come around pretty often at the start. With time, though, they were called back to their own lives. It was Natural Process; it was the slow shift of a pendulum's swing into a different plane. Or here was the law: as his life diminished, theirs burgeoned, requiring attention. There were romances now, travel plans. Old Chao won a car in a church drawing. George Lee eloped. More and more, Ralph became for them a funny set of ears that came up sometimes, a lesson about falling for foreign devils. And for Ralph, on his side, they became another lost family.

Except for moon-faced Little Lou, who not only kept track of Ralph, but came by every now and then, bearing gifts. A box of pork buns, a pan — and troubles, Ralph sensed, to rival his, although just what they were, who knew? Little Lou was such a stopped-up type that when Ralph was done with his news, they could sit for a quarter hour at a time in complete silence. This, with all their friends to draw on for conversation. Something was just not right. Ralph would eat and play with his hat. Little Lou would watch, blank.

And yet Ralph appreciated his visits. They were something solid to stand on, anyway. Respite. They were a breakwater against some black undertow in himself that could any moment snatch him away to its killing home. He felt himself to be small, barefoot, lacking friction. Nearsighted. Everyday events seemed magnified another power. Little Lou's dropping by became the concern of a boddhisatva. A pigeon corpse on his doorstep was Ralph's true self come to rot at his feet. Everything signified, everything blared and reverberated as though some adjustment was off, some knob turned all the way up. Exhausted, that's what he was. Gone out. Looking to the future, he saw no future; and who doesn't hurt when he sees his life fizzling, his life that should have climbed and burst, blooming, a fire-flower in the sky? Once Ralph could imagine his parents watching, breathless, amazed, but now . . .

And then there was another pain too, quieter, weightier, its roots in what everybody knows — that one day a person looks back more than forward, that one day he'll have achieved as much as he was going to, loved as much as he was going to, been as happy as it was granted him to be. And that day, won't he have to wonder — was it enough, what he's lived? Can he call that a life and be satisfied?

So it was that Ralph felt not only his future to have failed, but with it his past, the twin engine that might have sustained him. He missed his home, missed having a place that was home. Home! And yet his life there, no; it didn't begin to fill the measure of his hopes for a life. It was no golden time. He might gild it, but in truth it was lacking. Lacking what? Something, everything, he didn't know exactly. But he did know this — that the world he had lost had waxed valuable in the losing, like an unwon love. How perfect Cammy had become in his memory, how much more desirable for having stepped behind a locked door! He saw all of this now, with the terrible lucidity of a strained mind; and seeing it, wondered what there was to live for. His new job? His new job. Being Chinese, he had thought the safest place to work would be in the Chinese restaurants scattered like toys in around the legs of the el on 125th Street. Weren't people needed to wash dishes, wait table, make noodles? Ralph had no experience, it was true, but everyone started with no experience. And as it turned out, his lack of experience didn't matter.

"Please, may I speak to your boss," he'd say in Mandarin.

"What you say?" the answer would come back; or at least that's what he guessed, not understanding a word of Cantonese. *"Whaat?"*

Once or twice he tried asking in English, but it was no use. Talking wrong, he might as well have been a barbarian invader; the town gates were closed. Still he knocked, until finally a tiny girl perched on a stool in the fresh-killed meat store said, "Yes?"

In perfect English, this was. Off the stool she barely cleared the countertop, but she knew where her father was, and her father — also American-born, it seemed, a gum chewer — guessed Yeah, he could use someone. Sure.

Ralph's non-life began. At dawn he would get up, wash, put on his bloody clothes, and walk to the store basement, where by the light of a yellow forty-watt bulb, crates of animals surrounding him — pigs and rabbits against one wall, pigeons and snakes against another — he would kill and clean and pluck hours upon hours of chickens. The first week he vomited daily from the stench of the feces and offal and rotting meat. But the second week he only blanched, and by the third he worked as though indigenous to this world. Instinct — first the most sickly or troublesome of the birds. A practiced look through the ranks; he'd snap the victim's neck, bare its jugular, slit it. Into the barrel, still kicking, to drain. Later, a roll in hot water, to loosen the feathers. Then he would pluck and dress the body, working with such speed and authority that his boss no longer came muttering down the stairs, but only shouted from the landing for a count.

That meant, most of the time, that some restaurant was ready for a pickup. The times it didn't mean that were a disappointment. The times it did, the animals would nose at their wire walls. Ralph would wash his hands, a ritual. Scraping noises; and then, like the gates of the Western Paradise, the trap door would open, lowering into the basement an almost intolerable beam of light. The rabbits would freeze, eyes glowing red; the pigs would squeal. Ralph would compose himself, at the ready. A figure would appear — shadow, penumbra; and Ralph like a priest would proffer up through the unearthly shaft, through the snow of sun-spangled dust, his mute communication to the outside world — placing carefully in the hands of another human being, stooped down to receive them, these — his chickens, his doing.

Then the door would clang shut, and he would sit back down to work, seeing nothing — spinning halos, that was, spots of light, shapes — until his eyes readjusted.

How long did this go on? He couldn't have said. Ages. Until one evening Little Lou came to visit with news. Pinkus had been named chairman of the department.

"Go," he advised.

Now Ralph knew better than to let his hopes swell but still they surged like a rain-drunk river. He got his books out, studied a few days, called. Pinkus agreed to see him. Ralph dressed carefully for the visit, in clean clothes. He was there, on campus, an hour early. How beautiful it was! He had forgotten. He admired the columned buildings, august even in the rain. He admired the herringbone brick paths. He admired the sycamores, rising like important ideas from pedestrian plots of short grass. He admired the statue in front of the engineering building, though it was not of an engineer, but only a miner, with something that looked like a washcloth on his head.

Still he was early. He tried to relax.

Until he was late. Why hadn't he worn his watch?

A clean-shaven Pinkus glanced at his; but when he saw that Ralph noticed, said, "So you're a few minutes late, forget it. What are we, railroad trains, we have to run on time?" He said this quickly, though, like a man on a schedule.

Ralph stared at Pinkus's new office, twice the size of his old one, with five big windows spread over two walls.

"So is there something I can help you with?" Pinkus said.

Over his head hung a clock.

Pinkus tried again. "Is there something you'd like to ask me? Something you'd like to tell me?"

What could Ralph have said then? He shook his head, shamed.

"What is this, twenty questions?"

"I like," managed Ralph, "finish my Ph.D."

"You'd like to finish your Ph.D."

"I . . . I . . . "

"But your visa. How'd I know that? Your visa, right?"

"Visa."

"Please explain to me one thing," said Pinkus. "Please explain to me how this happened, with your visa."

Ralph shook his head.

"You don't know?"

"Don't know."

"You don't know, or you won't say?"

"Don't know."

Pinkus scratched his chin. "I tell you who to call. The Foreign Student Office . . . "

"Cannot do."

"You've asked them already?"

Ralph hesitated. "Yes."

"You've asked them?"

"Yes."

"And they said what?"

When Ralph couldn't answer, Pinkus swivelled in his chair and looked out each of his five windows, one after another, right to left. Then again, left to right.

"Listen," he said finally, slower now. "I don't like to tell lies and, excuse me, neither do I like to hear them. Let me tell you something. The best way to handle your problem is the honest way. I know, in China, everything's through the back door. You think I don't know? I have ears, I listen, I know. But China is China, this is America, and you see?" He waved his hand at his windows, his desk, his shelves of books. "Through the front door. Listen to me. You want to get somewhere, don't sneak around. And don't ask other people to sneak around for you." He looked thoughtful. "I don't mean I don't want to help."

Ralph didn't know what to say.

"You're a good man. I'm going to help you."

Ralph nodded.

"What I'm going to do is call up the Foreign Student Office."

Ralph said nothing.

"What I'm going to do is call up George Fitt and get him to straighten you out."

"Don't like me," managed Ralph.

"Who doesn't like you?"

"Mr. Fitt."

"George? Doesn't like you?" Pinkus looked out the window. "George is a man, he doesn't like a lot of people."

Ralph nodded.

"Give me some time, I'll give him a call. Not today, today is . . ." He looked at his watch. "But tomorrow, I'll give him a call, I'll get back to you."

Ralph hesitated. Should he risk it? "No phone."

"No phone? Then give me your address."

Against his better judgment, Ralph dictated.

"You reading the newspaper like I told you?"

"Sure," lied Ralph.

"Good," said Pinkus.

Every day Ralph ran to his mailbox, only to find it empty. Sometimes after he looked, he'd lift up the metal flap and feel inside, to be sure he hadn't missed anything; but all he ever felt were the heads of screws. In one way, he wasn't surprised. Pinkus had a big office, but Mr. Fitt was still Mr. Fitt. How could Pinkus stand up to him?

Yet still, each day, Ralph found his hope rising. In his mind he'd replay the scene, Pinkus's office growing larger and larger. At work he'd see signs of his luck turning — a run of placid chickens, a mistake in his wages to his favor — every time something new to fuel him. And each day he'd come away from the mailbox disheartened. This went on for one week, two weeks.

Finally, he stopped running. Little Lou thought he ought to go see Pinkus again, but Ralph knew it was no use. This was what happened when a son left his family in the hands of bar-barians. It was what a skirt chaser deserved.

Or so he said. When the phone calls started again, though — again — he looked in the phone book, found out where Pinkus lived, and took a room as nearby as he could afford.

"Only six blocks away!" he told Little Lou.

Pinkus, Pinkus, Pinkus. When Ralph thought about him now, it was in a kind of fever. Sometimes at work, he'd see Pinkus step out from behind the chicken crates, apologetic. He'd see Pinkus kneel down beside him, offer to help with the plucking.

No, Ralph would insist. No, no, no. You're a professor, this sort of work isn't for you.

But there Pinkus was, rolling up his sleeves, watching Ralph's hands. So show me.

And now Ralph spent whole evenings admiring Pinkus's house, a handsome three-window-wide brownstone on a clean street. A big lit globe shone on either side of the doorway, above twin frost-tipped yews, which in turn set off a short, wide stair-case. Up and down this tripped three teenaged children; a well-fed-looking wife; and Pinkus himself, who, Ralph discovered, carried an ivory-handled walking stick.

He tried to muster the nerve to go up to Pinkus, but he might as well have been asking him for a date. Perhaps he should approach one of the children, Ralph thought. They seemed less intimidating, particularly the youngest, a plain girl with bed-springs of bright orange hair. But though he followed her home a few times, he never said anything, thinking he could be arrested for that, and then he would be deported. No, it had to be Pinkus himself. Once he trailed Pinkus to the cleaners, once to the grocery store; and once he got so far as to start casually down the sidewalk when he saw Pinkus round the corner at the far end of the block. This would have brought them face to face if, five doorways from his goal, Ralph hadn't crossed the street.

Above him, the moon hid bright-faced in the trees.

He took another loop around Pinkus's neighborhood. He peered through the windows. Some people, he noticed, had taken their Christmas trees down, others still had them up. He took another turn around. And then, partly to warm up, partly to avoid seeing a certain policeman for a third time, he ducked into a bar.

Now this was a daring thing, almost enough to make up for his earlier lapse of nerve. He had always known about bars — Shanghai was full of them — but he had never actually been inside one before. Ralph shook his head. So many people in so little space that everyone had to stand up, with nothing to eat but peanuts and pretzels. And why didn't they turn some more lights on? Pressed against the radiator, he eyed a man banging his forehead against the rim of his empty glass. Once, twice. Was he crying? Ralph winced, turned his attention to another man, a man drawing a woman over to his stool. She gave him one of her bracelets to play with; he tried to put his hand through it; she kissed him, right there, for a long time.

Ralph stared, for a long time.

Saddened, he wriggled his slow way back to the door, where he almost bumped into a man with a walking stick.

"Hello?" said Ralph.

Pinkus looked down.

"I'm Ralph. Ralph Chang." Ralph's mouth seemed to be talking by itself.

"Of course," said Pinkus. "What, you think I don't know who you are?" He stepped aside to let someone through.

For the first time in months, Ralph smiled. "Hello," he said. "Hello!"

"Not only do I know who you are, I know what you are," continued Pinkus.

This time Ralph moved to let someone by.

"Not only do I know you're a liar, I know you're a sneak. You keep hanging around my house, you'll get arrested, you hear me?"

"Wha?" Ralph started.

"I gave you the benefit of the doubt, but now I'm onto you, you hear me? No more of this I'm a poor immigrant. I talked to George Fitt. I'm telling you now, I've called the police. My daughter's wearing a whistle."

Ralph edged back.

"Do you hear me? This is America you're in now. If you want to lie, you want to sneak around, you should go back to China. Here in America, what we have is morals. Right and wrong. We don't sneak around."

Ralph stared.

"You hear me?"

Ralph tried to nod.

"We don't sneak around!" shouted Pinkus. "We have morals! You keep hanging around my daughter, I'll shoot you!"

Just then another person tried to sidle through. The person stepped forward; Pinkus stepped back; and Ralph, ducking around them, ran.

At home, he took a cleaver, turned it over and over in his hand. He sliced a sliver off one of his nails, touched the blade to the center of his palm and pressed enough to open a triangle of skin like a tent flap into himself. Out of this trickled blood, which he watched meander to the edge of his hand. Then, tilting his wrist, he watched the blood cross back, no thicker, no more vibrant, than that of a chicken. He imagined a chicken in his hands, the practiced snap with which it became meat, a routine, a carcass to pluck to goose bumps; but first the blood must be let. He felt his neck for the vein he had slit countless times before. How easy to cross the line. One moment, one step, and a person was there, through the curtain to another world. How tempting. How amazing that the line wasn't crossed more often, if only out of curiosity. That curtain, it was like something someone made up. How could it be, in the real world, that a knife moved an inch in the wrong direction could — presto — transform everything?

He opened another triangle into his hand, next to the first. His hand, when he touched his pinky to his thumb, felt raw. The lines of blood crisscrossed.

Maybe he should wash his hands.

Was this his blood, all over?

He pressed his hand to his pillowcase. A red print, with no fingers — a mouth, evidence of a large kiss.

He was going to kill himself tomorrow, in front of Pinkus's house.

He woke up still holding the cleaver. Someone was knocking on his door.

"Phone call." Knock, knock. "Phone call."

Habit. Survival was such a habit with him that he put away his cleaver, moved down the block, this time to a building under siege by its owner's ex-wife. Sonya, her name was, her signature everywhere — broken windows, bashed doors. The moment the place was empty Sonya would break in again, sledgehammer a few walls, a floor.

But what did Ralph care? Once moved, he slept and slept, his days and nights marbled together as though so much vanilla batter, so much chocolate, cut into each other with a knife. He had stopped going to work; as much as he hoped anything, he hoped Little Lou would come and find him. But Little Lou didn't come, didn't come, didn't come; and then Ralph didn't care anymore if he came or not. He lay waiting to see what happened. Anything could happen, this was America. He gave himself up to the country, and dreamt.

DELIVERANCE

TIME spun on. Ralph slept.

Time spooled itself fat. Still Ralph slept. The sky cracked. Dust rained in his eyes.

He turned over.

Dust rained in his hair.

He turned on his side. Dust rained in his ear. He ignored it. A sprinkle more, seeking him; he plugged his ear with his pinky.

Through the ceiling came moaning, unmistakable.

It is a luxury to despair in peace. Who doesn't know it? Now plaster was hailing, in clumps so large that even after pulling the covers over his head, he could still feel them. "Oh Sonya, Sonya, Sonya," he heard. "Sonya, Sonya, Sonya."

Sonya.

"Sonya love, Sonya baby, baby."

More hailstones.

"Oh Sonya sugar, Sonya sweet, Sonya sugar pie!"

Pie.

"Oh! Oh! Oh!!"

Broom, he thought. He needed a broom, with a handle.

"Oh! Oh!"

He threw one of his shoes at the noise. A smile of lath opened amid powdery fallout. He lay back down, tried to sleep. Sugar. Pie. It was daytime.

And now that he was awake, he was hungry, he realized. His stomach burned. And his bladder — the old facts. He sat up slowly, blinked. Swallowed. Dust in his mouth. He tried to spit. He rubbed his face with his hands. What now? He walked his buttocks to the edge of the bed. A hand on each knee. He rocked himself up. Staggered a bit, crunching. Dark tracks trailed his bare feet.

Shoes.

He looked for his black shoes, found them plaster-dust white, tried to clean them off. The dust hung on, streaking. So what. In the bathroom mirror, he saw that his hair had been streaked white too. His clothes.

And outside, white. A conspiracy. White but warm, a day made for throwing off jackets. He trudged through the streets, hat and gloves on, studiously ignoring the broad blue sky, the winking sun.

He was not to be mocked.

Children yelped, exuberant. He ignored them. He ignored the icicles too, a whole row of glistening two- and three-footers dripping from a pipe. A boy accosted him. "Excuse me, mister? Do you have the time?" Not answering, Ralph shuffled aggressively on, stealing a look at the boy's surprised face — pink as a sweet cake. Ralph wished he'd been even ruder.

This was February. This was not spring. This spring was a false spring.

He thought. At the grocery he planned to buy what. Rice, but no place to cook it. Bread.

Rice, but no place to cook it.

From an open door, the smell of hot dogs.

Hot dogs! A step.

Ketchup. Another step. Relish. Pickle slices. Even the paper boat began to seem appetizing, glistening in his mind with left-over condiment and grease. Then he was there, fumbling in his pockets for change. Everything, he told the man, yes. The first he gulped down; the second, savored. Sweet, salty, juicy, soft, warm. Squish of the frank. Tang of the sauerkraut. Bun — here juice-soaked, here toast-rough. His stomach gurgled. Twenty cents each, he couldn't afford it. Still he had another. Another. His stomach started to heave.

Eighty cents! He swallowed manfully, and as the man behind the counter gave him an alarmed look — not here, please, not here — Ralph made his way into the street, his stomach contracting, relaxing, contracting.

Relaxing. For good?

A park. He cleared the wet snow from a bench with his forearm. The snow fell heavily, in a long pile like a sinking mountain range. And yet when he sat down, the bench was still wet. Wet wool. His under-thighs prickled. He took stock of his life. Three dollars and sixteen cents — more than he thought he had. He smoothed the bills out, lined the coins up on top of his thigh, in size order. On the other side of the balance — no job, no family, no visa.

A tall boy in a shrunk-up ivory sweater strolled by, hands in his pockets, singing. Then a girl teetered past in red heels and a red coat. For contrast the girl wore a large blue hat, fetching as a frying pan; Ralph watched as she took two steps, gazed up with rapture at the tree branches, then took another two steps. She twirled giddily, her handbag swooping. The handbag was red and gold, with a dainty gold-link chain. She held it by only two fingers. Was this temptation? If so, it was working. The bag swooped by again. How easy it would be to pluck it — quick! — out of the air. Instead Ralph pressed his fingers together and let the girl teeter on.

So. He'd passed the test. He felt momentarily pleased, like a man who, catching a chance glimpse of himself in a mirror, discovers a figure of some dignity. At the same time he wondered,

What test? Was he being tested? And who was doing the testing? And why him? That's what he really wanted to know. Why, of all people, him. From up the path, a black coat migrated his way, like an answer slow in coming. He squinted at it.

That there should be a purpose to suffering, that a person should be chosen for it, special — these are houses of the mind, in which whole peoples have found shelter. Ralph was not religious in general, but in times of hardship, gods grew up, some to test and prod, others to look in on him. Interested in himself, he believed himself a subject of interest; so that when, after months and months of calling, Theresa finally found him slumped there on that park bench, Ralph believed himself not so much rescued as delivered.

"So lucky!" Theresa said later. After all, she could've just as easily gone left instead of right, back around the pond instead of over the hill . . .

But what earthly luck could have produced this black coat, made it stop — could have made it talk Shanghainese, no less, could have turned it right before his eyes into a sister, his sister? Ralph was so astounded he couldn't talk, so astounded that in springing up to welcome her, he knocked her over, so that she fell to the sidewalk and sprained her ankle. Then he slipped too; and then they were both crying and not knowing what to do. Luck? How could it be only luck?

"Was miracle." This was Ralph's version of the story. "Miracle!" And even so many years later, anyone could still hear in his voice all that the word meant to him — rocks burst into blossom, the black rinsed from the night sky. Life itself unfurled. As he apparently, finally, deserved. How else could it be, that he should find himself lying in coin-spangled ice slosh, in America, embracing — of all people — his sister? Saved! Know-It-All in his arms! Impossible! So he would have thought; so anyone would have thought. But, heart burning, there he was just the same — hugging her, by Someone's ironic grace, as though to never let her go.

THERESA

AS FOR his deliverer — we turn now to her story, which curls from this sad truth: that as much as Ralph, growing up, should have been her, she should have been him. It was as if in some prenatal rush, they had been dressed in one another's clothes. With consequences for her too — who could imagine her salting a mother-in-law's soup just so? So smart, so morally upright, but she talked too much, in a voice that came from too far down in her chest, and she was *homely as a pig head three*, like her father. Drawn face, brown hair, big mouth, freckles. Plus she displayed her mother's worst tendencies, worsened. It was a paradigm of Western influence gone wrong. Her father had insisted on giving the children cow's milk, with the result that Theresa turned out a giantess — five seven! With feet that entered rooms before she did. Her mother, who regarded her own feet with dismay, looked on Theresa's with horror. And the girl's gait! In the convent school, she'd not only acquired this English name, Theresa, she'd also taken up baseball — with her father's permission — so that now she strolled when she walked, sometimes with her hands in her pockets. Her mother made her quit, sent her for dance lessons, strapped her to a stick-and-chalk contraption that was supposed to help her attend to her movements.

But Theresa would not care, being almost glad to be all wrong in some sphere. When Ralph laughed at her, she laughed with him. Wasn't she a misfit too! By day they shook their heads together, brother and sister, tears in their eyes. Only in the soft of the night, quiet, her pet cat in her lap, did she wish to be someone else. Like their younger sister, say, whose blessing was the blessing of blessings — to be who she was supposed to be, so in tune with her time and place that though she gave without calculation to others, she was invariably repaid severalfold. Her falling in love was typical. She helped a certain harelipped schoolmate with her homework, wrote her a part in the school play; and in return was introduced to that schoolmate's brother, a man gentle, handsome, and intelligent past imagining.

Not to say rich, which pleased their mother; and though it displeased their father that his wife talked of such things, it seemed that Theresa's sister and her beau were going to be allowed to marry. No one had actually said so; but neither was anyone matchmaking, and her lover's letters were permitted to arrive. Theresa tried to hint — she wouldn't mind if her sister married first.

No one would hear her. Her sister spent hours in the pavilion by the carp pond, composing replies. Her sister read poetry, searching out lines to quote. She admired her beau's handwriting. His absence bloomed in her until she grew absent herself, preternaturally agreeable.

Finally the news came that Theresa was engaged, to a Shanghai banker's son. There was only one hitch — her fiancé had asked to see her.

"Since when do boys come look?" fretted their mother.

Their father dropped his observation like a bomb. *"Modern type."*

But in the city, as the go-between pointed out, things were changing. She pressed delicately. Of course he would like what he saw.

"*Of course,*" their mother agreed. Still, in later negotiations, she tried to arrange things such that the young man might glimpse Theresa as she drove by in a car.

The go-between apologized, explained.

Their mother compromised. The young man could watch Theresa walk past a window.

Then, her final position. The young man could station himself by a certain park gate as Theresa strolled down a path some hundred feet away, carrying a parasol.

"*A parasol?*"

To protect her complexion from the sun. Their mother held firm; and as it would be unreasonable to expect a girl to take risks with her complexion, the matter was settled, except that Theresa refused to walk anywhere.

"*Meimei,*" their mother reminded her — Younger Sister.

They were standing in the shadowy arcade that encircled the cobblestone courtyard. Theresa hesitated, looked to her father, who nodded his head a little as he withdrew to his study. By this he meant, she knew, that she too should retreat to what study she could find.

Discipline. *At sixty,* said Confucius, *I was no longer argumentative.* Of course, she was only twenty-six. But still duty called to her, a voice like her own. *Meimei* — Younger Sister.

"*Anyway,*" she said, "*no parasol.*"

By the night before the walk, though, she had worked past that bit of pride too. Her outfit included not only her sister's shell-pink parasol, but also a new pair of silk shoes, a size too small, the idea being not so much to make her feet more acceptable — her fiancé would be too far away to tell — but to help her maintain a more ladylike step. Such indignities! She struggled to submit to them, only to be seduced. *A modern type.* Not the type to go along with his parents' designs.

Did that make him her type?
She placed her new shoes by her bed.

The path had been chosen so as to ensure that there would be
nothing small in the picture — no flowers, no low walls, nothing
for scale. Someone had proposed something about her sister
accompanying her on blocks, but that scheme was quickly
dismissed as too complicated. And so, as she started down the
path, she was alone. This was August. The heat wound itself
around her, stickily intimate. No danger of bounding. Theresa moved carefully, slowly — one step, one step — sweating.
Thinking, as she walked, of the way penguins cooled themselves,
sliding on their stomachs in the snow when a thaw was too
much for them. Biology — another thing her mother wished
Theresa hadn't learned at the convent school. She saw herself
as if in a textbook. *Instinct. The female of the species performs
her mating dance. This specimen carries her parasol on her left,
toward the gate and her fiancé, though the sun inflames her
right.*
 Her right shoulder burned.
 And yet so, paradoxically, did her left, her fiancé's gaze boring
through her thin silk shade like a second solar power. How hot
she was, caught in these cross beams! She was under fiery observation. *The female of the species performs her mating dance.*
And how her feet were swelling. One step, one step. She could
feel the ground radiating up through her finespun cloth soles.
 Her instep rose.
 A modern type.
 Sweating, she thought of her sister. How much easier for her
to dare hope!
 A modern type.
 Ahead, Theresa could see a bit of sky — a sheer blue wall,
undistinguished. Below, the cypresses looked dusty and dispar-
ate, like so many display pieces, badly grouped. To her right, a
discreet stand of sycamores, peeling.
 Her feet throbbed.

There were radical thinkers in the city these days.

Or so she'd heard. Sweat pooled between her fingers.

A modern type.

What if he'd just come back from France, or Japan, sleepless with ideas, only to find that he'd been engaged to some sweet country miss? *Of such fine family!* What then? He'd sit down with his father, his mother. *A capable girl, and so sweet-tempered!*

Of course, he was more probably a Shanghai banker's son whose grand ambition was to become a Shanghai banker.

Her feet grew vehement. *A capable girl, and so sweet-tempered, and so graceful!* How beautifully she did mince now, as though her toes had been bound with fire-strips. One step, one step.

She could not go on.

Still she took another step.

A cane. She should fold up the parasol, use it for a cane. The decision, when it came, opened suddenly, a crevasse. So let him see her! Let renegade not miss renegade for sheer lack of daring! Brave, she folded her parasol, hobbled off to the right, leaving the path. She did not look back to the gate, but only forward, toward the peeling sycamores.

Shade. She rested, her head spinning. So!

Then: What had she done? What — She tensed.

Nothing. Was it her imagination? Still she felt it, a presence behind her. A gaze, cool as the round marble inlay of a chair back. She tried to say something, but her voice dried in her throat.

He should say something.

But still he gazed, only gazed. Waiting.

What now? A bird shrieked. She saw it fly out from nowhere, its wings flashing black, then white.

She turned.

The report came back that due to an unspecified family crisis, the banker's son would be unable to marry for some years. In fact, Theresa found out, well before their date in the park, he had run off with his father's concubine. So what shame was there? What loss of face? It was his family who had been disgraced.

Still she grew vacant. The path; the brush; the rocks; the gate; and beyond the gate, sun-white, a small deserted clearing. Her spine twisted; in her dreams she twisted, turning toward that clearing again, again. A perverse tropism.

Her parents consulted, debated.

Finally she was sent to Shanghai, to some close friends with an invalid daughter; Theresa was to keep that daughter company for a few months. She was not allowed to bring her cat. When her sister got married, Theresa heard about it in a long, poetic letter, beautifully written. Then the Communists. Her parents' friends wrote, urgently. With tremendous good fortune and not a few connections they'd found a way to send their daughter abroad, on a student visa. What to do with Theresa?

The mail foundered with the government; they received no answer.

Hong Kong, Tokyo, San Francisco. Theresa picked the English name Helen for her delicate friend. Like Helen of Troy, she explained: also it sounded like Hailan, her real name, Sea Blue. They frolicked in a melancholy way, half giddy with freedom and travel, half fearful and lonely and worried, and irritated too, having gotten along in China, but as the simplest of friends. It was strange, learning to make decisions together. Years later, they laughed to see the girls, Mona and Callie, in a three-legged race. That's the way they were, they said, bound together with some old rope — their overlapping history, their parents' relationship. Things in common, that made it easier to talk to each other than to strangers, but hardly meant that when they did they would agree. And they didn't agree, though after a few near-arguments, each did her part never to let that show; so that they grew at once closer and lonelier, like colors that, when knit

together, gleam all the more distinct. Every day brought com-
promise so basic neither one would talk about it, as though such
prideless friendship belonged to a realm past conversation. "You
guys are so *formal* with each other," Callie told Helen once.
This was when she was in high school, trying to learn to be up
front.

Helen handed her a dish. "So many family members, I already
lost them all," she answered.

No elaboration. It was just before sunset, a time of day when
the sun stared blithely across the kitchen, instead of studying
the floor. Callie drew the curtains with a soapy hand, but even
so the light washed everything out.

THE
DELIVERANCE,
CONTINUED

"I CALL, call, call," went Theresa's version of the rescue. She spoke English for the benefit of the girls. "I don't know if this is right, this name, Ralph." Everyone in the room laughed. "I think, if Ralph's his name, how come no one has ever heard of this name? But I ask *Lao Chao*" — Old Chao — "and he says that's it, Ralph. So every day after class, I call every boarding house I can find. Or else I hunt for this friend, *Xiao Lou*" — Little Lou. "*Lao Chao* says *Xiao Lou* knows everything. But this *Xiao Lou* is just as hard to find as this Ralph. Anyway, I try. And one day, finally I find *Xiao Lou*! Only he won't say anything. He just looks at me like this." She stares, eyes wide. "As if he's afraid I'm a gangster, when I leave he'll never lift his arms up again." She paused. "You know, it's a very sad story about that *Xiao Lou*. Later on, he killed himself."

"How?" Callie wanted to know.

"With a knife," volunteered Mona.

"Mona! You're not supposed to say, you're supposed to let Auntie say!"

Mona giggled. "Like this!" She banged her fist into her chest. "Aargh!"

"It's not funny," said Theresa. Mona stopped.

"Was in the Chinese newspaper." Helen shook her head. "Really sad."

"Sometimes I think maybe he come to look for me, but cannot find me." Ralph's voice was sodden. "Nice person, Little Lou. Good heart."

"Sad," said Callie.

"Oh, *so sad*." Mona sighed heavily.

Theresa glared, but went on. "Anyway, so finally I call one place, and someone says yes, there's a Chinese man here named Ralph. She thinks she saw him go out for a walk."

"So happen," Ralph explained, "time I move there, I so tired, I forgot to ask them if someone call, please not to say anything."

"We were just lucky like that," said Theresa.

"Just lucky?" asked Mona, with an innocent look.

Theresa glared at her again, but before she could say anything, Ralph had already taken his cue.

"Not lucky, miracle!" he said.

And, of course, next came the black coat — and then, Older Sister!

First there was Theresa's ankle to take care of. Ralph tried to hail a cab, which he'd never done before. He put a tentative arm up; instantly one pulled over, in a rolling wave of black slush. Magic! Ralph marvelled at his own command. The driver leaned his head back. "Hospital?" said Ralph; and even before all the syllables were out of his mouth, the car lurched ahead, so responsive that Ralph was thrown against the seat. He straightened himself dazedly. At the hospital, Theresa was whisked into a perfectly white room; he was ushered in after her. She emerged on crutches, looking like a veteran.

Though it was after hours in Theresa's building — a women's residence — under the circumstances, Ralph was allowed in. He waved his thanks to the lady at the desk. *Clatt!* — the elevator doors. *Clatt!* They opened again, like the shutter of a slide projector; and in front of Ralph shone private splendor. Flocked wallpaper, moss green with gold, in a pattern of sinewy trellises; a matching moss-green carpet; and on the walls, electric torches. Flame-shaped bulbs spiralled up from gold-tone leaves. Ralph entered the hall reverently. Theresa stopped in front of door 9D. *"Push that,"* she instructed, and he did, with such a respectful press that he had to ring again, with more punch, to produce the noise that would make the door open. Still nothing. No matter — Theresa handed him her pocketbook. She had keys. But just as he fathomed the bag's knot-shaped clasp, the apartment door swung suddenly, wondrously, wide. Ralph stared, handbag agape. He'd readied himself for a comb, a mirror, a change purse, maybe some paper clips. Here instead stood a woman.

And around her, China. Ralph took in the scrolls, the shoes by the door, the calendar, the lidded cups of tea, as if they were part of her person, an extension of her clothes; he found them so familiar — found her so familiar — that even a half second later he could hardly have said what he'd recognized. Then she spoke (a soft, breathy sound) and he realized he didn't know her after all. That's why they were being introduced. Belatedly he began to register some specifics. Delicate feet. Sturdy calves. Slight figure overall. A contained way of moving; she seemed instinctively careful not to take up too much space. Shoulder-length black, curly hair (a permanent). A heart-shaped face that, with its large forehead, and small mouth, and slightly receding chin, seemed to tilt forward. She had large eyes, but mostly, it seemed, for his beat-up shoes. Shy, Ralph concluded hopefully. The considering type. Not a talker.

But Helen was not a listener either, so much as something else. Attentive. She sensed when a guest needed more tea before the guest did, expressed herself by filling his cup, thought in terms of matching, balancing, connecting, completing. In terms, that is, of family, which wasn't so much an idea for her, as an aesthetic. Pairs, she loved, sets, and circles. Shoes, for instance (he was right), and cartons of eggs — and, as it happened, can openers that rolled easily around a lid, never sticking. Not too much later, a clean Ralph, with all-new clothes, left a deluxe model on the kitchen counter, with a red bow.

Helen opened every can in the cupboard.

Theresa reported this back to Ralph.

Then it was belts, circle pins. Ransacking his trunk, Ralph found a tam-o'-shanter; socks; booties; a pen-and-pencil set; a hairbrush, hand mirror, and comb. All of these Helen used, displayed, wore, not once in a while, but every day, blushing. He spoke her dialect, that's to say; and she, certainly, his. Oxtail soup, she made him, steamed fish with scallions. Now that there were no servants, Helen was learning to cook. Would he taste-test for her?

He would, although, paradoxically, it inflamed more than abated his homesickness to try a mouthful of a dish and pronounce, after some prodding, that it was too salty, too sweet, too spicy-hot. Her cooking was so agonizingly close to that of his family's old cook that his stomach fairly ached with the resemblance, even as his mouth thrilled. More ginger, he coached. Less vinegar. More soy sauce.

One day, she had her crystal chicken just right, and her red-cooked carp too. Ralph proposed with a family ring Theresa had brought over, a single piece of spinach-green jade set in white gold. Not that he couldn't have afforded a new ring by then. From their friends at English language school, Theresa and Helen had discovered that most companies didn't care what papers their draftsmen came with; and just like that, Ralph had a job in an airy room, with his own tilted drawing board. Other people complained. The long hours, those hard wooden stools. If only the stools had backs, they said, then after hunching and hunching, they'd be able to rest a bit. And what were their prospects? Already they were beginning to discern what would be abundantly clear in another decade — that at the end of every project, they would all get laid off, and have to find new work at another firm, where, just as they were beginning to rise in the ranks, they'd be laid off again.

Ralph didn't mind, though. He was grateful enough to have

a place to go in the morning (with a doughnut shop on the way, no less), and every week, a paycheck.

Then came the possibility of Ralph's finishing his Ph.D. after all. This was serendipity itself; with the fall of the Nationalists, other Chinese students had become as illegitimate as he. "No status" — that was how they stood with the Immigration Department, suddenly naked as winter trees. What now? They waited. Rumor had it that, having kept the technical students here, the Americans were going to have to do something with them — probably send them all back to school. Sign-up sessions. Ralph went along with everyone else. No, he wasn't a Communist. Yes, his status was "no status." As for how he got that way, "English not so good, excuse please?"

"Say again, please?"

"Whaaa?"

The volunteer let it go.

So much to celebrate!

To save money, Helen rented a Western-style, white gown with a matching veil. The ceremony was in the side chapel of a college church; the reception in a small, carnation-wreathed social hall. Pipes clanked. Tables wobbled. Outside, it sleeted. Yet Ralph and Helen, in the simple way of newlyweds, were delighted with the food, with the decorations, with the guests, with each other; even, later, with the pictures, though in truth the majority were out of focus and overexposed. The photographer was a drunkard. But who wanted to say so? Helen hung the pictures up anyway. A shot of her and Ralph. A shot of each of them with Theresa. She even hung the shot of all three of them together, which looked like nothing so much as a triple-headed ghost. "The Mystery of the Trinity," Theresa would joke later. Yet at the time she admired it as politely as everyone else. It was a good likeness, she agreed, a fine family portrait.

PART II

The House Holds

HELEN,
FAR FROM HOME

HELEN'S LIFE in China had been in every way perfect. Though
a girl, she had been preceded by a twin sister who had died, so
that her own touch-and-go start was cheered breath by halting
breath; and in later life, she'd been blessed by just enough lin-
gering, sometimes serious illness, to win her much fuss. Well —
maybe some of the fuss she could have done without, for instance
the sort that involved her grandfather firing doctors; her mother
was always hiding with embarrassment, or else whispering at
the edge of Helen's bed, in a voice so low that Helen felt the
words more than she heard them. They were a sensation, a
stirring, something she could not have sworn came from outside
herself.

Still she was content, so sweet-natured that her two sisters
and three brothers, who might have resented her, instead vied
in their efforts to please. They carried her up and down the
stairs, sang her songs. She was a family pastime. Her life ambition was to stay home forever. The way Americans in general
like to move around, the Chinese love to hold still; removal is
a fall and an exile. And for Helen, the general was particularly

true. The one gnarl of her childhood was the knowledge that, if she did not die of one of her diseases, she would eventually have to marry and go live with in-laws. And then she'd probably wish she *had* died. How faint she felt, just listening to the stories other girls told — about a neighbor's daughter, for example, who walked all the way home from Hangzhou, only to be sent back. That was extreme, of course, but how about her friend's cousin who, married away into the countryside, was made to take baths in a big copper vat? Over a pit fire, as though she were a pork joint, in water that had already been used by her father-in-law, her husband, her husband's seven brothers, and her mother-in-law. *Don't worry*, Helen's parents reassured her, *we'll find you someone nice, someone you like too. No one's going to beat you.* But at best, Helen knew, she would be sent to scratch out some new, poor spot for herself, at the edge of a strange world, separated from everyone she loved as though by a violent, black ocean.

Now, America. For the first few months, she could hardly sit without thinking how she might be wearing out her irreplaceable clothes. How careful she had to be! Theresa could traipse all over, searching out that elusive brother of hers; Helen walked as little and as lightly as she could, sparing her shoes, that they might last until the Nationalists saved the country and she could go home again. She studied the way she walked too, lightly — why should she struggle with English? She wrote her parents during class, every day hoping for an answer that never came. She went to Chinatown three times a week, thinking of it as one more foreign quarter of Shanghai, like the British concession, or the French. She learned to cook, so that she'd have Chinese food to eat. When she could not have Chinese food, she did not eat. Theresa (who would eat anything, even cheese and salad) of course thought her silly. *"In Shanghai you ate foreign food,"* Theresa said (*da cai*, she called it — big vegetables). *"Why shouldn't you eat it here?"* Still, for a long time, Helen would not, which they both thought would make her sick.

She was not at home enough, though, even to fall ill.

This could not go on forever. Eventually, faith faltering, Helen studied harder, walked more, bought new clothes, wrote her parents less. She did continue to spend whole afternoons simply sitting still, staring, as though hoping to be visited by ghosts, or by a truly wasting disease; but she also developed a liking for American magazines, American newspapers. American radio — she kept her Philco in the corner of the living room nearest the bedroom, so she could listen nonstop. She sang along: "The corn is as high as an el-e-phant's eyyye . . ." She did not insist on folding all her clothes, but used the closet too. She began to say "red, white, and blue" instead of "blue, white, and red" and to distinguish "interest" from "interested" from "interesting." She caught a few colds. And she married Ralph, officially accepting what seemed already true — that she had indeed crossed a violent, black ocean; and that it was time to make herself as at home in her exile as she could.

A
NEW LIFE

NOT THAT HELEN would ever be at home anywhere but her real home. And yet sometimes she couldn't help but be infected with a bit of Ralph and Theresa's enormous enthusiasm for their new arrangement. How right it all did seem! That Ralph should marry her, friend of Theresa — it was just as their parents would have had it.

"*Don't you think she's just like our little sister?*" Ralph asked Theresa once.

"*There's a resemblance,*" said Theresa.

Helen blushed.

"*Such a coincidence,*" said Ralph. "*You know, someone at school was talking the other day about a person who took his house apart, and moved it, and then rebuilt it, just the way it was.*"

"*That's like us, and our family,*" Theresa agreed.

"*The odd thing was that that house had a leak. So why did the man move it, if it had a leak? That's the question. Also, he had always hated the inside of it. Too small.*"

"*Well,*" said Theresa, "*leaks or no leaks, maybe he was used to it.*"

"I guess," said Ralph, uncertainly.

Helen sighed. At home, room had always been made for her in the conversation; people paused before going on, and looked at her. Here, she had to launch herself into the talking, for instance during a lull, as now.

"You know that saying about a wife's ankle?" she put in softly.

"What?" said Ralph.

"Don't interrupt," said Theresa. *"She's talking."*

"I can't hear her."

"That saying," Helen said louder. *"Do you know that saying, about a wife's ankle? Being tied to her husband's?"*

"Of course," encouraged Theresa. *"With a long red string. From the time she's born."*

"Well, I think maybe my ankle was tied to my husband's and sister-in-law's both."

"Ah no! To both? To my ankle too?" Theresa protested, laughing. Then, in English, "Are you trying to pull my leg?"

They all laughed. *"Good joke!"* cried Ralph.

"Good one!" Helen agreed.

Weren't they happy, though? At least until it was time for them to move to a run-down walk-up north of 125th Street, whose air smelled of mildew and dog. It was the kind of place where the poorest of students lived, where the differences in housekeeping between the halls and the rooms were as dramatic as the occupants could manage. An economy. Ralph and Helen and Theresa had agreed on it. Yet they were belatedly shocked. So many Negroes! Years later, they would shake their heads and call themselves prejudiced, but at the time they were profoundly disconcerted. And what kind of an apartment was this? This apartment sagged. Theresa poked a finger in a soft spot of plaster, occasioning a moist avalanche. *"We're not the kind of people who live like this,"* she said.

But their super, it seemed, thought they were. That Pete! He expected them to stand endlessly in his doorway, his half German shepherd jumping up on them as he rambled on about the boiler. As for their situation — Was it an "urgency"? he'd ask. Only, yes or no, to not be coming — not to see about their plumbing problems, not to see about their ceiling problems, not to see about the crack in the back bedroom wall that seemed quite definitely to be widening.

"Leaks," said Ralph, batting the dog away. "Paint come down. Big crack." Politely at first. Then, with more vigor, "You do nothing! This building falling down!" The result was that Pete once said he'd "swing by sometime," once explained that his boss, the owner, had some months ago done a bit of work on the roof.

"So?"

"Well now, I don't know that ever'thing a body says has got to have a *point*," he said.

Fan tong, Ralph called him — rice barrel. Helen and Theresa laughed. And here was the most irritating thing: fly open, feet up on his legless desk, dog at the door, he'd often be thumbing through course catalogs, exchanging one for another, sometimes working through two at once. Should he be a lawyer? A doctor? An engineer? As if he could be an engineer! As if he could get a Ph.D.!

A man, Pete said, was what he made up his mind to be.

"That man is fooling himself!" Ralph shook his head.

Helen, meanwhile, hired a plumber, scraped the loose paint so it wouldn't hang, walked Ralph's file cabinet into the back bedroom to hide the crack. Could this place ever be a home? Next to the file cabinet she put a tall bookcase, and straddling them, a small, wide one that only just cleared the ceiling.

"Smart," admired Ralph.

"I saw it in a magazine," she told him. *"This is called* wall unit."

"Wall-unit," repeated Ralph. And later he observed that it was exactly in solutions like hers that a person could see how well they Changs were going to do in their new life.

"Not like that Pete," he said. *"He's fooling himself."*

Entertainment: Ralph took to imitating Pete's walk. He'd slump, a finger cleaning his ear, only to have Theresa gamely cry out, *"No, no like this,"* and add a shuffle, turning out her knees as Helen laughed. They studied the way Pete blew his nose, that they might get it right; they studied his sneeze, his laugh, the self-important way he flipped through his calendar. "Well, now, let me have some look-see," growled Theresa. "Typical Pete!" Ralph roared in approval. "Typical, typical Pete!" Ralph even mimicked Boyboy, Pete's mutt — strutting around, barking showily, calling himself "Ralph-Ralph." He paced back and forth, guarding the door with wide swishes of a brush tail; he jumped up on Helen and Theresa as they tried to dodge by with grocery bags. And pretty soon, no one knew quite how, "typical Pete" turned "typical American" turned typical American this, typical American that. "Typical American no-good," Ralph would say; Theresa, "typical American don't-know-how-to-get-along"; and Helen, wistfully, "typical American just-want-to-be-the-center-of-things." They were sure, of course, that they wouldn't "become wild" here in America, where there was "no one to control them." Yet they were more sure still as they shook their heads over a clerk who short-changed them ("typical American no-morals!"). Over a neighbor who snapped his key in his door lock ("typical American use-brute-force!"). Or what about that other neighbor's kid, who claimed the opposite of a Democrat to be a pelican? ("Peckin?" said Ralph. "A kind of bird," explained Theresa; then he laughed too. "Typical American just-dumb!") They discovered stories everywhere. A boy who stole his father's only pair of pants. A mother who kept her daughter on a leash. An animal trainer who, in a fit of anger, bit his wife's ear off.

"With his mouth?" Ralph couldn't believe it.

But it was true. Helen had read it in the American newspaper, which was honest enough to admit, one day, that they were right. Americans had degenerated since the War. As for why, that was complicated. Sitting in the green room that was the living room and Theresa's bedroom both, she read the whole article aloud. Ralph and Theresa listened carefully.

"*That's what we were saying,*" Ralph commented finally. He looked to Theresa, who nodded.

"*Americans want to loosen up now, have a good time,*" she said. "*They're sick of rationing.*"

"*Would you read it again?*"

Helen would — glad, she supposed, to have in the family at least this one rickety seat. And sure enough, there it was once more, evidence of how smart they were. Imagine that — that they could see, in a foreign country, what was what! Above them, the ceiling light dropped haloes in their hair as they listened on. Everything, they heard, was going to be okay.

The only question was why Ralph lay awake whole nights, listening to Helen asleep in the next bed. It wasn't just the strangeness of rooming with a woman which kept him up with the streetlights. Not anymore; he was already used to the company, or almost used to it — to the way she dressed in the morning, under the covers, reaching to the bureau with a lithe, bare arm; to the way she and his sister sometimes talked to each other through the door. He was more or less used to saying *wife*, to being called *husband*, whatever that meant. He was even used to sex, which he no longer wanted twice a day. Once was enough; already the fumbling had become memory. An ease had set in. He'd cross to her bed; a touch, and she'd turn over. A few touches more; buttons; then quiet, quiet, listening to be sure they weren't waking his sister. It was easy. Quiet. Quiet.

But Helen never said anything, or even seemed about to make a noise. She was so quiet he worried, not just in bed together, but all night, in their own beds, like this. Was there something the matter with her? She hid things, he'd discovered — keys, batteries, letters. She kept magazines under her mattress. What else might she be keeping from him? Maybe an illness, he thought, listening hard. For she didn't just breathe; she inhaled, then stopped, then expelled the air in a little burst. Squinting up at the ring-stained ceiling, he tried to make the sound she was making. A slight popping, as if she had been holding her breath. Or as if there were some obstruction . . . where? In her chest? No, in her throat. Right at the base of his own throat he thought he could feel a little door that might stick. He envisioned visits to the doctor. Cancer. An operation. Where would she want to be buried? He didn't even know. Or worse, he pictured a wife with no throat. How would she breathe? How would she eat? He swallowed. Would he have married her if he had known this would happen? And should he have married her if he wouldn't have?

He wished there were someone to ask, someone who could tell him how much love was the proper amount for a pair of newlyweds, how enthusiastic they should feel about their new duties and responsibilities, where they fell in the spectrum of human attachments. Did they talk to each other more than average? Less? Did they kiss enough? Fight too much? What mattered? He wished he were in China, where if there turned out to be something wrong with the marriage he could always take a concubine. That was a better system, he thought, more sure. Although now that he was thinking about it, he wondered if he would even know if something were wrong. For this was the odd thing — all his life, he'd known he would get married, and yet he'd never stopped to consider what it would be like once he was. Marriage, as he'd thought of it, was the end of a story, much like a Ph.D., except that the marriage story was shorter, and less work. Not that life wouldn't take up again, but it'd be in other realms. At home, the husband would command, the wife obey. They would find harmony under their pillows the way that children, New Year's morning, found chestnuts.

So he'd thought. But instead here he was, listening. Now she half turned, so that she faced away from him. He couldn't hear her at all. Had she stopped breathing? He sat up a little. A truck hitting a pothole, rumbling on. A distant radio, a soprano, very faint. He worked his pajama top out from under his back.

Nothing. He stilled himself, lay himself out, patient as land;

until finally, like a wandering rain, it came to him, not the sound he awaited, but something else, a recognition — that what he wanted more than anything was to secure her. He did not want her to float away into history, into the times, an upswelling of the masses. He wanted her to be permanent, an edifice whose piles touched the heart of the earth.

Still nothing. He got out of bed and crossed the cold aisle to hers, shivering. How attached he was already — it was frightening how attached — just to her sound and presence, to her simple animal company. To her ways of doing things — the way she rolled up the washcloths, the way she dusted with a feather duster. What a privilege it was to know another person's habits! To know when she set her hair. To know that she hid things. He wished she wouldn't hide things. But even so; yes, already he was attached. He could not imagine how he was going to feel in twenty years. And how about fifty? How was he going to let her walk around on the street then? He was going to want to keep her in a satin-lined box.

He fingered the hem of her pillowcase. The light in the room arced up to the ceiling, a half vault of stripes, below which he could almost make out the rise and fall of her body. Still he warmed his hands in his armpits; then gently picked up her head. It was heavy in his hands, and harder to grip than he'd expected — her hair. One of his thumbs slipped into the hollow of her ear. Yet he managed to turn her face back toward him. Ahh; her breathing again; better. She yawned, seemed to stir.

Had he awakened her? He froze, hunched over, listening.

Was she settling down?

He would count to ten, then move, he decided. One, he started, two.

But when eleven came he was still poised, waiting — holding his breath when she did, letting it go as she let hers.

With morning, though, once more came day. Ralph asked if Helen had something to tell him; and when it turned out that there was nothing wrong (or nothing, at least, that she would admit), childish love turned into adolescent embarrassment turned into manly tyranny.

"*This way,*" Ralph demonstrated, inhaling, exhaling. "*Even. Do you see? You should breathe this way.*"

Helen mimicked him, timidly. "*That one right?*"

"*Right,*" pronounced Ralph. "*Again.*"

Helen did it again.

"*Again,*" he commanded. "*Again.*"

Helen thought a moment, then experimentally let her breath catch.

"*No,*" said Ralph. "*That wasn't right.*"

"*Show me once more?*" She tilted her head, and was pleased to see the pleasure with which Ralph authoritatively obliged.

So it went, back and forth, Ralph playing at husband, Helen at wife.

Later, the game over, Ralph approached Helen as she chopped vegetables. He had in the meantime gone to school to meet with his new advisor, who was not Pinkus — he missed Pinkus, who was consulting full-time now — but Pierce, a Professor Rodney S. Pierce, who with his greased goatee looked more like an artisan than an engineer. A bird-boned, finicky man. Anyway, Ralph had gone to meet with him, as he was supposed to, and had walked back, and now was supposed to be studying. And he would be, if Pierce's voice were not roaring in his ears. The ocean in a seashell. "Detail, Mr. Chang." So now what was he going to do? "It's a matter, shall we say, of inclination." Inclination. "There are engineers and there are engineers. I wouldn't presume to predict. But I should tell you. A favor, believe me. Nothing you don't realize yourself."

Nothing he didn't realize himself. This was, consequently, his fourth trip to the kitchen in an hour. The first trip he had tasted the soup; the second, he had asked Helen to make him a cup of tea; the last, he had had more soup. "*Needs salt,*" he had said then. To this she'd answered affectionately, as she tasted it herself, "*What do you know?*" She'd called him a *fan tong,* just what his father used to say. Of course, she was teasing. She wasn't a big teaser, but sometimes she did tease, and then she called it "ribbing." An odd word; sometimes he wondered whether she kept words like that among the other secrets of her drawers. Anyway, this time she had her chin stuck out over the sink in case she dripped as she ribbed, and when he'd tickled her Adam's apple, she'd laughed, which gladdened him.

But now, as he stood in the doorway again, homing to her presence, he thought he saw her shoulders rise with apprehension, her elbows draw in. *"No more, no more,"* she said without turning around, or at least that's what he thought she said; and when he came in anyway, she said, *"More soup?"*

He shook his head and simply stood, wanting to tickle her Adam's apple again but not knowing how to get to that. There was a way, he knew, but he knew it the way he knew that boat captains could navigate by the stars. He gazed up at the fluorescent circle blinking overhead. Unfathomable. *"Sure,"* he said, after a moment. *"Soup."*

She ladled him some.

"Needs salt." He smiled.

But this time she didn't call him a *fan tong*. Instead she said okay, in English, patiently, and reached for the salt shaker. She was going to add salt. What wasn't proper? Still, as he watched her salt with one hand, scratch the side of her nose with the other, he felt himself to be, not the head of the family, a scholar, but a child on a high wooden stool, helpless, bright air all around him. He heard a patient voice. *Your father will beat me too.*

The room resounded with patience.

"Not right."

"Not right?"

He heard himself talking. *"Your breathing."*

Their marriage so young, yet already it was easier to say what they'd said before. *"Show me again,"* she said. No tilt of her head. He demonstrated. She imitated him perfectly, chopping carrots.

"What's so interesting about those carrots?"

"Not right?" Still chopping.

"You didn't even look."

She watched.

"Good," he said then. *"I want you to breathe that way all the time."*

She agreed. But ten minutes later, he caught her holding her breath again.

"You were listening?" asked Helen. *"From around the corner?"*

He nodded, barely.

"Is there something wrong?"

"You hide things," he said.

"Hide what?"

"Everything. There are things you don't tell me."

She scraped a ragged peel off a turnip.

"Say something. I want you to say something."

She thought. *"Would you like some soup?"*

"No."

"Would you like some tea?"

"No."

"Would you like some —"

"No!" he yelled, and left.

What kind of love was theirs, that it brought strife instead of peace? They fought again a few days later, and then again the next week, and then again and again, until they were practiced at it — until it had become the kernel of their married life, the form of intimacy they knew best. Sad refinements: Ralph knocked at Helen's skull. *"Nothing to say? Anybody there? Come on, open up."* Knocking made Ralph feel fierce, but it made Helen go blank — which made him knock more, and command her to breathe, and accuse her of holding her breath on purpose (which she wasn't, really, she wasn't, she wasn't) until she ran away into another room. Sometimes she would blockade the door; he would bang and bang, unable to stop himself. He had never dreamed a person could be so powerless in his power. But there he'd be, yelling, *"I'm the father of this family! Do you hear me? The father, not the son!"* She would start crying. Then usually he would back off, apologetic and tender. These were some of the most passionate moments of their lives together, the most searingly entwined. How central Helen felt then, how naturally indispensable!

As opposed to the hours and hours she seemed to stand outside of something deeper than mere marriage. Was it natural or unnatural? Helen didn't know, and tried not to be jealous, but she couldn't help but notice how Ralph hung on to Theresa's every word these days, even if what she had to say didn't particularly interest him. *"We're wrong to say typical American,"* for example. That was a new theme with Theresa. Over and over she explained that Pete was just a person, like them, that Boyboy was just a dog. *"Really?"* Ralph had no idea what she meant, but he listened as though trying to discover his essential human worth. He cocked his head. He beetled his brow. Once he even cleaned out his ears with his pinkies, as if what stood between him and some more vital, degree-holding self was wax.

What could Helen do but place her hopes in time?

A

CHILL

YET, when in time, Ralph's love for his sister took another turn too, Helen found herself half-glad at best.

March was on them like a bully then, raining and blowing between bouts of snow, and sleet, and hail; and indoors things were no better than out. Ralph's work dipped and peaked with the barometer. Some days he stayed home. He began to complain about Theresa, who was studying for medical school. How *nuli*, he observed — how diligent. He began to call her Know-It-All again, first behind her back, then to her face. It was as if their past, in the eternal way of pasts, had been shipped after them by sea mail — arriving in spectacular condition just when they'd forgotten it entirely.

"*Pressure*," was all Theresa would say. "*The pressure is too much for all of us.*"

Helen watched the roof leak. During the worst squall, she had counted thirteen containers scattered around the apartment, each with its own rhythm and pitch. Some pingged; some plopped; others plisshed, or splashed. She was waiting for the ceiling to come down. Once she'd even climbed through the trap door onto the roof, to have a look around.

"You went up the trap door?" Ralph said.

"It was nothing, really. You should try it," she said, nonchalant, though in one way, she was taken aback too. How much, how fast she was changing! There was at least that much to be happy about, she supposed. The same girl who had never so much as drawn her own bath was now sprouting mung beans in jars with holes punched in their screw lids. It was as if, once she'd resigned herself to her new world, something had taken her over — a drive to make it hers. She made her own Chinese pancakes now. She made her own red bean paste, boiling and mashing and frying the beans, then using them to fill buns, which she made also. She made curtains; she made bedspreads; she rewired Ralph's old lamp. She couldn't help but feel proud. Too proud, really — she tried to bind that feeling up — recognizing still, though, that in her own way she was becoming private strength itself. She was the hidden double stitching that kept armholes from tearing out. And all because she'd discovered, by herself, a secret — that working was enjoyable. Effort, result. Twist, the cap comes off. Water, the plant grows. Having never done things before, she was entranced by these small satisfactions; she was astounded when, pausing at the sink, a door of sun opening and shutting on her wrist, she realized — yes. Just now, waiting for her bucket to fill, she felt strong. Just this moment, plotting how not to leave footprints on her clean floor, she was at peace.

Of course, it was still important that her hands be too delicate to wield the mop, or the rust-spotted butcher's cleaver. Once, in an effusion of sympathy, a strange American woman had squeezed Helen's hand (typical American no-manners); the American had wondered then at how soft and smooth Helen's skin was. "Really?" said Helen. But actually, she knew it. She knew how tiny she was too, how unmuscled in the arms; she appreciated, as if in a mirror, that she was amazing. And that mattered, the way it mattered that she be busy but not busy at the same time — that, while competent, she be a Chinese girl. Theresa's work might be her life. One part of Helen, though, still lounged in her pink-piped pajamas, under a shimmering silk comforter, clapping while her brother performed magic tricks. Scarves out of his shoe! And how did he know she was holding the ace? Later he had showed her how it all worked, the secret marks and folds, the way he distracted her eye. *Standard stuff*, he shrugged, in his brotherly way. He flared his nostrils at her, a sign of affection. *Anybody could do it.*

Now there was no one to show her anything anymore; the tricks, in her dimming memory, glowed with magic again, like an old mirror resilvered by candlelight. After work, though, still came what she thought of as "doing nothing," a proper Shanghainese-girl activity. Without Theresa and Ralph knowing, she spent large parts of her afternoons listening to the radio, or reading the magazines she kept under her mattress. She loved the advertisements especially, so gorgeously puzzling. Which part of the picture was the "velvet"? Which the "portrait neckline"? Also she liked the insights into American home life — the revelation that most Americans showered every day, first thing in the morning, for example. (This amazed Helen, who took occasional baths, in the evening.) Sometimes she talked on the phone to friends from the English language school. Juliet Shon and Pauline Hu, every now and then. More often, Janis Chao. These were the hours in which she sang a little; breathed however she wanted; and simply kept quiet — more important now than ever, as she had a hunch she might be pregnant. It was only a tingling in her breasts so far, an odd pressure that might almost be a mood; still, if her mother were here, Helen knew, she'd be telling her at every minute to *man man zou* — go slow, take care. A calm mother, she'd be saying, makes for a calm and happy child.

Who could take it easy with Ralph home, though? He was elated when she told him the news, but for the most part slept on the couch like an oversized roll pillow. Everything he took badly.

One day Theresa heard that the super's dog had been sent to the veterinarian, something serious. Then, the next day, more — Pete had had Boyboy put to sleep. *"Cancer,"* Theresa said.

"Asleep?" Ralph said. So much fun he'd made of the dog; still, now he turned mournful. *"Boyboy? A dog can get cancer?"*

There was nothing anyone could do, explained Theresa.

Ting bu jian — Ralph did not hear her. *"You're glad,"* he accused, as though, bearing the news, Theresa had something to do with it.

"I am not glad," she said.

Not too long after that, she came upstairs waving a letter. It was only a state school, but she'd gotten money too, a scholarship.

"You are glad," insisted Ralph. He moved from the couch to his bed.

Now the radiators clanked extra-loud, several times — so loud, they woke Ralph up. Something the matter?

"Nothing," Helen answered.

That was wrong. At first it wasn't noticeable. Then, by morning, it was.

"It's cold in here," said Ralph.

When Helen and Theresa went down to Pete's office to complain, they found it deserted, and his desk tipped over. Several of its drawers were gone; gray and pink gum wads barnacled the underside of the kneehole. The office window had been smashed.

Theresa shook her head. *"Who knows what happened."* She righted the desk.

"Left?" said Ralph, upstairs. *"Pete? No heat?"*

It wasn't so bad. They put on extra sweaters, feeling hardy. Typical American unreliable! They agreed Pete would come back. Or else the owner would come. For the rent, they agreed. That was in two weeks. If they knew the owner, they would call him, but they didn't. They asked around. Did anyone know him? But the only person anyone knew was Pete.

Day three. Ralph opened the windows. It was colder inside than out, he maintained. The curtains, usually limp, furled and billowed, magnificent with life.

"The rain's coming in," observed Theresa.

"How stupid of me not to have noticed," said Ralph.

Day four. Still no super, still no owner. Ralph doubled up his blankets and slept to one side of the bed.

Helen pulled Theresa into the hall closet. *"What should we do?"* Theresa blinked in the green darkness. What are we doing here among the hangers? she wanted to know; but instead, responded carefully — *"Whatever we can"* — and when Helen didn't say what that was, thought hard. Her relationship with Helen had always depended on silence. Restraint. Only now did she appreciate how much it depended on sight as well. How else, after all, to know how to read those silences? For instance, this one, now, coalescing in the air like a queer humidity. She considered, trying to ignore the jangling hangers, with their cold, quick touch. Then, experimentally, she said, *"You know, I've been thinking of getting married."*

"Really!" said Helen. Her voice burst with surprise. All the same, it was a response; Theresa sensed herself on the right track.

"Do you think that will make a difference?"

Helen couldn't help but agree.

Later, though, Helen clopped down to the basement in wonder. All she'd wanted had been for them to throw up their hands together. At Ralph; at the cold; at the rain. It had been a feeling she'd been after, a convivial solidarity; she'd hoped to murmur to one another, as if sitting at the edge of one of their beds. But instead look what had happened. She gripped her flashlight tightly, fitting her fingers to its ribs, though in fact she didn't need it at all. The basement, it turned out, had a light switch. And what lights! A paradise of bulbs. Flames and rods and tubes and circles, not to say ordinary bulbous bulbs of every size and wattage and color, dangled like fruit from an ecstatic entanglement of wire vines. Helen was transfixed. There were no shadows in the room. She blinked. What else didn't they know about Pete? Had they in fact known anything at all? And how warm it was here! She could feel the heat of the lights on her face as she continued down. She unbuttoned her coat a little, squinting. Her eyes watered. She shaded them with her hand, turned, glanced back up. Was there a way to shut some of the lights off?

Just the one switch.

Down some more. The wooden steps were bouncy, with a loose railing to one side. Careful, the baby. A few steps more. She was relieved to feel the hard concrete floor through her slippers. The boiler was straight ahead, a giant, white, curvaceous beast, with a rough asbestos hide. She circled it, feeling as though she were in a movie. A what — a Western. She tried to focus. Gauges, with spindly needles all at zero. And, on the beast's belly, a door. Bold, she unlatched it. Leapt back. No flames. She leaned in a little, careful. Nothing, just a cavernous bowl. Dark. She clanked the door shut, circled again, more surely this time. On top of the furnace, a pile of paper plates, some with scallop-edged pizza crusts. And attached to a pipe with a bit of shoelace tied to a piece of wire tied to a length of string — a grimy, coffee-splashed booklet, its edges soft with age. In English, naturally: OWNER'S INFORMATION MANUAL — SERIES 200 OIL BOILERS — RETAIN THESE INSTRUCTIONS FOR FUTURE REFERENCE.

She read.

Ralph was dreaming hard. He wanted to sit up, but could not sit up. He wanted to move, but could not move. It was as if the gravitational pull of the earth had been multiplied; or as if he lay on the bottom of the ocean, all the massive waves weighing on him. He kicked off his covers. Too warm. Back to sleep. Then, awake. Warm?

"Is the heat back on?"

Helen nodded.

"*Heat,*" marvelled Ralph. He reached out, questioned the radiator with his hand. "*Is Pete back?*"

"*Not yet,*" said Helen.

"*We have heat.*" He wiggled his toes. "*Heat.*"

A miracle!

"*How did you do it?*" Theresa wanted to know.

Helen haltingly described how big the boiler was, how intimidating. How she found the instruction manual. How complicated it was. How many terms she didn't understand. She savored the details.

"*You fixed it?*"

"*Then I called the phone number at the back,*" finished Helen. "*There's an oil tank under the ground that needs filling every so often.*"

"*Really!*"

"*Pete has an account to pay for it.*"

Theresa shook her head. "*That was pretty smart,*" she said.

Helen modestly declined the compliment. Still Theresa mused all night, and the next day too. She'd always respected Helen, but she had never felt the kind of overwhelming admiration for her that she did now. What different kinds of intelligence there were in the world! Who was to say which mattered most? One couldn't say, couldn't begin to say, although this much was certain — what mattered in China was not necessarily what mattered here.

The third day, she came home resolved. In front of the apartment door she dabbed at her eyes with an onion peel, then entered in tears.

"*What's the matter?*" Helen asked. "*Sit down.*"

Theresa balled up her handkerchief. "*My scholarship has been cancelled,*" she lied.

"*Cancelled?*" said Ralph.

"*Cancelled!*"

"*Impossible,*" Ralph sat up. "*How can it be!*"

"*It does seem impossible, right?*"

"*Unfair!*"

"*That's what I said. It's horribly unfair.*"

Helen made tea and filled a hot-water bottle for Theresa. Everyone went to bed early.

But Ralph lay awake in the dark, wide-eyed. "*I can't sleep,*" he told Helen.

"*Really.*"

"*Maybe I've been sleeping too much,*" he said. "*I'm tired of sleeping.*"

"*So get up,*" she said.

PLANS
FOR THERESA

"*HE'S STUDYING AGAIN,*" Helen reported the next day, on the phone to Janis Chao. "*Everything's okay.*"

"*It's about time.*"

Janis Chao was exactly the sort of person Helen would probably never have known in China. Not that her background was so bad, but her father had died when she was young, so that her mother had had to support the family by selling jewelry; if some rich woman had a few pieces she'd tired of, Janis's mother would show them around to other women, on consignment. This hardly made her a peddlar. Her daughter, Janis, though, grew up seeing more of Chinese society than a nice girl should. She knew where the boundaries lay; she knew that social reality was not reality at all, but so many rules people could not imagine breaking. Helen at first hadn't quite trusted her. In America, Janis was the class organizer — friends with everyone, especially people who once would've looked down on her. *The type of person who, when a wall is falling, comes to help push,* someone said. But was that true? Janis wore no jewelry at all, ever; a sign of some sort, Helen thought. And when Helen quit school (after filing for permanent residency under the Displaced Persons Act), she was disarmed by Janis's efforts to stay in touch. Weren't they genuine? Janis was so easy to talk to, having so much to say herself; any awkwardness she smoothed over with accounts of all kinds of Chinese-student affairs. Picnics, dances. She invited Helen and Ralph to everything. *"You should go out more, see more friends,"* she said. *"Don't lock yourself up in the house."*

They never went. Helen wasn't sure exactly why; it had something to do with the fact that Janis's husband had not only been sponsored by the Chinese government to come to the United States, but was almost done with his Ph.D. already. *"A record,"* ventured Helen.

"Hmm," said Ralph.

"If he's done by next September that'll be only five years. Including his master's! Of course, he was able to transfer a lot of credits from China."

"Hmm," said Ralph again.

"Janis says you and her husband are old friends. Classmates."

"Really?" Ralph scratched his head. *"What's his name again? Henry Chao?"*

Did that mean Helen shouldn't be too friendly with Janis? Helen didn't know — which was to say that Ralph was aware that they were in touch, but not that they chatted some three or four times a week, nor that she had visited Janis's place, and that Janis had visited hers. No husbands involved, Janis had said, proffering the idea as though it were an hors d'oeuvre. And Helen had agreed, reluctant but excited — it would almost have been rude to refuse — though a part of her wondered if Janis's husband did know, not only about their visits, but about everything she told Janis. Her throat dried to think that she might have revealed things about her husband to another man.

Yet such was the pleasure of confiding, of sharing the daily stuff of her existence — it made her feel somehow accompanied in life — that for the most part she relegated Henry Chao to a kind of netherworld, in which he was not so much a person and potential threat as a spirit that could be scared off by a good loud noise. This was especially easy on the telephone. On the telephone, even Janis sported a flickering reality. And when, after all, would Henry and Ralph ever meet? In China, Helen had been taught enormous circumspection; the world there was like a skating rink, a finite space, walled. Words inevitably rebounded. Here the world was enormous, all endless horizon; her words arced and disappeared as though into a wind-chopped ocean.

A relief. *"The only thing I worry about is, what if he finds out that Theresa's scholarship wasn't cancelled,"* said Helen. *"Of course, maybe he won't."*

Clinks. Helen could hear Janis washing dishes in the background. *"You know what they say,"* Janis said finally. *"Not even an earthworm can stay in the ground forever."* A few clinks more. *"Your sister-in-law should get married before he finds out."*

"She knows it herself."

"Does she?" Janis stopped doing the dishes.

"She said so the other day. That she should get married, I mean." Helen hesitated. Her words did not meet her understanding.

But there was no chance to find better words. *"I know just the person,"* said Janis.

Was Theresa ready to look? Too polite to object, Helen found herself listening. In China, friends were always *arranging things* for each other; Janis's reaction felt familiar, a form of goodwill Helen knew how to accept. A friend of Henry's, Janis said. A Ph.D. *"But, well, he was born here,"* she finished.

"Born here?"

"Well, I should say he's completely American," said Janis.

"You mean . . ."

"Well," said Janis. *"He loves Chinese food."*

"A foreign devil?" said Helen. *"A long nose?"*

That was the end of the matter.

Or so it seemed. A few days later, another candidate surfaced. Born in China. Barely tall enough, and not much hair, some of it white, but he spoke Shanghainese and had a Ph.D.

"*I don't know,*" said Helen at first. Janis asked so many questions that Helen couldn't answer, though — wasn't it natural for women to marry? what could it hurt to ask? — that in the evening, she mentioned the man to Theresa, casually.

"*A friend of Janis Chao's?*" Theresa dropped her book to her lap.

"*He has a Ph.D. —*" started Helen.

"*You told Janis Chao?*"

Helen's mind flooded then with questions of her own. How could she have embarrassed her sister-in-law that way? Who was she becoming? She did not raise the subject again.

And so it was that by the time *arranging an introduction* came up once more — Theresa broached it this time — the old Shanghainese with a Ph.D. was taken.

Janis had just one last bachelor in stock, her landlord. Short. No Ph.D. "*American born,*" she told Helen. "*Owns lots of property besides our building, and does other business too.*"

"*Is he Cantonese?*" Helen didn't want to sound prejudiced, but at the very least, his dialect was a consideration. "*What does he speak?*"

"*English,*" said Janis. "*This is America. His family has been here for so many generations, I don't think he even knows what province he's from. And what does it matter anymore? He's rich. You should see the shirts he wears! All nice and starched. His shoes shine like mirrors. And he has a maid, this one. Think of it — no housework!*"

A short, American-born, English-speaking businessman with no degree — for Theresa? It was a joke; but in the end, dinner was arranged, for fun.

THE
IMAGINEER

HOW TO CONVINCE Ralph to come along? Helen considered her approach, her tone, her timing, only to discover it all (like so many things, too many things) wasted on him. *"Supper? At Old Chao's house? Sure,"* he said, blithe as a new frog. So what if last week he'd been a tadpole? He was changed.

Could she have known that?

The earth by then had revolved and rotated, at its certain speed, its certain angle; it had kept to its course; and as a result, the world that had been mud, now was sun, forsythia, daffodils, and flowering quince. Still, Ralph considered his rise from the couch a separate miracle, his own. Lightly hitched to society, he imagined himself bound to grander forces. He construed his deliverance from the park to have to do with the heat coming up, and that to have to do with the cancelling of Theresa's scholarship, which he now chided himself for having celebrated. These days, he almost wished Know-It-All success in her work — no, did wish it. The world was giving to him, he did not mind giving back. Most recently, for instance, Professor Pierce had given him, of all things, a book. Ralph had risen from the couch, and three days later, a divine gift.

Not that he'd recognized its divinity at first — not in this flat rectangle wrapped in checkerboard paper; its attached clump of gray ribbon curlicues looked like the head of a mop. "You might open it," Pierce suggested. Ralph had ripped, smiling warily. *The Power of Positive Thinking.* "Ah," said Ralph.

"I had hoped to get hold of the young people's edition." Pierce's goatee wagged. "Thinking, you know, the English. However, it was out of stock, so you have in your hands the genuine article."

"Ah."

"My wife's suggestion. I've been plagued over the years with headaches, you know. Not that it should concern you. But when they made their return — this is about the time you reappeared — she said — well."

Ralph read, an arduous process. He did not see ideas, but shapes that became letters that he sounded out into words he then had to look up. He'd decipher a phrase, read it over again, pocket it while he worked on the next, until a whole sentence, a whole page was his. His alone! Of course, the book was a best seller, as he knew from its jacket. But how many people knew the book by heart? As per the author's instructions, he'd written down a statement to carry in his wallet: "I can do all things through Christ which strengtheneth me." He could do anything! It was a matter of faith; and of imagination, a thing Ralph had never considered before. A matter of "imagineering." He needed to picture — with faith, with all his heart — his ideal. For a man was what he made up his mind to be. Which was what? Surprisingly, Ralph wasn't sure. An engineer, certainly. A powerful man. Like his father, he thought one night. But the next morning, in church (which he occasionally attended with Theresa, though he'd never converted), he stared up into the multicolored air, and knew: he wanted to be like that man-god. More realistically, he pictured a kind of assistant to the man-god, say a half step up from an apostle. He pictured himself able to do what he would.

And to an amazing extent, his imagineering worked. No bread and fish, but he noticed that his bit of athlete's foot had gone away; that he thought more clearly; that he could will certain foods to appear in the icebox. He willed Professor Pierce to go on vacation, and he started making plans. A fellow grad student, Pierce's favorite, dropped out without warning, improving Ralph's prospects.

So it was that when Helen broached the subject of going to Janis's for supper (his older sister, marriage, their obligation and so on), he thought, Old Chao's house? Sure!

The day of the dinner, though, he got stung by a bee. Walking down the street, minding his own business, he stopped to retie a shoelace and got stung, right between the eyes. How was it possible? He was an imagineer! Yet when he held his hand to his face, the skin was pounding hot. He could hardly see. His whole brow was swelling as though with a third eye.

LOVE
AT FIRST SIGHT

AZALEAS. Ralph blinked gingerly as they walked. The bee sting was still swollen, so he could not properly appreciate how beautiful his sister looked with her hair out of its bun, though Helen told him. "*Softer, don't you think?*"

Theresa's hair fell from her navy blue hat sleekly to her shoulder, then mostly curled under, except for one section on the right side, which presented passersby with a little bristle bouquet. Luckily, Theresa was oblivious to the offering. She walked carefully, swishing her stockings. Against her better judgment, she'd bought a new pair of vermilion high heels, the voluptuously curvy kind; not that she had her hopes up. But the day before, on the way home from class, these shoes had snagged her — so vital, there in the store window, that they did not look like shoes so much as some highly adapted life form, mimicking shoes the way lizards mimicked desert rocks. Whereas the shoes she'd had on were plainly the real thing: worn out, dried up, cracking. Like their owner — her reflection in the window was spindly and stiff, separated just this way, by a pane of glass, from some more vibrant world. At the center of her image, the red shoes had seemed to pulse, like her own true heart.

Now she regretted buying them. In the store, they had appeared glowing but dignified. With her blue-black *qi-pao*, they bordered on desperate pink. Good thing she didn't care what this short businessman thought. Though why *had* she gotten high heels?

She tottered.

Yellow-brick cube with modern sliding windows. Inside, the lobby was quiet; it was Sunday, they were eating at three o'clock, American-style. A novelty. Steel elevator, automatic.

"Welcome! Come in!" Janis, pregnant, waved from her doorway. In a fit of daring, she had had her hair cut short and curled all over in the latest style — the poodle, this was called. To go with it she wore a turquoise-and-gray-striped apron and matching backless slippers. A large shadow appeared behind her.

"Old Chao." Ralph tried to sound hearty and enthusiastic, but his voice struggled from him like a half-drowned river rat.

Old Chao's sallied forth like a navy. *"Little Chang!"*

Old times. Old Chao seemed genuinely delighted to see him. This made Ralph feel all the worse. How Old Chao towered still! Inescapable. His hair seemed longer than Ralph remembered, almost wayward; his eyebrows darker and shaggier. But, as of old, his smooth face fairly shone with affable ease. Even as they stood there, Ralph suspected him of secretly prospering.

"So long since we've seen each other," said Ralph.

"Too long, too long. Come in! Ah yes! And this, if I'm not mistaken, is your Older Sister."

"How did you know?"

"When I was looking for you," explained Theresa. *"Remember? We met then. He was very helpful."* She nodded and smiled.

"That's right, you should thank me," joked Old Chao. *"If it weren't for me and your Older Sister, you'd probably have landed up a beggar."*

"Ah," said Ralph.

"*Well, maybe not a beggar,*" put in Helen, comfortingly.

"*That's right! How could you land up a beggar? Don't listen to him!*" Janis gestured with unusual vivacity. "*He thinks this is China! As if there are beggars here!*"

"*There are beggars here,*" said Old Chao.

"*Ah,*" said Ralph. "*Have you met my wife?*"

Janis nudged Old Chao. "*No, no, we've never met,*" he said then. "*Pleased to meet you!*" Helen blushed. Ralph appraised her with a sideways look. "*Come in, come in, come in!*" Old Chao went on. "*What happened to your face!*"

While Ralph explained about the bee, Theresa stationed herself on the far side of the triple-tiered hall table, so that her feet wouldn't show. Both watched Helen; with her hair drawn back into a low horsetail, she did look "darling," just as Janis was saying. In her best, rose-colored dress — this combined a mandarin collar with a circle skirt — she also looked perceptibly pregnant. Thickened, buxom. Who could believe, though, that in a few months she'd be like Janis, distinctly preceded wherever she went? Already they clasped their hands over their bellies in almost the same way; their heads tilted toward one another like two halves of a drawbridge.

They're old friends, Ralph realized. Good friends. She didn't tell me. He wished he hadn't come.

"Let me introduce —" Now Janis, in the living room, was speaking English.

Ralph had so forgotten the point of dinner that when the man stood — a handsome, burly, breezy man, about his height, with large teeth, one of them gold, and a powerful jaw — he, Ralph, stepped forward, as though to be presented.

Janis was thrown off. "Let me introduce . . . " she repeated. "This is, ah . . . ah —"

"Grover," offered the man, helpfully, flashing a smile. "Grover Ding." He wore a three-piece suit with a carnation on his lapel, and looked around at the company confidently, as if at friends. "So whose acquaintance do I have the honor of making here, eh?" He winked deliberately at Helen. "It is certainly a pleasure." With a bow, he extended his hand to her.

"Oh, nonono." She blushed, radiant. "Please to meet my sister-in-law."

Theresa lifted her head shyly.

Grover craned his solid neck up, then down. His hand curled like a cooked shrimp. "Nice shoes," he said finally.

"New ones," Helen volunteered.

"Very darling," said Janis.

"Darling," echoed Helen.

Theresa's collar tightened.

"Very darling, indeed," agreed Grover. He placed his hands in his pockets. Then he winked again, a gleam in his eye, at Helen.

Dinner was ten long courses. These Janis served one after another, banquet-style, more because she had only three working burners and two hands than for formal effect. "Shredded Beef with Peppers," she'd announce, forehead damp, or "Squid with Button Mushrooms." Everyone would exclaim; Theresa and Helen would stand, set aside their napkins, insist they were going to help — Janis was too pregnant to be doing this, really she was — only to have Janis describe how her kitchen was too small for one person, much less two or three. Sometimes this involved pushing her guests back into their chairs. "No, no, your job is eat," she'd say, disappearing again. "Do you know she's think maybe write a cookbook?" Helen asked once. Everyone agreed that Janis certainly could, or should, except Old Chao, who shook his head. "She just like to run after every crazy idea," he said. Everyone agreed with this too. A more politic subject was tried. Another, but over and over, with a collective sigh, the company was dragged back to its apparent fate, congratulating Old Chao on having received a tenure-track job offer just that afternoon.

"I think you heard more than enough on this particular subject," Old Chao kept saying. As indeed they all had. Anxious that they have some kind of conversation, though — it was a matter of face — Theresa especially responded with such keen interest that Old Chao had no choice as a host but to keep talking. He did try digressions — wondering if certain aches he'd been having might be arthritis, for example (Theresa assured him they were not) — but none of these proved sustainable. "And do you know, the department interviewed sixty people — that's six-oh, sixty — and by the end, only two people received so-called offer." This was after the soup, at the fourth course, Lion's Head. "Myself and one very smart guy, much smarter than me, I should say" — a wondering shake of the head here — "who got his doctorate from MIT."

"From MIT! Really!" chorused Helen and Theresa; and, faintly, Ralph. He couldn't eat.

Old Chao hesitated, apparently aware that he was displaying more self-satisfaction than was seemly. But as the silence mounted, he impulsively described another smart guy who didn't get an offer at all. "Can you believe it? Turned down, and he got his doctorate from CaliTech."

"From CaliTech! Ohh!"

Only Grover said nothing. Here everyone was, speaking English out of consideration for him, and he was too occupied to listen. He removed his jacket, chuckling to himself. He put it back on. He took it off again. He folded the napkin on his lap. He played with his chopsticks. He rotated his plate a quarter turn. Helen eyed him surreptitiously as she nodded in Old Chao's direction.

Theresa ignored him. As it was, she could feel her curls unceremoniously uncurling; she forced herself to converse, that she might not see herself in a small, strange room, ever shrinking with shame, far away from everyone else. Lucky thing there was Old Chao — stretching on like taffy, but in an effort to save her, it seemed. And the way he inclined his head her way, pressing his chest to the table edge — wasn't he behaving politely?

As opposed to Ralph, who, head tilted, mouth slack, looked for all the world like someone in love. Theresa saw it; anyone could have seen it. Especially when Grover, whistling, stood to leave the table. What Ralph would have done then to leave with him — good-by, Old Chao and his tenure-track job offer! Good-by, social nicety! Ralph could only ogle, though, helpless with envy, as Grover balled up his napkin. He did not push his chair in, but left it angled out like a door in midswing.

Janis came out with Strange-Flavored Chicken.

By Ants Climbing Trees, Grover hadn't returned. His jacket hung on his chair back; his napkin uncrumpled slowly beside his plate, blooming like something out of a time-lapse photography sequence. All the same, Old Chao spoke in English, as though Grover hadn't left.

"Of course, for the back and forth, I had to buy a new car," he said. "You remember the old one, I won it in the church lottery?"

"Sure!"

"Well, now I trade it in for a new one."

Shrimp in Hot Sauce. Still no Grover, but they knew that the car was a barely used 1950 Chevy Bel Air DeLuxe, buttercream yellow. It had a full chrome grille, whitewalls, mud flaps, a push-button radio, the new stove bolt six engine, and a black convertible top that worked like a dream. It did not have Powerglide automatic transmission; Old Chao had had to settle for manual. He reported that Janis was begging to learn to drive too, which he opposed. "She run around too much already."

By dish ten, a steamed fish, everyone was groaning. "Too much, too much." Janis took her apron off. "Maybe I should . . . ?"

Grover was in neither the living room nor the bathroom, but in the bedroom. Janis knocked. Her guest emerged, coolly explaining that he had needed to make a few phone calls.

In the dining room, he pulled his chair close to the table. "I do appreciate your saving me some of your, ah, *old chow*." He grinned significantly at his host. Janis spooned some food onto his plate. "Good shrimp." He tried another dish. "Good pork." No one else said anything. "Did I interrupt the conversation?" Looking around, he winked at Helen, rakish; and when this time she stared stonily down at her near-empty plate, he simply turned and winked once more, at Ralph.

GROVER
AT THE WHEEL

IT NOW seemed that they were going to have dinner all over again. Grover began to eat desultorily, and as Janis hadn't had anything yet either, everyone else nibbled to keep them company. The dishes had all gone cold. Strikingly, Grover did not fidget at all; what was more, he participated in the conversation with as much alacrity as he had formerly shut it out. Would Old Chao consider giving them the lowdown on his new job? Grover said he knew how reluctant Old Chao was to talk about himself. But was it true that one of the candidates turned down had gone to (he gasped) *Cal Tech?*

And what about the other guy who'd gotten an offer? Hadn't *he* gone to M (Grover breathed) *I* (he breathed again) *T?*

Old Chao answered from between clenched teeth.

"We-ell," said Helen finally. "I've had enough." She gave Janis a look. "Such a delicious food."

Janis pushed her chair back, about to stand up. "Everyone finished now?"

"And did I hear you bought yourself a new car?" Grover lit a cigarette.

Silence. "Yes," Old Chao said. "That's right."

"Well, I'll be damned." Grover blew a smoke ring. "What kind?"

At length it was determined that the men should go out and see the car in person. Janis tendered the suggestion; the relief was almost audible.

"And what will you girls do?"

"Oh," said Janis, "talk girl talk. Be down in a couple minutes."

Neither Ralph nor Old Chao nor Grover said anything in the elevator. Outside, though, they began to talk a little. The weather, the traffic. It had just rained. The sewer drains thundered liltingly; the streets shone like glazed candy. And before them, now — the car. A long, curvy, ample machine, it sported some chrome — a front grille like a bulldog's jaw, a back bumper. But mostly it was a heartwarmingly plain, sincere machine, promising good fun and few breakdowns; the sort of car that, especially in soft yellow, looked like nothing so much as a bar of soap.

Grover patted it as though it were a racehorse. "She's some gal," he said, between pats. His diamond ring clanked enthusiastically. Old Chao watched nervously, and when Grover turned, inspected the metal for scratches.

"Beautiful!" Ralph touched the car with one respectful finger.

"How's the top work?" Grover asked. "Can we get a look?"

Old Chao started to say no, something about how he didn't like to fold it up when it was wet, but Grover started to clank some more.

"Well, okay." Old Chao unlocked the door in order to demonstrate how the roof unlatched, how it accordioned. The snaps that held it in place, the cover that fastened over that. "What you think?"

Ralph and Grover oohed.

"You see this?" Old Chao showed them the spare tire, which rode in its own metal case on the rear bumper. Ralph and Grover ahhed. "You want to sit inside?" Opening the door, Old Chao seemed to have forgotten his irritation.

Grover settled into the driver's seat. Ralph sat beside him.

"How about the radio there?" asked Grover. "Does it work?"

"Sure." Old Chao reached back into his pocket for the keys. "You got to turn on the engine."

Ralph and Grover tested the radio, the windshield wipers, the lights.

"What an auto-mo-bile," said Grover. "You're one lucky guy."

"I guess I am," said Old Chao, a little surprised.

All three of them shook their heads a moment.

"How'd you get so lucky?" asked Grover. "You got a secret?"

"Oh, I don't know."

"Nothing you'd care to divulge, huh."

"I just work hard, you know."

The car hummed.

"I just do what people tell me, and don't ask so many questions." Old Chao said this pointedly; but then as if remembering himself, continued in a more amiable tone. "Maybe that's the trick. You know, American people, they always ask this, ask that. Not me."

"When people tell you to hop to it, you hop, hop, hop."

"That's right. That's the Chinese way. Polite." Something in Grover's tone seemed to have set Old Chao back on edge.

"When people ask a question, you answer. No fooling around."

"Right."

"Hmmm," said Grover. "How do you release this brake here?"

"Just pull on the handle." Old Chao answered civilly, modelling his manners.

Grover pulled.

"I wish I have car like this someday," said Ralph.

"And how do you drive?" asked Grover, hands on the wheel.

"First you put the car in gear," answered Old Chao. "Then you step on the pedal."

Grover put the car in gear, then stepped on the pedal.

"Hey! Stop!" called Old Chao as the car sped away. "Not funny! Hey! Not funny!"

By the time he'd started running, though, Grover and Ralph had already turned the corner; all he got for his efforts was the dwindling sound of the pair of them, laughing.

"Maybe we better go home," said Ralph, after a few minutes. Grover kept driving. "Where are we going?"

"Where do you want to go?"

"Home," said Ralph. He explained where he lived.

"You like it there?"

"Some things I like, some I don't." Ralph told Grover about Pete the super and Boyboy.

"Hmm," said Grover then, or at least that's what Ralph thought he said. He couldn't hear anymore. Since leaving the traffic on the George Washington Bridge they had sped up; now they were headed straight west, fast. Later Ralph was to notice how Grover loved motion in general and speed in particular — obliterating speeds; and how, just when the rest of the world packed its tools away, at twilight, he seemed to come most alive. He didn't ever seem to need to see better than he did.

For example, now. The sun was huge and low, directly ahead; it looked like a moongate leading to a fiery garden. Ralph put his visor down. "I can't see," he said. "Can you see?" Grover did not answer. How fast were they going? Ralph squinted, straining to see the speedometer. It seemed to say a hundred miles an hour. Surely not, he thought; though he could barely move, jacketed as he was to his seat by the wind. "We better go home," he tried to say again. "Where are we going?" And, "I'm cold." But he could not force his words into the air — *shuo bu chu lai*, literally. He was captive. What could he do but watch Grover drive? Ahead, the moongate stretched wide, just as a cloud cover lowered itself out of nowhere. Lower, lower. It hovered above them like an attic ceiling. The town ahead, squashed, became all broad, bright horizon; and when the clouds went gold, it seemed to Ralph that the buildings kindled violently. Such live reds and oranges! And now, as though on cue, it all turned — in an instant — to writhing cinder. Ralph felt smoldery himself. Yet Grover drove through the whole grand catastrophe undistracted, as though the torching of a place simply did not matter to him, or as though it were no more than some histrionics he'd ordered up. Background, say, for some larger drama.

Ralph watched him closely. Before this, he'd known only two kinds of drivers — the kind who hunched up, both arms bent, pulling on the wheel as though to keep it from retracting into the dashboard; and the kind who sat so far back that in order to drape one casual wrist over the top of the wheel, they had to stiffen their elbows and curve their spines. Grover was neither. He was, rather, a natural driver, for whom the wheel seemed a logical extension of his hands. Anyone would have thought he'd invented the automobile. For how else could it be that he never had to slow down or speed up? He did not move and consider, move and consider, like other drivers, but only moved. As the cinder town began to deepen, cooling to mere scarlet, Ralph began to discern the familiar road again — to reassure himself that they were indeed on an ordinary highway with other cars. It had seemed that they were hurtling down a straight line; actually, though, they were snaking their way through traffic. He began to see that Grover was directing the slither — not by craning his neck and putting on his blinker and swearing, but simply by glancing, passing, glancing, passing.

Then night, the quick pour of roofing tar that changed everything. Still they drove. Ralph marvelled as the stars came out; the car moved so fast, yet they stayed so still. And how many of them there were! He'd never seen so many, he'd never seen such an enormous sky. "What do you say? Don't see stars like that in the city, now do you." Grover was speaking. Ralph was surprised how easy it was to hear him. "If you don't get out for a spin every now and then, you forget all about them. And will you look at those trees." They were driving through forest. "Look like leaves and branches, right? But every one of them is an opportunity. You just have to see it." He nodded to himself. Ralph nodded too. And one truth, he found, led to another: "I'm hungry." He had hardly eaten anything at Old Chao's.

"Me too!" Grover boomed his agreement, a buddy and friend. "Ravenous!"

They pulled so smoothly into the diner parking lot that Ralph took a moment to realize they'd stopped. The lot was empty except for one other car.

In the diner they slid into a green vinyl booth. There were no other customers. "Have what you want," Grover said. "Whatever strikes your fancy."

"Anything?"

"You like to eat," he said sagely. "I can tell."

A freshly painted sign over the counter put closing time at nine-thirty; the clock next to it read nine-twenty-five. Still, the waitress took their order as though she'd be more than glad to stay as long as they liked. Would they like breakfast, lunch, or dinner?

They had dinner, then lunch, then breakfast.

"My treat," Grover kept saying. "It's on me."

Ralph politely began with a hamburger, plain.

"Nothing to drink?"

Ralph shook his head no.

His hamburger arrived. Grover reached across the table and removed the top half of its bun. "Nobody," he said, "eats a burger naked." He piled on top ketchup, mustard, relish, a tomato slice from his own cheeseburger super deluxe, a few rings of onion, five French fries.

"That's good!" Ralph said; and when Grover ordered a black-and-white ice cream soda, Ralph shyly did too. And when Grover ordered a fried clam plate *and* a Salisbury steak, just for fun, Ralph ordered a list of side dishes — onion rings, potato salad, coleslaw. Plus a chocolate milkshake. "What the heck," said Grover, approvingly. Ralph laughed. They ate at whim, taking a bite here, a bite there. When their table was full of plates, they moved to another one, where they ordered desserts — apple pie, cherry pie. Black Forest cake.

Ralph groaned. "I'm full."

Grover roared, "I say we order more!"

"Nonono," Ralph protested, thinking, fleetingly, Typical American wasteful.

But when Grover ordered bacon and eggs, Ralph did too. It was a game. French toast. English muffins. German pancakes.

"We're going to have to haul it all home," said Grover, "in a doggie bag."

"A doggie bag!" Ralph laughed. Everything had begun to seem funny.

"What haven't we ordered," wondered Grover.

Ralph roared. "Chinese pancakes!" he said. "How come there are no Chinese pancakes!"

"Good point. How astute of you," Grover burped.

Ralph belched. Grover loosened his belt a notch. Ralph loosened his belt and undid the button of his pants, saying, "Hope the waitress can't see."

"And so what if she does?"

"We tell her we're just get comfortable."

"We'll tell her," winked Grover, "that we're getting comfortable, so she better watch out."

Ralph roared again. What an adventure! He pried off his shoes; loosened his collar; slumped in his seat like an opium smoker. He was glad, though, that the waitress was nowhere to be seen; and when Grover, getting restless, suggested that they simply go back into the kitchen to see what was left that they hadn't tried, Ralph hesitated before padding after him, holding his pants up with his hand.

The waitress reappeared. "Ah," said Grover. "We were just

saying how we were getting comfortable, you'd better watch out."

"Were you?" To Ralph's surprise, she did not blush.

Grover caressed her earlobe. "Nice earring you've got there." She giggled. He pulled her to him.

"What do you say?" Grover winked at Ralph again. "To the kitchen?" Hands on the waitress's hips, he began to walk her like a puppet in front of him.

"Ah," said Ralph. Then suddenly polite, "Nononono."

He drifted back to the dining room alone, buttoning his pants. Flies buzzed over the tables of half-eaten food. One got stuck in some orange pancake syrup. Ralph tried the counter stools, one after another, for squeaks. Then the booths, for spring. In, out. From the kitchen came the sound of pots thrown to the floor. *Cronng.* Dishes smashing — *ack! ackk! asssh!* Then laughter. What were they doing that they laughed as they did it? He and Helen never laughed. More dishes. Screeches. He counted the ceiling lights. Then came what sounded like sobbing. Sobbing? Ralph shook his head to himself. Who was going to clean up later? And what about the dishes? And who was going to pay for all the food? Somebody, he thought, was going to have to pay, and though Grover had insisted all along that he would, Ralph began to wonder now if he was going to have to pay too.

He was brooding about whether to call home when Grover emerged, dusting himself off, though he didn't look dusty. "What a mess," Grover said.

Ralph heard the metallic scrape of a car starting up outside — the waitress, leaving.

Grover surveyed the dining room. Morose, he examined his hands. "So." His vest was open, his shirt rumpled and misbuttoned, his carnation wilted.

"So," said Ralph.

Grover felt his pants pocket for a handkerchief.

Silence.

Finally Ralph asked, "So where you from?"

"From?"

"Your hometown is where?"

"Hometown!" Grover laughed, instantly recovered. "You've been here how long? And still asking about people's hometown." He shook his head. "I'll let you in on a secret. In this country, the question to ask is: 'So what do you do for a living.' "

"So what you do for a living?"

Grover laughed again.

How did people get so that they could laugh like that? "I'm work on my Ph.D.," Ralph offered. "My field is engineering. Like Old Chao, except my specialty is so-called mechanics."

"Is that right."

"So your field is what?"

"What? Field? My *field*" — Grover flashed his gold tooth — "is anything."

"Anything?"

It was almost past understanding: Grover was whole or part owner of any number of buildings and restaurants. A stretch of timberland. "You make a few bucks in one business, then you branch out." He described mines he was in on, and rigs. A garment factory. A toy store. "What with babies popping out all over, toys are getting to be big business."

"Whooo," said Ralph. "That's a lot."

"Think so?" Grover preened, straightening his shirt.

"How come you own so many parts of things instead of one big thing?"

"Good question. And the answer, if you understand me, is that that way it's just a mite harder for people to get a fix on you."

"I got you." Ralph nodded. "That's Chinese way."

"What?"

"All the Chinese guys, you know, outside they look like they live some lousy place, but inside, beautiful."

"No kidding."

"Otherwise government ask them pay tax."

"It's the same story here. The government is a pain in the neck."

"Big pain. Make you be crazy."

"You know," said Grover, squinting. "You got some first-class gears twirling around in that upstairs of yours."

"Think so?" Ralph sat up a little. His waistband pulled.

"I'll tell you who you remind me of."

Ralph waited.

"Myself. You remind me of myself, back when I was nobody."

Slouching again, Ralph twiddled his spoon.

"You know, back then, I worked every lousy job in town, you name it. I was a jack-of-all-trades. I painted houses. I drove cab . . ."

No wonder he drove so well! thought Ralph.

". . . I washed dishes. I even sang in a music show, get that."

"Show!"

"My authentic Chinese face got me in the door. *South Pacific,* a local production. You know, 'Happy talk, keep talkin', happy talk.' "

Ralph clapped.

"That's what you are in this country, if you got no dough, a singing Chinaman." Grover paused. "True or false?"

"True," guessed Ralph.

Grover smiled enigmatically. He explained how he got his break — how he kept his eyes open until one day he met this guy who needed somebody he could trust. "We happened to get to talking, just like we're talking now, and the next thing — bang — I'm a millionaire. A self-made man. What do you think of that?"

"Millionaire! Self-made man!"

"In America, anything is possible."

"Just from one day, happen to get talking!" Ralph was dazed. "Like we're talking now."

"Understand me, I was already the can-do type."

"Doer type. I got you."

"I had the correct attitude. Very important."

"Positive attitude, right? Use imagination?"

"You got it."

" 'I can do all things in Christ who strengthen me,' " quoted Ralph.

"Well, I'll be damned. The engineer's done some reading."

" 'Prayerize,' " said Ralph.

" 'Picturize,' " said Grover.

" 'Actualize.' "

Grover slapped his two hands on the table, grinning so that his molars showed.

"A man makes his mind up who he's going be." Ralph grinned with his molars too. "So what business was that?"

"What?"

"Your first business, that you became millionaire."

"That business?" Grover leaned forward conspiratorially. "That was fats and oils. I still have a hand in it." He explained how his factory took leftover cooking grease from restaurants and turned it into nice, white soap. "We make it smell good, you know? That's the important thing, the smell. You can sell anything if it smells right."

"Interesting."

"That's a secret. I'm telling you a secret."

They went on to other secrets. How a self-made man should always say he was born in something like a log cabin, preferably with no running water. How all self-made men found what they needed to know in bookstores. How he should close some deals with handshakes.

"A couple of big deals. No contract. And favors. Favors are important or the story's not right."

Risk was the key to success. Clothes made the man. Ralph wished the night would go on forever. But finally Grover was winding down. "And one last thing."

Ralph cocked his head, already wistful.

"Keep your eyes open."

"Eyes open."

"Keep your ears open."

"Ears open."

"Know who you're dealing with."

"Know who I'm deal with."

"And keep moving." Grover stood up and stretched. "Keep moving." He seemed to be talking to himself. "I'm going to call us a cab."

"What about the car?"

"It's out of gas anyway."

"The bill," Ralph said. "The mess."

"Forget it," said Grover. "I own this place." He called a taxi, and when it came — a bright yellow Checker, with a loose muffler — he directed the driver to Ralph's address first.

"How do you know where I live?"

"By your able description, remember?" He smiled winningly. "Your landlord's a buddy of mine."

Ralph gaped.

"You'll get that new super one of these days."

They drove home as they'd come, in a deafening wind — Grover had seen to the opening of all four windows. Now, though, instead of magic, what seemed to be flying into the car was everydayness. Grit, chemical smells. As the dark slowly gave way to light, they saw that the day was going to be hazy. Ralph propped his feet up on one of the jump seats, the way Grover had. His bee bite, he noticed, was finally gone. They arrived. Ralph lowered his legs; the jump seat popped right back vertical as though it had already forgotten him.

Grover shook his hand. "Good-by."

"Thank you." To his surprise, Ralph felt his eyes begin to tear. "So much you told me, I know you don't have to."

"Maybe I took a liking to you."

"Did you?" Ralph gripped the door handle. "The way your fats and oil boss liked you?"

Grover laughed. "Come on now. Time to call it a night."
Ralph opened his door.

"But here. My card," said Grover.

"Thank you. Thank you!"

"Give me a ring."

"Good-by." Ralph climbed out. "See you again!"

Who closed the door? It seemed to slam itself shut. Grover leaned back, disappearing from view as the gay yellow cab puttered away, its muffler clattering forlornly after it. Ralph waved at the empty street awhile; even the gas fumes seemed to be evaporating before he was ready. Then his feet turned, and shuffled a few steps, and began climbing the long staircase home.

WAITING

MEANWHILE, Theresa and Helen and Janis had come down-stairs to find Old Chao pacing back and forth. He swung an arm as though to loosen a frozen shoulder. Explaining what had happened, he worked his fingers, casual. He rotated his wrists. He adjusted his pants, running his right hand flat along the inside of his waistband so that it sat properly on his equator. He laughed — haw haw — a man pitting style against horror.

Ha ha. Theresa joined in, carefully. Then, Janis and Helen, together. Ha ha. With brightness. "*Joking!*" they joked. Ha-hahaha.

A slight wind rose, lofting their hopes.

"*Maybe they've run out of gas.*"

"*Maybe they've taken a wrong turn.*"

Only Theresa knew they hadn't.

"*That's the car!*"

A convertible drove by, but it was white and a different make.

Darkness began to materialize, a black coat for each of them. The streetlamps blinked on, buzzing. At what point did they realize they were in crisis? Under the elbows of a new-leaved tree, they were illuminated in pieces — an ear, a finger, a bit of torso. They'd become their emergency selves, in which lopped-off state they felt humanity stretched smoothly between them like one long wash line. They chatted quietly about the schools in the suburbs, how coats were marked down Columbus Day, whether the United States was doing the right thing in Korea. Old Chao consulted Theresa on a pain he'd been having. It was as though they were gathered around a bridge game, an activity that set the social level for them, so that they did not have to gauge and give out, gauge and hold back, but could relax, companionable. What friends they were! Unexpected as always, happiness flapped through, brushing them with its soft wing. When Old Chao suggested they might take a walk around the block, just to have a look, they did, all four of them. Then Old Chao suggested they try the neighboring blocks too. They each set out in a different direction, making a cloverleaf, meeting back at the apartment. They made phone calls.

No answer. No answer.

Real worry took a chair. They huddled out the night together, until Helen's hair had straightened like Theresa's; Janis's likewise was turning into a lion's mane. Helen and Theresa borrowed slippers. It began to seem that the room smelled like cigarette smoke. But no; they ascertained that the smell was coming from their clothes. That Grover! Finally, at dawn, news. The car had been found, abandoned at a diner in Pennsylvania.

"They must of drove it 'til the gas run out on 'em," said the sergeant.

What about Grover? Ralph?

The sergeant was sorry.

It was better to have known nothing. Their fears began to circle the abandoned car, then to pile into it, tense new passengers with theories in their laps. Who met Ralph and Grover by the roadside, and what for? Where were they all headed? Was this what Grover was up to, making those phone calls in the bedroom? Helen began to sob in short, ragged bursts, like hiccups, gnawing so hard at the base of her thumb that she drew blood.

Theresa called a taxi for them. It was a sticky morning, foggy, with no sunrise that they could see.

"I wanted to go home," explained Ralph.

"You wanted to go home."

"I asked him where we were going."

"You asked him."

"I asked, but we weren't going anywhere. We were driving around."

"Ah."

"I had no choice."

"You were kidnapped?"

"Kidnapped," he affirmed.

"Ah! Did he give you liquor?"

"Dinner," said Ralph. *"We had dinner, then lunch, then breakfast, in a diner. He owned it."*

"Dinner, then lunch, then breakfast?"

"I had a burger, with ketchup and mustard and relish and a tomato and onion and French fries. And a black-and-white ice cream soda."

"So much!"

"And some other things," finished Ralph.

"How come you didn't call?"

"I thought to call. But I couldn't."

"How did you escape?"

"He called a taxi to take us home."

"There was a phone."

"There was."

"And the taxi took both of you home?"

"It dropped me off first."

Theresa, frowning, stood up to put on some tea.

"It was all Grover's fault." Helen offered this conclusion as though they could make it the truth; all they had to do was agree on it.

Theresa pursed her lips.

And that bit of story-making allowed the family to go on.

"It was," said Ralph, with relief.

Later, though, he regretted having given in, as he thought of it. Was that what a self-made man would have done? Hunched over his small wooden desk, he knew what he should have said instead. He should have said, with sonorous finality, *I'm the father in this family.* For he *was* the father, and could do whatever he liked — to remind himself of which, he ripped his soft, gray desk blotter in half and wrote, in large red letters, AC-TUALIZE. What exactly did that mean, again? He thought he had better reread that part of the book. In the meantime, he tacked the sign up on the wall in front of him. Then he took out Grover's card. He was an imagineer, invisible, dialing. Se-cretive, like Helen. Grover's phone was ringing. What was he going to say? Hello. That was right, yes. Hello, and he'd like to be a self-made man too.

No answer.

He let the phone ring twenty times, thirty, tried the line again, let it ring forty times. But Grover didn't answer that day, or the next day, or the next week. Was the card a phony card? Was the number a phony number? Ralph couldn't believe it. He was an imagineer! This wasn't supposed to happen. Should he check the number? He could check it, he supposed, with the new super, a tough-talking veteran with a pit bull.

Ralph, though, never did. Partly he was afraid of what he might find out. Mostly, though, he wanted to have faith. Wasn't imagineering a matter of faith, like going to church? And indeed, in church, he often considered Grover. He worked to dispel his doubts about his friend as though to pass another test, like his ordeal in the park. He sat with his eyes closed in the pew. He felt his knees.

News: Janis and Old Chao's child had been stillborn. *"Dead?"* said Ralph. *"A little baby?"* Helen cooked pots of food. Janis wouldn't eat. *"She cries all day,"* Helen reported. *"She doesn't change her clothes. She doesn't wash her dishes."* Then, *"She doesn't want me to come visit anymore. She thinks she's bad luck."*

Ralph began to think then of what children meant, and how Helen ought to rest more. *Man man zou,* he told her — go slowly, take it easy. *Xiuxi, xiuxi* — rest.

And he bought a new desk pad, that, like a real father, who needed to make a real living, he might apply himself to the doctorate on which the future of his children depended. "Crack Stress of Airplane Bodies by Computer Analysis" — he was looking for a numerical solution to analytically insoluble equations. Every day he punched cards, punched and punched, trying to avoid instability, divergence, distortion.

HELEN
IS HOME

HELEN by that time was growing more and more still. She was her resourceful self, but she was also an instinctive counterweight to Ralph's activity — a fixed center. Though she did not know Ralph had become an imagineer, she sensed it — sensed that if it weren't for her and Theresa, he might not have come back from that long night with Grover. There would have been nothing to come back to. A decade later, she might have likened their family to astronauts, floating in space; that was how ungrounded they were. If one person were to go wandering off, it was important that someone else stay put.

Which was all right — it made her feel nearer the center of the household, whatever that meant anymore. And she was too tired and too encumbered to move much anyway. Not to say too hot. Now that she had breasts and a belly of a size to contend with, she also had a new deep crevice between them, fiery as a steam hole. Into this Ralph would sometimes fit a cool, balled-up washcloth, as a special attention. They were closer than they had been. For all his dismay over her friendship with Janis, he had been in no position to say much; and he seemed to have his own secrets now, a barrier between them that was at the same time a kind of bond.

Was it enough? She hoped so, prayed so, haunted as she was by her latest, most dangerous secret: that the night Ralph disappeared, she'd worried not only after him, but also after Grover — winking, rich, handsome Grover. What a scoundrel that man was! She knew it. Still she saw herself as though in a magazine. A lady again after all, and more — she saw herself wildly in love. He lived for her, only for her. And in her dreams, she lived for him too, this man her parents would never have picked.

Callie — in Chinese her name was Kailan, Open Orchid — was two weeks early, a blizzard baby. The storm curled along the coast like a question mark; all over the city people braced themselves. Food. Blankets. Helen and Ralph and Theresa stocked their cupboards like everyone else, only to have to leave them. It was a hard delivery, long and painful; Helen felt as if she were giving slow birth to a rock. Outside the window, the sky mocked her with its spectacular spill. Until finally — finally — there was a sliding and a bawl. A girl! Theresa didn't mind, but Helen and Ralph were disappointed until they held her, and saw the way she nestled her plump cheek into her shoulder, as though she had no neck. And then they could not imagine how parents drowned their daughters, as they knew farmers in China often did — *bathing the baby,* it was called. They were won over by her extremities. Her mashed-in nose, her downy ears, her miniature fingers with their miniature nails and wrinkly knuckles. Her toes — five stubs, like a little stub family, on each fat foot. Her head was conical, an extremity too, and so thick with black hair that she almost needed a haircut. What wasn't perfect? Gently trying her working parts — her elbows, her wrists, her knees — they decided they'd have their boy next time, who'd be a scholar, and maybe a millionaire too. . . . How much more work a boy would have been anyway, all that schooling. As it was, they had their hands full just learning how to fuss. Proper bundling was important, that she not catch cold. Were all babies this floppy? They experimented with different techniques.

PROGRESS
AT LAST

GROVER then was a man better not mentioned, meaning that it was he as much as Callie that made them, finally, a real family. Something to protect, something to protect against. The group strengthened like a muscle. More than ever they teased each other. Helen's Chinese astrological sign was a cow; Ralph's, a pig; Theresa's, a dog. But Ralph joked that he was the real dog and also the pig. *"How could you be a dog?"* he asked Theresa. *"Too smart!"* They mooed at Helen. There was no more talk of marrying Theresa off; and though Helen did call Janis to let her know the baby had been born, the things that had changed between them didn't seem to be changing back. Poor Janis! In what free time she had, Helen thought of her friend, but there weren't many minutes. Callie was colicky and allergic to formula, the sort of baby who hollered more than she slept. In between school and schoolwork, Theresa pitched in, happy to get away from her cadaver. How much better a living baby smelled! Helen was grateful for the help.

As for Ralph — by the time Callie was crawling and making nests for herself in the laundry basket, her father had moved on to writing up his results. And by the time Mona was born (so vigorous and wriggly that she managed to get herself dropped on the floor first thing; Helen named her Mengna, Dream Graceful, all the same), Ralph had finally finished. Hands were shaken, backs slapped.

Graduation was ninety-eight humid degrees, the sort of day when even the rare breeze feels like the fond approach of a hairy, panting animal. Still Ralph heard every word of every speech as though it were the crystalline note of an ice chime. For the occasion, Theresa had borrowed a second camera, so they would not be relying on one picture-taker for the big moment; now Ralph, accepting his diploma, hesitated, to be sure to give the women a good shot. Everyone was clapping. He turned to the audience and waved a little, like a movie star. He, Ralph Chang, was now Doctor Chang!

"Congratulations," said the president of the university, loudly, again. He was a tall, narrow man, like one of the marble pillars, except that, sheathed in sweat, he gleamed more.

Ralph shook his hand a second time. "I'm sorry," he said. "I'm just wish my father, mother, could be here."

The president mopped his brow patiently. "I understand," he said.

The pictures came out so beautifully that Helen hardly knew which of them to frame, and finally had two of them done, professionally, as well as his diploma. She hung these in the living room, near the wedding pictures. Level? Ralph backed up to look. "*Level*," he affirmed. Then, to his amazement, he started crying. "*Father*," he said. "*Mother*."

"*They would have been so proud!*" Theresa turned emotional too. "*You know, in the pictures, you look like Father*."

"*Do I?*" Ralph didn't think so until Theresa pulled out some old photos; then it was striking that in profile, he did.

Helen hung one of these photos next to Ralph's. This was followed by a picture of Ralph and Theresa's mother, to keep their father company; and by pictures of her own mother and father, with a little shelf, for flowers. Not that their parents were dead — they were not to make offerings to the pictures, as if their parents had become ancestors. But when, shortly after they hung the shelf, Ralph was blessed with a tenure-track job (Old Chao had put in a word for him), they thanked their parents for whatever help they might have been.

They did this again when Theresa got her M.D.

By the time the fall semester began, Helen had found a new, larger place, in Washington Heights. Solid ceilings, she enthused, a room for Mona and Callie, and a dining room that could be made into a room for Theresa. The girls helped by unpacking the boxes almost as fast as Helen could pack them. But finally Helen had crumpled her last piece of newspaper; Ralph had rented a truck. How excited they all were! — though at the last minute, unexpectedly afraid and sentimental too. So long, old apartment. Mona and Callie kissed all the walls good-by. They kissed the stove too, and the radiators, and the crack in the back bedroom, which had gotten much worse. Once the file cabinets were walked away from the wall they could see that actual slivers of sky shone through it, lustrous and white.

Helen and Ralph furrowed their brows for a long time. Then Ralph climbed up the trap door to the roof, returning to report that the building really needed a turnbuckle or something to keep its corners from falling outward. Like this — he drew a diagram on a napkin. Mona and Callie shook their wispy-haired heads in imitation of everybody else.

"House could fall down?" Callie asked.

"Any day," Ralph said, patting her. And to Helen, *"Any day that corner could have fallen out, especially with those heavy files there."*

Helen shuddered at the idea; Callie shuddered too. Mona laughed.

But as it happened, the house had held, and now they were moving on.

PART III

This New Life

CHANG-KEES

IN MANDARIN, change is handily expressed: a quick *le* at the end of the sentence will do it, as in *tamen gaoxing le* — now they are happy. Everywhere there are limits, but the thin fattens, the cloudy clears. What's dry dampens. The barren bears.

Thankfully! It had already been nine years since Ralph had touched foot in the United States. Theresa had begun her internship; they had all studied up on the three branches of government, and so advanced from permanent residents to citizens. Ralph and Theresa had sprouted their first white hairs. Helen had developed muscles in her arms after all, it was carrying children that did it. They celebrated Christmas in addition to Chinese New Year's, and were regulars at Radio City Music Hall. Ralph owned a Davy Crockett hat. Helen knew most of the words to most of the songs in *The King and I,* and *South Pacific.* It was true that she still inquired of people if they'd eaten yet, odd as it sounded; Ralph invented his grammar on the fly; even Theresa struggled to put her Chinese thoughts into English. But now she had English thoughts too — that was true also. They all did. There were things they did not know how to say in Chinese. The language of *outside the house* had seeped well inside — Cadillac, Pyrex, subway, Coney Island, Ringling Brothers and Barnum & Bailey Circus. Transistor radio. Theresa and Helen and Ralph slipped from tongue to tongue like turtles taking to land, taking to sea; though one remained their more natural element, both had become essential.

And yet feeling truly settled was still a novelty. How easily they woke up now, and with what sense of purpose! They might or might not have counted themselves happy, though; happiness as they conceived it then was a thing attained, a grand state, involving a fiefdom to survey from the plump comfort of their dotage. It was only in retrospect that they came to call plain heartsease a happiness too; and though they sometimes thought that a shame, other times they thought differently. For if they had been able to nod and smile and say, How unruffled we are, then too, they might have been able to fret, We fear it all ending. Instead, this way, they were all innocence, all planning. They were, as Ralph thought of it, "going up," every day, with just enough time to take in an occasional movie or ball game, and to be glad that Mona and Callie were happy.

What a life those girls were going to have! Toddling Callie, wobbling Mona; they seemed to be always emerging from under the kitchen table — Callie on a mysterious errand, Mona forever chasing that sister gone around the corner. Helen and Ralph had agreed that they would have a second family in a few years, another two, who with luck would be boys; but in the meantime, Mona and Callie were as soft as their brothers would be, as enigmatic, bullheaded, goofy. They were a lively, durable luxury, to be "love-loved!" as Helen would say, tweaking their feet. She taught them to *jiao ren*: Though there was only one relative to name, Helen would ask, *Who's that?* as Theresa entered the room. And Callie would answer, properly, *Gugu!* — meaning her father's sister. Mona would clap.

This was how Callie knew herself to be clever, like Theresa. Everyone said so; she even knew that while her American age was three-and-a-half, her Chinese age was a year more. Mona at one was good-natured, like Helen.

"And which is like me?" Ralph would joke. "Ah?"

"Memememe," the girls clamored in English.

They climbed over him and pulled at his fingers, his nose, his ears, as if to take them for their own. Mona reached into his mouth for his tongue.

Ralph, jaw agape, laughed.

"Won't come out," Callie told her sister.

Still Mona pulled, giggling, until finally Ralph extricated her wet fingers and closed his mouth firmly and bounced her on his knee to distract her. "No tongue," he scolded. "My tongue not so good anyway. You should go pick Auntie's."

Callie, standing, pressed against his other leg. "Am I your little girl?" Her voice was plaintive.

"You are," Ralph reassured her. "You're my little girl — and you too." He hugged Mona, who had begun to twist. "I'm the father, and you both are my little girls."

"No-o-oo," Callie said then, singsong, laughing to have set her father up. Mona copied her, in her piping pitch. "No-o."

"Ye-e-ess," said Ralph, mimicking them.

"No-o-oo!"

"Ye-e-ess!"

"No-o-oo!"

"Ye-es!" cried Mona, by mistake.

"Mon-a." Callie tweaked her sister's foot the way her mother did. "You're supposed to say 'No-o-oo!' "

"No-o!" said Mona then.

"What's the racket going on in here?" demanded Helen, coming in.

"No-o-ewww!" yodelled Mona.

They all laughed.

"No! No! No!" Mona was yelping now.

"Yes! Yes! Yes!" laughed Helen, and then Theresa was behind her, crying, "Yes! No! Yes! No!"

"No! Yes!" said Ralph.

"Yes! Yes! No! No!" Callie shouted. "Yes! Yes!"

Then everyone was laughing some more, until it was time for supper. Theresa began to talk about moderation, and how too much laughing upset the digestive process, but that was funny too. Even she laughed as she talked; her words meant nothing. They were not like words at all, but like soap bubbles, or like the kisses blown around by a starlet in a motorcade. Was this, finally, the New World? They all noticed that there seemed to be no boundaries anymore. Helen, for instance, had become friends with Janis again, who had happily given birth to a son, Alexander, about Mona's age. No one seemed to mind that Old Chao had not only been granted tenure but was now acting chairman of Ralph's department. And what their super said or hoped didn't matter any more than the way Helen breathed, or how much Theresa talked. *"You know why we used to say typical American good-for-nothing?"* Theresa said at supper. *"That was because we believed we were* good for nothing."

"You mean I thought I was good for nothing." Ralph could laugh about anything these days.

"Well . . ." Theresa tactfully nibbled a slice of stir-fried hot dog. *"Anyway, now that you are* assistant professor, *life has a different look to it, right?"*

"Everything looks different. It's true." Finishing his rice, Ralph handed his bowl to Helen without so much as glancing her way; absentmindedly, elbow on the table, he awaited its return. He had his hand stretched palm up in the air, like a man trying to determine whether it was drizzling.

"I must confess something then," said Theresa. *"Do you remember that scholarship that was cancelled?"*

"Your scholarship?"

"It wasn't cancelled. I just told you that to make you feel better."

Ralph's forearm thudded to the table. Helen gingerly placed his steaming bowl in front of it. *"Well, it did make me feel better,"* he acknowledged finally.

"*Also Helen has something to tell you,*" said Theresa. "*About the furnace.*"

"*Ah, nonono!*" said Helen.

"*What furnace?*" said Ralph.

Helen turned her attention to Mona. "Open wide — good girl!" Mona poked one finger in either nostril as Helen fed her.

"*Eh?*" said Ralph. "*Something else you didn't tell me?*"

"Uh oh." Callie, precocious master of the helpful disturbance, knocked her chopsticks to the floor. "Took the elevator."

"I'll get it." Theresa ducked under the table.

"*Anyway, I don't mind,*" said Ralph.

"*Now that you are an* assistant professor, *I didn't think you would,*" said Theresa, feeling among the shoes.

"*Just like now that you are a* medical doctor, *you mind less that you have no husband, right?*"

Ralph's tone was teasing; still Helen held her breath until Theresa surfaced, brandishing the retrieved chopsticks. "*I mind less, it's true. Anyway, since I have a home here, why should I have another one?*"

"No reason," they all agreed. "No reason!"

"If she marries, she will bring the man come live with us," proclaimed Helen.

"Sit here," Ralph joked, pulling up a chair.

"Ya-aa-ay!" cheered Mona and Callie.

"Family member means not allowed to leave." Ralph wagged his finger at the girls.

"We are family," echoed Helen.

"Team," said Ralph. "We should have name. The Chinese Yankees. Call Chang-kees for short."

"Chang-kees!" Everyone laughed.

Ball games became even more fun. Theresa explained how the Yankees had lost the Series to the Dodgers the year before; they rooted for a comeback. "Let's go Chang-kees!" This was in the privacy of their apartment, in front of their newly bought used Zenith TV; the one time they went to an actual game, people had called them names and told them to go back to their laundry.

They in turn had sat impassive as the scoreboard. Rooting in their hearts, they said later. Anyway, they preferred to stay home and watch. "More comfortable." "More convenient." "Can see better," they agreed.

These were the same reasons Ralph advocated buying a car. *"Seems like someone's becoming one-hundred-percent Americanized,"* Theresa kidded.

"What's so American? We had a car, growing up. Don't you remember?" Ralph argued that in fact this way they could avoid getting too Americanized. *"Everywhere we go, we can keep the children inside. Also they won't catch cold."*

"I thought we agreed the children are going to be American," puzzled Helen.

Ralph furrowed his brow. When Callie turned three they had decided that Mona and Callie would learn English first, and then Chinese. This was what Janis and Old Chao were planning on doing with Alexander; Janis didn't want him to have an accent. For Ralph and Helen, it was a more practical decision. Callie had seemed confused by *outside people* sometimes understanding her and sometimes not. Playing with other children in the park, she had several times started to cry, and once or twice to throw things; she had lost a doll this way, and a dragon. Also, one grabby little boy had, in an ensuing ruckus, lost some teeth.

"Not a lot of teeth," Helen tried to tell his mother.

Now Ralph drummed his fingers. He stopped and smiled. *"And what better way to* Americanize *the children than to buy a car!"*

Theresa laughed. *"Plus this way they won't catch cold, right?"*

"Health is very important," put in Helen.

"And," said Ralph, *"it so happens Old Chao is selling his, to buy a new one."*

"Ahh!" said Theresa. *"But since when do friends sell each other cars?"*

"Dear Older Sister. Please allow me to explain —"

"I know. This isn't China."

"So smart," said Ralph.

RALPH
AT THE WHEEL

NINE-THIRTY, Saturday mornings, Ralph took driving lessons in the convertible with a special instructor a neighbor recommended. "Used to be an inspector himself," the neighbor said. "He knows all the tricks." Ralph called him up. And not long after that — mirror adjusted, brake off, blinker on, traffic clear — Ralph was pulling away from the curb, as solemn as a boy leaving home. He returned to a hero's welcome. *"Tell us!"* Helen would fling open the apartment door. With Mona on one knee, Callie on the other, he'd modestly recount that day's encounters. An enormous pothole. A blinking yellow light. A fire truck. He had conquered the three-point turn. Hand signals would fall to him anytime.

"Of course," he reminded them gently, "the lesson is one thing. The test is something else. First time, most people fail it." They nodded.

And yet when he did fail, they were almost as disappointed as the driving instructor, who had contracted to provide as many lessons as were needed to pass.

"Okay, okay," the instructor said, when he heard. A long-nosed dandy with a rubbery grin, he was not grinning now. "First thing let me tell you is mirrors. You can't just look front, you gotta look back."

"Look back," said Ralph.

That wasn't all. He had to open his eyes up when he looked so the inspector could tell. "Here. Do this." The instructor bugged his eyeballs. Ralph bugged his eyes out too.

Still, two months later, he flunked again. "Went on the curb," he explained. "Car conked out."

The instructor rubbed his nose. "Well, okay. Now listen here. First thing let me tell you is mirrors."

"That's last time you told me. 'Before anything, look back.'" Ralph bugged his eyes.

The instructor rubbed his nose again. "Well, okay," he said. "First thing let me tell you is signals. You gotta signal like you know what you're doing."

The third time Ralph flunked, the instructor lit up a cigarette. "You know what you are?" he said. "You're what we call a losing proposition. I tell you this because I'm a nice guy."

The car was filling with smoke. Ralph rolled down his window. The instructor had flipped open the shiny chrome ashtray in the arm of his door, and was flicking his ashes into it.

"You're never going to get your license. You know why? Because you don't inspire confidence. I know the inspectors, these guys're friends of mine. They take one look at you and you know what they see?"

"I already paid this car," said Ralph.

The instructor drew hard on his cigarette. "Accidents," he said. "You want to get a license, there's only one way. I'll explain it to you simple. Being a nice guy."

Ralph spread his hand over the horn.

"It's called grease. This is how it is in America. Certain American palms require a certain American —"

"Understand," Ralph gripped the wheel as though removing himself to some other place were a matter of steering.

"What I mean is —"

"You know," said Ralph, slowly. "In China, my father was government official. Scholar. One-hundred-percent honest type."

"So my father's a priest. What —"

"My father was big shot." Ralph opened his door and climbed out, feeling strong, almost athletic. "And I am his son." He crossed to the passenger side of the car, opened that door too.

The instructor slid out of his seat. His brilliantined head gleamed like a bowling ball.

"Thank you. I do not need any more your help." Ralph gave the door a good push.

Had he done the right thing? Ralph retook the driver's test by himself in June; and every day after that, as soon he came home from work, he'd rifle through the family mail, hoping. Sometimes he'd wander outside to look at his car, rev the engine, play with the mirrors. He'd flash the headlights, considering the postal system. How many letters did they lose a day? He imagined the bins they used for sorting. He imagined the clerks, up all night. He imagined the letter from the Department of Motor Vehicles, that one most important letter, flipped so that it whizzed close to the right bin, but landed, finally, in the wrong bin. He thought about selling the car.

One day, though, the letter finally did arrive — an ordinary letter, come without incident through the ordinary channels, with a large ballpoint X just where he wanted it. Ralph took the whole family out for a drive to celebrate; even Theresa came, though she'd been up all night at the hospital.

"Are you have fun?" he said.

"Fun?" they answered. Then, "Yes, we're having fun! We're having a great time!"

It was relatively bearable out for July. Too bright, too warm, and too stuffy, but the street garbage did not seem to be emanating gases the way it sometimes did, and most people were wearing clothes; only a few men sauntered around in their pot-bellies. Helen and Mona and Callie bobbed on the springy front seat with Ralph. Theresa, in the middle of the back, bounced less; though sitting forward, she said, she could see and hear as well as anyone — really!

Hands at ten of two, Ralph maneuvered the car around the block. "Can you feel when I switch gear?"

The passengers closed their eyes. Ralph took extra care to let up slowly on the clutch.

"Can't tell at all!"

Ralph beamed. "Important to use mirror," he informed them. "Before do anything, look back."

"*Am I in your way?*" asked Theresa in Chinese.

"*No, no,*" said Ralph, although it was also true that when he looked back, all he saw was her.

Around the block again. When a bum senselessly gnashed his gums at them, Ralph sped up. "*Let's see something nice!*" he said. They headed for Central Park, crossing and recrossing it, stopping once for Good Humor ice cream. Then all the way down Fifth Avenue. Of course, Helen and Theresa and Ralph had all been to Fifth Avenue before, but it was different from a car. Now they beheld more than they experienced, observing how it was a lot like Shanghai, only newer. And with no rick-shaws, and no one starving in public.

Downtown some more, to Chinatown. English-speaking or not, Mona and Callie knew this much Chinese: *da bao* were big buns with chicken and egg and juicy chunks of Chinese sausage (unless they had a red dot on them, those were sweet bean paste); *cha shao* was roast pork. *Zongzi* were lotus leaf–wrapped bun-dles of sticky rice — the girls liked the savory ones, which came tied up in pairs. "More! More! Buy more!" they urged Helen. *Jiaozi* were the pork dumplings they went down the block to eat with *jiang you* and vinegar, counting. "I ate six!" "Ten!" "Eleven!"

As they left Chinatown, Ralph braked a moment, nodding

casually toward a fresh-killed meat store. "I used to work in a store like that."

"Where?" Callie said.

"Really? You never told me that before," said Helen.

Ralph slowed down again on the way home, partway up the West Side. *"This is where my advisor used to live."* He was surprised how unimposing the brownstone looked now. The yews sprawled, yellowish and ungainly; the stone steps had the grimy, unswept look of a city institution. And what color was that door? A kind of gloomy, once-was-green. Ralph shook his head to himself. The door swung open.

He drove on quickly, up through Harlem, slowing a third time in front of some dilapidated old buildings.

"How come we're going here?" Callie demanded.

"You forgot already?" wondered Theresa.

Like Fifth Avenue, their old block looked much different from the car than it had from the sidewalk. For one thing, they could now see that the building next door was missing two groups of three or four windowpanes; it looked as though it had been shot in the eyes. Also, their building was missing its nose. Had it always been that way? They circled.

"Look!" Theresa exclaimed. *"Look! Look! Look!"*

Ralph braked. That corner of their building with the crack had actually fallen off, exposing a cutaway section not only of their old back bedroom, but their living room too.

"Don't tell me," said Helen.

"So dangerous, and we didn't even realize it."

"Terrible."

They stared.

"We were just lucky."

They stared some more.

"Same old ugly wallpaper," Helen said finally.

They passed Old Chao and Janis's building, a more solid affair.

"Old Chao and Janis just bought a house," said Ralph. *"Everybody says he's going to be* full professor *next year."*

"*Already!*"

"*A record. Now I'll take you on the highway,*" he announced.

"*I thought we were going home,*" said Theresa.

"*After the highway, we'll go home.*"

"Can we put the top up first?" Helen couldn't help but consider her hair.

"*Nonono,*" said Ralph. "*No fun with the top up!*"

On the highway, they went faster.

"*Where are we going?*" Theresa shouted.

Ralph didn't answer. They were speeding recklessly. Twice they cut other cars off, and once they almost hit a truck. "Hey, watch it, buster!" the truck driver yelled out. "You're going to kill somebody!"

"*Little Brother,*" Theresa tried to say, "*I wonder how fast you're driving?*"

"*Faster!*" Ralph answered. "*Faster and faster!*"

Mona and Callie clung to the dashboard as though to their lives, while next to them, Helen took a more adult tack — knees and hands clasped together, lips pressed tight, she seemed to be trying to control the situation by going dead rigid.

Ralph refused to get the point. Until luckily, the sun clouded over, and everyone began to get goose bumps. "*The girls are catching cold,*" Helen shouted.

"We are!" Mona and Callie played along. *Gan mao* — to catch cold — was one Chinese phrase they understood completely. "We're freezing! We're dying!"

"*Better put the top up,*" Theresa advised.

Ralph pulled off at the next exit.

"*Where are we?*"

"Connecticut."

"What's Kencut?" Callie wanted to know.

"Another state," Theresa answered in English. "We're in another state."

"Isn't this near where Old Chao and Janis are moving?" Helen asked.

"*Not too far,*" said Ralph. "*This is where Grover Ding lives. One of his houses, something to do with tax.*"

In later years, when Helen taught the girls *how to talk,* she'd teach them when *not to continue,* as she put it. It was a polite way of making a point, she said, but the way she said it, the girls knew that by point she meant barb. How come, though, when *they* fell silent, no one seemed pricked? "American kids, their mothers teach them nothing," Helen said. "Typical American, what can you say."

In their household, on the other hand, silence had teeth. Now, when, at the mention of Grover, no one *continued,* Ralph looked to see what the women meant. He glanced toward Helen, checked Theresa in the mirror. Then, civilly, he took them around for a tour.

Connecticut would have been beautiful any time of day. But so breathtaking were the streets that late afternoon, with their sentinel trees and tender gardens, that the sun itself seemed to waver, unsetting, reluctant to leave; it was the onlooker whose presence weighted everything. Colored it too, with banner greens, strawberry golds, every fairy-tale hue. And such peace! Such stillness! Perhaps after driving so long, they would have found any bit of ground fabulously unmoving. In any case, they sighed — a *hometown* — and feeling themselves to have arrived somewhere, parked the car.

When did they realize that a town like this was their destiny — that if they drew out the line of their past it would pass through this point, that however it curved afterward, for some time they would dwell in a house like one of these, with a yard and garage? Their collective longing thickened in their throats, Helen's especially. "*Beautiful,*" she whispered, over and over. Through the windows, she saw curtains, candlesticks, cupboards; and in one, a woman moving among her chosen objects. "*Beautiful, beautiful, beautiful!*"

"*It is,*" agreed Ralph.

"*It's almost as nice as China,*" said Theresa.

"For America —"

"It's beautiful," insisted Helen.

"So clean," agreed Ralph.

Mona and Callie romped on the sidewalks. "We're skipping!" cried Callie. "Skip!" echoed Mona, stumbling.

"It would be nice for the children to have a place to play."

"A backyard."

"It's a good place for family."

They mused up the streets. Down.

"What town is it Old Chao and Janis are moving to?"

"Tarrytown."

"That's Westchester."

"Ah."

"Next time, maybe we'll go over there, look around," said Ralph.

Helen's heart fired up. *"Next time!"*

ARDOR

THEY CAME every weekend. Not that they were, as Helen said, "looking to buy." A real estate agent had convinced them that they shouldn't do anything until Ralph had tenure; otherwise they might find themselves "overcommitted." Anyway, they had no money for a "down payment." And so they "just looked."

Avidly, though. Helen soon knew traditional from contemporary, split-level from ranch from center-entrance Colonial. Tudors, bungalows, A-frames, she explained. Stucco, brick, shingle. Clapboard.

"Extras," she'd say. "Double garage with separate entrance. Finished basement. Sliding glass doors."

Theresa was amazed. *"How your English has improved!"*

"Bu, bu, bu," said Helen modestly.

"And how do you know so much?" Ralph shook his head.

"I'm picking it up."

They "just looked" some more. Until one day, at breakfast, Helen said, *"Maybe I should go to work, save up some money for a* down payment."

"To work?" Ralph was shocked.

138

"*Janis is going to study real estate, become a* broker."
"*You want to work? Outside of the house? For strangers?*"
"*Sure she can go to work if she wants to,*" said Theresa. "*Why not?*"
Helen uncovered her cup, checking to see if her tea leaves had sunk all the way to the bottom yet.

Ralph suggested they try to *xiang banfa* — to think of a way.
"*What banfa?*" Helen sat up in bed.
"*I don't know,*" he said. "*But maybe there's someone we could ask to help us, some smart guy —*"
"*What smart guy?*"
"*Well, for example, that man, you may remember him, Grover Ding . . .*"
Helen did not continue.
Or not that night, at least. Another night some months later, though, she wondered, "*What exactly does Grover do?*" She did not really expect an answer when she asked this; Ralph was snoring.
But at the name Grover, Ralph stirred enough to answer, "*A lot of things. A lot of real estate too.*" He rolled over to face the aisle between their beds, his blankets twisted around him. "*He knows everybody.*"
"*Do you know how to get in touch with him?*"
"*What about Older Sister?*"
"*I didn't mean we should do anything.*" She retreated quickly to her restless sleep.

Ralph dug through his old papers, sneezing as he explored one box after another; somehow they'd grown dusty in the move. He could still envision Grover, the morning mist, the taxi door slamming. He could still hear the door slamming too, and there, that clatter, that was the muffler pipe. He could smell the exhaust. Grover's crisp card lay in his hand that morning; the raised letters shone. He pictured it in his hand again — he was an imagineer, about to find it, he was sure — when Theresa shuffled into the room, her old slippers rasping against the floor like sandpaper.

"Are you all right?" she asked. *"You sound sick."*

"No, fine," said Ralph lamely. *"Just looking through some old boxes."* He sneezed again.

"Doing a little cleaning, huh."

"That's right."

"Ah." Theresa hesitated.

Ralph turned red. Dust hung in the air.

"Okay," said Theresa then. Resignation crossed her face; it was not so much an expression as something that appeared to emanate from her pores. *"I just heard you sneezing, that's all."*

Ralph blinked; she turned to the door; and as her angular form began to soften and disappear in the bright hall light, it occurred to him that she really had just come to see about his sneeze. It occurred to him too that he'd never seen anyone look so tired. How long her training had gone on already; when would there be an end to it? She might as well have been swimming across an ocean. Days at a time, she was gone, and when she returned she sometimes went straight to bed without washing her face or brushing her teeth. Yet even so, she had come to see about him — she who saw patients all day, every day — because he was her brother.

"Older Sister," he said.

Her slippers grew quiet.

What had he meant to say? He flushed again.

"You have something to say?"

"If we buy a house, will you live in it with us?"

"I was hoping to."

"Good. I just wanted to be sure. You know — whole family together."

"You have to know how many bedrooms, huh."

"Exactly."

"Are you going to buy soon?" She was surprised.

"*Not too soon.*" He shrugged. "*No* down payment."

Theresa considered him. What was he so awkward about? Then she thought she knew. "*Well, I hope I can chip in on the* mortgage payments. *I'll be done training pretty soon, you know, and then I'll have a good salary.*"

"*Oh nonono,*" said Ralph.

"*Why not? I chip in for the rent.*"

"*Nonono, this is different. A mortgage is a big commitment.*"

"*So? I'm going to live there for a long time, right? And because of me, we'll have to buy a bigger house than we would otherwise.*"

What if you get married? Ralph wanted to say, but didn't have the heart. "*I'm the father of the family,*" he explained instead. "*It's my job, the house. You are only —*"

"*I'm only what?*"

Ralph swallowed, chagrined.

"*Don't worry, I'm not going anywhere. You'll see. Thirty, forty, fifty years from now, I'll still be here.*"

"*Will you?*" Ralph wasn't sure what to think about that.

"Once a Chang-kee, always a Chang-kee," she quipped.

"*Good one!*" exclaimed Ralph. "*That's a good joke!*" — and for a moment he was laughing, his heart full of family feeling, that tremendous, elemental solidarity.

This time, though, when she disappeared into the white hall, he was glad enough to let her go.

EXAMINATIONS

WHAT was Ralph doing, that he didn't want her to see? Theresa's lashes caught at the corners of her lids; and as she closed her door and began to undress, something about removing her layers and hanging them up proved too much to bear. What was it? The way her blouse creased from the waist down, having been tucked in all day. The meekness of the wire hangers, with their twisted throats and bent heads — they waited too patiently, too neatly, every one a spinster.

This was what she suspected about herself, as she looked in her green-tinted mirror, with its brown spot, and many-forked streak, and chipped edge — that she really was, after all, just wrong. Every day in the pitiless hospital light she saw how patients deceived themselves — about their weight, their drinking, their shortness of breath — only to find herself now, in her estimation, worse than any of them. Cold kiss of the stethoscope; she was doctor and patient both, asking and answering. Was her life her own fault? In China, a person's character was believed written in her face; a prospective bride's picture was studied under good light. Turned this way and that. Theresa had once judged this silly. Now she pondered her image with seriousness. She looked inward too, at the quality of her heart, its constrictions, its deposits. Its vessels were clogged with words, she discovered. An unexpected finding. When she first came to America, her English teacher had admonished her, not for speaking too much, but too little. "Speak up!" Her teacher had lifted her arms through the air like a priest ordering a congregation to stand, so that her slip showed, gray and raggedy. "Speak up! Speak up!" At the time Theresa had not dared to; and though later she'd learned to talk professionally — to present cases — past differential diagnoses and treatment plans, she managed nothing. Her teacher, it seemed, had exposed her lingerie to no use.

Except this — that Theresa now, too late for class, fairly burst with what she had to tell. About having to parade herself through parks in August. Or what about that dinner? Her indignation came to her in English, even as she recalled a Chinese saying, *Lao xu cheng nu* — constant shame becomes anger.

Her heart was indeed a fist, just as it was described in the texts.

If she slept more she might be able to contain herself better, she thought; she imagined rest and sleep to be like the clay flood walls villagers built in China. Lacking rest, though, she was the Yellow River, roiling, threatening to become the sorrow of millions. She envisioned Grover, bloated, somersaulting in the water, his eyes spongy with fungus . . .

What kind of a way was this for a doctor to think?

Years later, she might have recognized anger's place in her life to be like that of a poison color in needlework — Callie could have told her this. She might have seen it to be the garish shade that could bring a planned composition to life. Now, though, she tried to box herself up. She had always been nice about her morals; she grew nicer still. How dangerous a place, this country! A wilderness of freedoms. She shuddered, kept scrupulously to paths. Once she had allowed other residents to wink at her, and had sometimes even winked back. Now she stiffened and turned away.

Only to come, not too much later, to a surprise. Life heaves these things at us, chance gifts from its green waves: she'd noticed from the chart that she was about to see a thirty-six-year-old Chinese male, height five-ten, weight one hundred seventy pounds, blood pressure on the high side of normal but entirely normal nonetheless, in good health, reason for visit suspected bleeding hemorrhoids (why did people come into the emergency room for hemorrhoids? but of course they did, for sunburn too, and gas) and already it had occurred to her that there might be a certain awkwardness, there always was, when this hemorrhoidal Mr. Chao realized he was about to see a woman doctor. Still, she was prepared for it. So authoritatively did she sweep into the room, eyes on the chart, so coolly did she inquire, "So what brings you here today?" that she might not have noticed to whom she was talking had he answered back.

The fluorescent light buzzed. She lowered the clipboard. *"Old Chao!"*

Old Chao was blushing so furiously that he seemed to be swelling, his very blood cells agitating to escape. Nothing in his upbringing had brought him toward this. He sat down, blinking. *"I have, ah, corns,"* he said finally. *"Foot corns."* He nudged his bulging briefcase under a chair. *"Haven't seen you in a long time! What a surprise!"* He said, *"A woman doctor! You! They didn't tell me. They told me, Dr. Chang. I think they should tell people if they are going to see a woman doctor. My regular doctor is Dr. Blumberg. A man. He's on vacation. I thought you were in medical school."*

"I'm in training."

"Really? My doctor is away."

Theresa smiled professionally. *"On vacation?"*

"On vacation." Old Chao seemed to relax a bit, as though, walking in the dark, he'd reached out and found a railing.

"Would you like to see another doctor?"

"Oh, nononono," said Old Chao; but then he stood up as if to leave.

"Would you like to go?"

"Oh, nonono." He sat back down. The chair wheezed.

"Well. Shall we have a look at those, ah, corns?"

"Sure." Old Chao nodded his head, once, twice, three times. He untied his right shoe.

"Let's have you up on the table."

Old Chao changed seats, wing tip in hand. Theresa peered politely at his cornless foot. She cupped his heel. Dead skin flaked into her palm. *"So how are things at the department?"*

"Things at the department. They're, ahh — right there, do you see it? — they're going very well. Of course, we're very happy to have your brother even though he's —"

"Here?"

Old Chao puckered his face into a semblance of pain.

She let his foot down gently. *"So things at the department are ..."*

"Very good, yes, thank you, and Ralph's doing very well, except, you know, that he may be 'climbing a tree to catch fish' ..."

If Old Chao was trying to divert her attention from his foot, he'd succeeded. *"What do you mean? What tree? What fish?"*

"What do I mean?" Old Chao seemed to be pulling his usual self back on with his sock. He applied himself to his shoelace.

Theresa smiled. *"Well. I suppose I'd be pleased to write out a prescription for your corns."*

Old Chao retied his other lace, for good measure.

"Those corns," she said again, pointedly. *"I've never seen such corns."*

She thought she saw a blush rising; but a moment later, Old Chao had both his shoes on. In English, he said, "You play hard, you Chinese girls."

Now Theresa blushed.

"Okay, a favor for a favor."

Ralph wasn't going to get tenure; or at least it wasn't definite. Space, Old Chao explained. Satellites. Rockets. Mechanics was out. *"What matters now is plasma. Fluids. Ralph is making a big mistake. I've been trying to tell him."*

In the end, Old Chao left without any prescription at all. Theresa began to write him one, but he waved his hand at her to stop; and when she didn't see him, he impulsively picked her pen out of her hand. *"No need,"* he said. He threaded the pen back through her fingers, gently.

Ralph, meanwhile, was explaining himself to Callie and Mona. "You know what your father is? Your father is scholar." He drew them a pyramid. At the bottom were the graduate students. Then there were lecturers, then there were assistant professors, then there were tenured professors. "I am grade three," he explained. "A grade-three scholar."

Callie oohed and ahhed. Mona drooled. "And when will you be grade four?"

"Soon, soon. Though of course grade three is okay too."

"Very fine, are you kidding?" said Helen proudly.

Tenure, tenure, tenure. If Ralph gets tenure, this, they said. If Ralph gets tenure, that.

"Of course, it is possible I won't get it," Ralph said one morning.

Helen swept this dust ball away. *"But won't you?"*

Theresa did not comment.

"Don't you think?" Helen was sure. *"If nothing else, Old Chao —"*

"Is that what his wife says?" asked Ralph.

Helen picked an eyelash off Mona's cheek.

"It's not up to Old Chao," he went on. *"Plus, I don't want to get it because of him. I want to get it by myself, the honest way."*

As, honestly, he thought he would. Not because he was so

brilliant, but the government had just announced plans to send a satellite spinning around the earth, and most of his department seemed to be planning on being launched with it. Wasn't the school still going to need someone in Mechanical Engineering, though?

"*Hmmm*," said Theresa.

"*Are they crazy?*" said Helen. "*How can they make such a big machine stay in the air forever? Even airplanes have to come back down to refuel.*"

Ralph drew pictures. Fields, he explained, forces. Curves, velocities, orbits.

Helen was impressed.

"*Yes, theoretically, they can do it. But it's not easy. Of course, Old Chao is going to work on the space program anyway. You know Old Chao. He doesn't ask questions. Everyone says the space program is great, he goes to work on the space program. But you know what I think? I think the world will always need mechanical engineers. The world will always need machines, right? Factories? Gears make everything turn.*"

"*Very true.*"

"*You think I'm afraid to start over in a new field? I'm not. But I'm a mechanical engineer. That's what I am, that's all.*" He banged the table hard, as if he were arguing with somebody. "*Let everybody else go up in the air. That's what I am! That's what I am!*"

Theresa worked through her last admission. She had already done seven earlier in the day; she would not finish for another hour. There had been two car accidents. In one, a motorcyclist had broken his spine. In the other, a teenager had come in with no heartbeat. Her belly had been opened to locate the bleeding, and her chest too, for open heart massage. Theresa did an arterial stick, as the resident crunched through the patient's breastbone with a bone cutter. The room stank; a medical student fainted. The resident, swearing, began to work the heart — a gruesome sight. Theresa looked away, noticing that though the girl's jewelry, like her clothes, had been removed, her nail polish remained. This was a summery, watermelon pink, just the sort of color that a carefree young lady with her life in front of her might pick. Theresa shuddered.

And yet what was hardest about training was not such horrors. It was not the hours. It was not the responsibility, or the pain, or the patients, or the politics, or the masses of information tumbling and reeling in her head like cars on a circus ride. It was not the mnemonic devices, as hard to recall as the facts. ("The Argyll-Robertson pupil accommodated but did not react." What was the joke, though? Something about a prostitute.) It was not the fatigue. Or not exactly. What was hardest about training, for Theresa, was having to sleep in that dank, little room the interns all shared, with men. "If there were more women . . ." someone had explained, with a shrug. Now, as weary, she headed that way — finally, finally done — she thought about how soundly the men slept. She thought about how the men snored and tossed. They cried out. They moaned. They farted. They scratched themselves, and worse. Even the still ones, who slumbered soulfully, who curled up neatly, even they disturbed her; she could feel their radiant presence, against which she had to stand guard. Maybe they bothered her most, the sweet ones. So peaceful, but what dreams they might stir up in her if she slept, all throbbing, and sliding. A spinster's hot heaves; how pointed her needs were, it was impossible to sleep. It was impossible to think about people witnessing her sleep. What if she moaned, and cried out, and scratched herself, or worse?

And so it was that when Old Chao phoned, Theresa was lightheaded with fatigue. Taken aback, she not only dropped the receiver but admitted to him that she had — a small intimacy. Who would have predicted the larger ones to follow?

"So clumsy," she said. *"I don't know what's the matter with me."*

He laughed. The conversation could have loomed, a mountain range of awkwardnesses. Instead, it rolled. Anyone would have thought they spoke on the phone all the time. *"And I don't know what's the matter with me either,"* he said. *"Do you know, I managed to leave my briefcase in the examining room. Under that chair."* They agreed on a time for him to come pick it up.

But she could not find the briefcase. The next day, she called and left a message at the department.

"What message?" Old Chao adjusted his belt in the hospital hallway.

"Anyway, since you're here, we can have another look around for it."

The examining room was occupied. They waited in adjoining chairs, chatting. The weather. His various ailments. And, at one point, *"Why isn't your Little Brother attending the conference next month?"*

"What conference?"

"The space conference. Everyone else in the department is going."

The door opened. No briefcase, and no one they asked had seen it. The lost-and-found was closed for the day.

"We should have tried there first," Theresa lamented.

"It seems I'll have to return tomorrow," said Old Chao.

She was surprised, Theresa told Ralph, that he didn't go to more conferences. She herself was rather looking forward to going to conferences, she said. She wondered, Did schools pay for engineers to go to conferences the way hospitals sometimes paid for doctors?

"They do," said Ralph shortly. *"In fact there's a space conference coming up that Old Chao wants me to attend. But I'd rather finish this paper I'm working on."*

"He has a paper to write," Theresa reported to Old Chao. *"He thinks his time would be better spent on that."*

They went together to the lost-and-found. There it was! Old Chao's briefcase. Old Chao rifled through the manila folders.

"Nothing missing?"

"Nothing!"

To celebrate, he treated her to a Spam sandwich in the cafeteria.

Was Ralph right or wrong? Was he headed for disaster? Theresa couldn't decide. All she knew was that, crossed with shadow, their family life took on a poignancy sharper than she could stand.

"Brew." Mona was blithely pointing at a red turtle.

"Red," said Callie. "Red."

"Brew." Mona gnawed on her knee.

"Mona, it's red. Red!"

"Brew."

As if she could tell from her sister's tone that there would be no setting her right, Callie diplomatically went on to the next page, a green horse.

"Brew," said Mona.

"Green."

"Brew."

"Green, Mona, green!"

Mona looked bored. Callie turned the page impatiently; Helen had to yell to be careful with the book. But then the girls settled into a sweet disharmony that brought tears to Theresa's eyes.

"Purple," said Callie.

"Brew."

As if her sister had agreed with her, Callie simply turned the page. "Yellow."

"Brew."

Ralph made up stories for them. One about an ant climbing a tree. Another about a monk hiking a mountain. Up, up, up, he said. Higher and higher.

And every time he told a story, as if to counterbalance the motion, Theresa's heart sank.

What should she do? Theresa analyzed the relative merits of action versus inaction until her choice seemed not so much between paths, as between going blindly left or right in a featureless wood. How tired she was! The problem began to expand to levels at once more profound and absurd. How had they come to this crisis? What use was reason to her now? Why try to alter fate?

It was a release to be paged for a phone call.

"I've forgotten my briefcase in the cafeteria," said Old Chao. *"Not really!"*

"I don't know what to think." Old Chao's voice was strangely rough, perplexity cut with cheer. *"I can't seem to keep hold of it."*

LOVE
ANIMATES

EARTH, SPACE. Invisible forces. Things gravitated toward one another, sometimes successfully, sometimes not. Theresa came home to find Helen lost in a panoply of analytical tools, all laid out on the kitchen table. How love did animate! Helen had never been lazy that Theresa could see, but she had always seemed to possess a certain amount of energy, *e,* which she could expend on any projects, *x, y, z.* Now, suddenly there was no equation; *e* was no longer a constant. Notebooks, she had, index files, tables, graphs, maps. There were several colors of pencils, even a slide rule, at which she was frowning. A newspaper lay open on her lap.

"*Working?*" joked Theresa. She shut the door behind her.

"*Figuring.*" Helen turned the slide rule over. "*Is that right? No.*" She turned it upside down and shook her head. "*That can't be right either.*"

"*This way.*" Theresa showed her. "*You set this scale above this scale.*"

"*Oh, right! I remember now. Like this.*" She tried two times two and triumphantly produced four. "*We so appreciate your offer on the* mortgage, *by the way. Really, you shouldn't.*"

"I'm just sorry I won't be making a real salary sooner. Then you could buy a place right away."

"Oh, that's okay."

There had been a time, Theresa remembered, when Helen had held the paper gingerly, to avoid getting her hands full of newsprint. Now she grasped the pages with enthusiasm, her fingers so black they left their prints in the margins.

"Two bedroom cape with add-on potential. Nu to market, builder's special. Contemporary ranch with extras galore." She looked up. *"Today Janis took me to this house with a winding walkway. Really darling! However, it was very overpriced, they're going to have trouble selling it for anything near what they're asking. And yesterday I saw a breakfast nook with built-in benches —"*

"Be careful you don't fall in love," laughed Theresa, wagging her finger.

Helen laughed back.

Six weeks later, though, Theresa came home from yet another lunch with Old Chao (her fourth) only to find Helen aglow with dismay.

"Oh! You'd have to see it. It's beautiful, perfect, brand-new, and you wouldn't believe how affordable. Janis says no one in her office has ever seen such a good deal, ever. It's on an odd lot, which makes it a little cheaper to begin with, plus the builder wants to sell quick. The only reason he has it is because the original buyer's mortgage didn't go through, and he's got a shopping center going so he needs cash." Three bedrooms, one and a half baths, a walk-out basement. *"And so many extras!"* A nook off the kitchen. A brick planter. A big backyard. *"Plus the location's perfect, on a dead-end block, very quiet, with all young families."* Helen stopped. *"We'd fit right in. And good schools."*

"This one's the one."

Helen's eyes misted over. *"Of course, there'll be other houses.*

But not like this one, not at this price. We'll never be able to afford one like this. I guess I really didn't expect to find anything.''

"*No one knows what she's going to find.*" Theresa sighed heavily as she unbuttoned her coat.

Once, while Theresa was taking his history, a glittery-eyed patient grabbed her waist and put his mouth to her ear — or so she gathered later. What she remembered better was her scream, the scream of someone she didn't know and didn't trust, a screech so bloodcurdling that even the emergency room, whose very livelihood was disaster, stopped dead still. As the chief resident joked later, it was as if Theresa were Vesuvius, and the rest of the staff, Pompeii. "Never knew you to be such a show-stopper," he quipped. And, "You sure do know how to get a man's attention."

What she would have done then to get him to leave her alone! He didn't seem to realize how shamed she felt. How exposed. Everyone saw me, she kept thinking. Everyone saw me, everyone heard me. Yet he continued, with just that sort of relentless bantering she seemed to attract from men who were married; until finally, happily, it did begin to seem almost all right, what had happened. This was months later. In the end she'd felt grateful for his help, that was true, for the help of all married men. What was the harm of their flirting?

Or so she'd thought. Was Old Chao in love with her? And was she in love with him? It seemed to her that great harm could indeed come of *their* flirting. If to sit and talk was flirting — if, indeed, it was anything at all. She should talk the situation over with Helen, she thought; but then said nothing. And what about Old Chao? Had he said anything to Janis? She plucked up the nerve to ask him. He answered, quietly, no. Conspirators, they were then. She would not have guessed him a conspiring type. But then she would not have guessed many things about him. That he loved to watch ice skaters, for example, and surfers on

TV, and that he could skip stones — one of his students had taught him how on a field trip. So much he knew about water, about its freezing, its surface tension, its turbulence and flow; he once explained to her about eddies, and how they broke away in certain alternating patterns as they drifted downstream. Yet he could forget his learning too, baldly enjoying the phenomena produced. She had realized this slowly. She had admired it, deeply.

Was this "getting to know someone"? How little she'd understood the joy of it! Here she could envision a man's skeleton, his musculature; she could describe the workings of his lymph nodes. But what he remembered, valued, feared — all this was news. Listening, she revelled. His mind was nothing like hers; she tried to understand in which ideas his maleness lay. She spoke too, and was heard; she spoke more, surprising herself with what she said. What more could anyone ask? Their talk was enough for her, more than she'd dreamed of. She did not consider passion. Passion! Guilt kept its cold grip on that pleasure.

"If only I could do something!" Theresa lamented, trying to console Helen. *"Do you want me to go see it?"*

That would only make things worse.

"Maybe there's some other way?"

Helen shook her head, practicing acceptance. She was pretending she was ill. There was nothing to do but rest. *"Don't ask me how I could get so silly over a house, anyway,"* she said. *"A house! What is it? Four walls and a roof."*

Three days later, Theresa found Helen jumping up and down.

"A special kind of loan," Theresa told Old Chao, glumly. *"A new program to encourage people to move to the suburbs."* She explained how they only had to put ten percent down. The monthly payments, however, were quite high. *"For our income, they figured out how much I'll make, added that to how much Ralph will make once he gets tenure."*

Old Chao was surprised the bank would agree. *"Don't they realize —?"*

"Janis arranged it."

Old Chao played with his fork. *"My wife, you know, will do anything for anybody. Everyone has to like her. Everyone has to like me."* He set the fork on its tines. Their booth was so close to the kitchen that their napkins leapt and settled to the bursting rhythm of the swinging doors, which did not so much swing as boom. *"So what are you going to do?"*

"I don't know. Ralph, you know, thinks his life is going to go up and up and up."

"Maybe I should tell him . . . ?"

She frowned. *"No, I don't think so."*

"You're sure?" He grasped her hand. His touch was firm and warm, his reaching out somehow unextraordinary.

"If there were some way he could save face," she began; and before she knew what she was doing, she had removed her hand from Old Chao's, that she might massage her brow.

The first time in her life a man had ever touched her, and all she'd done was fret about her brother! She felt veiled in cobwebs, a woman wedded to her family.

"Say Ralph found some kind of job," she said the next day, *"for which he got paid something like what he gets now. Then if I moonlit in the emergency room in addition to my practice, we could manage it."*

"How could you moonlight on top of your practice?" asked Old Chao. *"When would you sleep?"*

"I'm used to no sleep. I don't sleep now." She wished Old Chao would put his hand on hers again.

"And look at you," he said instead, gently.

"It's my duty."

Old Chao called for the check.

THE
NEW HOUSE

HOW LUCKY they were! How many people came to this country
and bought a house just like that? Time passed too slowly and
too quickly; Ralph and Helen and Theresa could not wait to
move and yet had barely grasped that they were going to, when
they had. Enormous as the moving van seemed, the new house
was more enormous still, a split-level, with an attached garage.
No longer did they store their teacups on the windowsill. Now
Mona and Callie had a room, Theresa had a room, Helen and
Ralph had a room, and in addition they had a living room and
a dining room both, and a closet that could be made into a
study, and a basement that could become a playroom; not to
say a kitchen, of course (with that nook Helen loved), and gold
shag wall-to-wall carpeting, and their own half flight of stairs.
The stairs had a black wrought iron railing on one side that
Mona and Callie at first wouldn't use, the wall seeming more
familiar; but this being their wall now, and not everybody-in-
the-entry's, when Helen showed them how even hands that
looked clean left prints, they stopped, and took to running up
their five steps without touching anything. It got to be a game.

They would hop up, take the steps by twos, jump them backwards, all without using their hands; and then they would bump down on their stomachs like alligators. Up and down, up and down, up and down. Mona liked the going down part, even though she got rug burns, but Callie preferred the going up. She liked the work of it, the feeling that she was getting somewhere; and she liked the view that was her reward, a tunnel of impressions that moved from their plaid sofa to their cardboard-box cocktail table, and from there on out the picture window, through which she could see almost everything going on at the Kennedys' across the way.

Theirs was the last house in the neighborhood to be built, but when they moved in the area was still so new that local maps showed it as woods. The just-paved dead end was shiny black as the enamel walls of their oven, and all the yards were staked off with twine, as only the Kennedys had real grass (their rich uncle having had sod installed for them). Everyone else had spotty coverings of skinny, peapod-colored seedlings that they watered two, three, four times a day, depending on the weather. Rainy days were days off; sunny days it was back on the job. Some of the more ambitious neighbors had planted bushes and trees too — squat, well-spaced bundles of leaves and scrawny, solitary saplings — but the grass was the true binding hope of the neighborhood, and it was when the Changs spread their lot with lime and peat and 6-8-3 that they started to get to know everyone. Mrs. O'Connor lent them her Rototiller; Mr. Rossi, his spreader; Mr. Santone, his abundant advice; and soon their sprinkler was casting its bit of the community spell, crossing and recrossing the soil in concert with its fellow magicians up and down the street.

What had they understood about America? Evenings, they shook their heads at themselves. *We didn't realize.*
We thought we knew. But we didn't know.
We thought we lived here.
But actually knew nothing.

Almost nothing.
Completely nothing!

They would eat supper; then fortified, go on — *really, nothing; nothing really* — finding, to their pleasant surprise, that the deeper their former life sank in the black muck of ignorance, the higher their present life seemed to spring. So bright it shone, so radiant with truth and discovery! It was as if the land they had been living in had turned out to be no land at all, but a mere offshore island, a featureless mound of muddy scrub and barnacle-laced rock, barely big enough for a hospital, an engineering school. Whereas this New World — now this was a continent. A paradise, they agreed. An ocean liner compared to a rowboat with leaks. A Cadillac compared to an aisle seat on the bus. Every dream come dreamily true.

Except, that is, that their corner of paradise seemed after a few days to be carpeted not with plush grass, but birds. A whole flock of birds; and not loopy-plumed songbirds, but scrappy, raucous brown birds with teeth. Callie swore they had teeth. Helen tried to set her straight gently. "Birds don't have teeth." "In America they do," Callie answered. "I saw them! These are American birds, with teeth!" So insistent, that after a while Helen found herself going out to have a good look herself. Teeth? She was on her hands and knees on their flagstone walk when their neighbor Arthur Smith strolled by.

"Problems?" Arthur Smith, once a slender man, now was slender still except for the beach ball he sported under his shirt. He squinted, pursing his lips. His hair was cut so short Helen could see sweat beading on his pink and brown scalp.

"So many birds," Helen said weakly. She casually wiped her hands against each other, brushed her knees off.

"That's life." He continued to stand there.

"Maybe there's something wrong with that seed we used?" Mr. Smith considered the birds. "You folks Japanese?"

"Chinese."

"There you go," he said. "That's what I told Marianne. I told her, it ain't Japs moved in. Them Japs is farmers. These don't know dirt from dirt."

Helen smiled weakly.

"You ever raised up a lawn before?"

"No."

"There you go, I told Marianne that too. I could tell that just from our living room," he boasted. "Watching through the window."

Did he really watch them through the window? By day, Helen moved self-consciously through the yard. By night, she watched back. This was how she found out he kept a gun. *"A long one,"* she told Ralph. *"He cleans it and shines it while he watches TV."*

The grass wasn't coming up. They waited.

More birds.

Until one bright day, at long last, a green shadow appeared; Helen had to examine it back on her hands and knees again (hoping Arthur Smith wasn't watching) to be sure it wasn't moss, or mold. Seedlings! So what, that one of their neighbors kept a gun? In among the birds, there were seedlings! Then there were fewer birds; and after that there was grass of an unearthly green, so bright it glowed far into the twilight, like a luminescent clock dial. Who wouldn't shake their heads to see it? The Changs agreed — a lawn like this was more than just nature, just life. A lawn like this was America. It was the great blue American sky, beguiling the grass upward. It was the soil, so fresh, so robust, so much better quality than Chinese soil; Chinese soil having been prevailed upon for too many thousands of years. The blades were a bit skinny now, but they would fatten. Of course! After all, this was top-quality grass, grown out of top-quality soil.

Just as a top-quality family was growing out of a top-quality house; or so Helen believed. Taking her afternoon rest on the living room couch, her feet on the cardboard cocktail table (she was saving up for a new one, and maybe for a love seat too, to go in her nook off the kitchen), she couldn't help but wonder — could a house give life to a family? A foolish idea. And yet, the house did seem to have filled itself, to have drawn out of the family roomfuls of activity. Moving day, she remembered, they had clumped together in the living room like a pork ball; for a long moment, she'd almost believed they were always going to find themselves there, just inside the front door, their own intimidation sweeping toward them like a tide of soup. The moment passed, though. A relief. They were people, not ground pig shoulder. But would they always move about the house as if in a department store, trying to make sure that no one got lost? How real a possibility that seemed then; the space seemed like a threat, a challenge.

Whereas now, what would they do without it? So much livelier they all were! Helen had never seen the children run so much, touch so much, shout so much. They did not contain themselves. Why should they? Theresa talked to herself, Helen noticed, sometimes loudly; Ralph swung his arms around when he walked, sprawled when he sat. Even his papers had begun to proliferate. As for herself, she'd begun leaving the radio on all day, and cooking big complicated meals involving multiple bowls. Also, she breathed more. Or differently, so that for the first time in her life she noticed smells. She still didn't believe she breathed as oddly as Ralph claimed. But it did seem possible that in the city, she hadn't wanted to take in the fumes and gases, everyone else's exhaust; that air was like garbage air. Compared to this. She loved the aromas of the dirt, the grass, the flowers; the rain. Who would have thought the rain would smell? The seasons had their smells too; and indoors, she smelled clean house, soapy children, a medicinal sister-in-law, a sex-strong husband. How amorous Ralph had grown since they moved! He winked at her, he flirted in front of the children. "How many boyfriends you think your mother had before me?" he would ask them; and they would answer, "A thousand," or "A million," or "Ten zillion trillion," the highest numbers they could

think of, only to have him always say, smiling at her, "More."
Finally they would turn to her. "So why'd you marry *him?*"

And she would answer, "Because he was the best," or "Because he was the smartest," or "Because he was the handsomest."

He would add, "And the luckiest."

And later they would laugh about that, about how strange it was that their marriage should have turned so loverlike after so many years. "*My mother used to tell me it would be this way,*" she told him once. "*But I didn't believe her.*"

"*What way?*" he said.

"*She used to tell me that marriage would be like a pot of cold water put on the fire. For years it would be cold, she told me, and then slowly it would come to a boil.*"

"*It was like cold water?*" Ralph sounded hurt. "*For years?*" But a few minutes later, the light was out, and his outspread hand was in her pajamas, circling. "*Boil, boil,*" he whispered. "*Are we boiling now? Eh? Are we boiling?*"

She pressed herself against him, stretching. "*Let's have more children.*"

"*As many as you want.*"

"*Two more.*"

"*Boys, right?*"

"*If we can manage.*"

"*Boys coming up,*" said Ralph. "*Does it feel like boys?*"

"*A boy, anyway.*" Helen laughed.

"*Hmmm,*" said Ralph.

What couldn't the house do.

In the fall, Callie started kindergarten. Helen bought her a navy blue jumper with a duck for a pocket, a light blue blouse with a Peter Pan collar, matching light blue stretch ankle socks with lace trim, and a pair of marine blue tie-up Buster Browns with such perfectly smooth pale tan leather soles that Callie wouldn't wear them home from the store. "Beautiful!" she said, kissing them. "Look, Mommy, beautiful!" "They are beautiful," Helen agreed; and that night she allowed Callie to go to sleep with one hand in each shoe, while envious Mona looked on.

"Can I have one?"

"Tomorrow," Callie promised.

"I want one!"

"Tomorrow!"

"I want one now! Now!"

"Okay," said Callie. "Baby."

The next morning, the shoe was gone.

"Where is it!" screeched Callie. "Where is it!"

"Come on, Mona," said Helen. "We got to go."

"It's in jail," said Mona.

"In jail! Where in jail? Where?"

Mona giggled.

"My sho-oe," wailed Callie.

"Mona!" said Helen. "Where's that shoe! Give it to me! You hear me? Right now!" But even when Helen spanked her and called her a bad bad girl, Mona refused to produce the shoe, and in the end Callie went to school in one old shoe and one new one.

"You're a dirty rotten," cried Callie.

Mona shrugged, diffident.

"Come on, now," said Helen, already out on the front step. "Time to go."

"You're a baby!" yelled Mona as they left.

"You are!"

"You are!"

"Come on!" shouted Helen. "We got to go! Right now!"

"See you later, baby," said Callie.

As the door slammed, Mona's hair whipped across her face and caught in her mouth. She chewed on it.

Ralph came up behind her. "Taste good?"

She didn't say anything.

"Maybe you should have something else to eat?"

She shook her head.

"Some" — he thought — "some candy bar?"

Mona burst into tears.

He took out his handkerchief. "Ah, Mona." He dabbed gently at her eyes. For a special treat, he allowed her to play in his office, usually off limits, and when she crawled into the kneehole of his desk, he hung an old shirt down the front of it, making a tent. "Ahhrr!" Mona roared, emerging. "I'm a dragon!" Ralph pretended to be scared until Mona grew bored. Then he let her rummage through his desk drawers, rearranging them however she liked.

TENURE

THE NEXT DAY, Callie's shoe was found in the washing machine. The next month, Helen began playing bridge with Joyce Genovese and Amy Halloran and Tobey Long down the block. The next February, they had an extra-elaborate Chinese New Year's dinner, with cunning little dumplings, and balls, and buns, in addition to the usual hot pot with gold-chain bean threads. The next spring, Callie learned to read. The next June, Theresa began her specialty training (obstetrics). And the September after that, after a squabble with Helen about the lawn (he did have to cut it soon, she was right, it was looking like a jungle), Ralph was presented with a large, lidded cardboard file box, into which he was to collect all the materials "pertaining to his case."

Of course, he had always been convinced he would get tenure. It was the kind of confidence, though, built to keep terror at bay. Now, every morning, every afternoon, every evening, he considered that file box, until its nervous scattering of tan speckles began to look like so many clods and crumbs of dirt flung indifferently upon a sad destiny. His sad destiny — which was not only to have to rest himself in a box (and a tiny box at that,

smaller even than a pauper's box), but to have to embalm himself
first. How lifelike he had to look, how perfectly, robustly pro-
fessorial! For the gatekeepers of heaven were to review him in
state, that they might make their decision: *Would this man be
a credit to the empyrean? Can you imagine him a colleague of
yours? A colleague of yours — for eternity?*

Some of them nodded their long white locks yes. Some of
them shook them no. About half and half, Ralph figured.

Would he ascend or descend?

In only months, he would know.

Meanwhile, he hammered at his statements with the small
obsession of a woodpecker. He thought he should write them
in Chinese, then translate them, but when he sat down, he per-
versely found that he wanted to compose in English. Was one
way better? He'd try it the other way too, then backtrack, then
rewrite what he'd written, again and again, until he couldn't
even tell if what he was writing was different from what he'd
written before. Sometimes he considered that he could not be
too careful. At the same time he wondered if, being overcareful,
he would never finish his statements at all. In fact, he dreaded
finishing; as long as he hadn't finished, there was still hope. (*He
doesn't look as well as he might, but you know, the embalmer's
not done.*) He found that whereas when he began his statements
he could spend hours on a paragraph, after some practice he
could spend days, even weeks; and then he needed to consider
what Old Chao would think of it, or Ken Freedberg, who was
probably going to vote no, no matter what. . . . So Ralph wished
he could believe, at least. Because the times he thought there
might be something he could say to change Ken's mind, or Neil
Nixon's, or Lou Radin's, or Chris Olsen's, were the times he
agonized most. What was the word that would do it? If only
the word would occur to him! If only he were a person to whom
it would occur!

Instead what occurred to him were ways of telling people off.
It may seem to you that others are transfixed by the clarity of

your mind, but actually we are just afraid if you don't get your way you will cry. He liked that one. More often, though, the ideas that flocked to him lacked real sting. *Your mother would be ashamed to see how mean you've become.* Or, *So you voted no, you have the brains of a dung fly, and what's more, you have no manners.* It was less than satisfying; and yet as his due date neared he kept on, sometimes all night.

In your next life, I hope you are a sea clam.

For a break, he analyzed. At four in the morning, hunched over the kitchen table, he made lists. He listed all of his papers. He listed all of his papers graded as he thought the various committee members would grade them; he listed all of his papers with the grades they properly deserved. He listed the various committee members and what they thought of him. He listed the various committee members and what he thought of them. He listed which committee members he would've voted yes on if he had sat on their committees, noting that this list was remarkably similar to the list of committee members he had guessed would vote in his favor. He listed how many of those people were working feverishly on space. Sputnik! What trouble the Russians had made for him. And all this nonsense now about monkeys and rocket-powered airplanes. Weather satellites. Everyone was in love with the moon. Moon rockets! He wished he were a doctor, like his sister. What had happened in medicine since the polio vaccine? Nothing! He listed how many people knew anything about machine tools.

Why should I listen to you, with all that hair in your nose?

In the daytime, he continued to teach, and to grace meetings with his most authoritative manner, and to hold office hours. He continued to smile and nod agreeably when people spoke. "You're right! I agree one hundred percent." He strove to appear sure he would get tenure. When people asked how he thought the decision would go, he answered, "What decision?" He was surprised how easy this was. He tried not to avoid any members of the committee, even if he thought they were going to vote no. If anything, he was friendliest to them. How were their children, he asked, their wives?

No children? Not married?

Such stumbling was rare. Except that the world buzzed and that he shook all the time, he thought he was doing remarkably well. Who else could hear the world buzzing, after all? Every now and then, he would ask, casually, "Do you hear a buzz?" No one else could hear it. *(Ting bu jian!)* As for the shaking, he simply kept stones in his pockets — a rough one in the right pocket, a smooth one in the left. These he grasped, loads to dampen the vibration. He thought they must be working. No one said to him, "Ralph, you're shaking." They said only, "You must be nervous, with your decision coming up."

"What decision?"

May. Helen was deadheading the rhododendrons. Time to present his file to the department. At home, he was alarmed, picking it up, at how light it seemed — bodiless. He imagined the committee gathered around a scale, shaking their heads. Outside, though, as he loaded it into the car, he was surprised to feel a sudden surge of confidence. Maybe it was only that he had worried himself out. In any case, he felt the morning flow into his mind through his ears and nose and mouth, even through his eyes; and when he considered his box — that same too-light box of just minutes before — he believed, Yes, it would indeed be returned to him with congratulations. He could not lose his job, and with it, this solid house, with its ever-growing lawn and maturing ornamental shrubbery. He would not imagine it. What he imagined instead was handing his file to Old Chao, who told him, *Don't worry. You'll get it.*

Really?

Everyone agrees. We might not even bother to vote. The feeling's that unanimous.

Really?

But at school, Old Chao's office door was closed. Ralph could hear Old Chao talking to someone inside. He put his free hand in his coat pocket, to weigh it down with the stone. Dampen the vibration. He decided to come back later.

No sooner had he settled into his own office, though, than he heard Old Chao's steps in the hall — a firm patter, deliberate, squeaky. He jumped up. Old Chao had just turned the corner at the far end of the corridor. Ralph hurried after him. As Old Chao was walking briskly himself, Ralph was not gaining ground. Should he run? Unprofessional. File in arms, Ralph chased Old Chao down another hall, then another, then another. They crossed a wing that the chemistry department had recently abandoned and headed toward a seldom-used lounge.

"An affair!" Ralph told Helen.

"Impossible," she said. *"Chinese people don't do such things."*

"Then Old Chao isn't Chinese anymore."

"You're sure?"

"I saw them."

"What did she look like?"

"Chinese."

"You're sure it wasn't Janis?"

"Skinnier. I couldn't quite see because the door swung shut. Also, I was so shocked, I dropped my file box."

"On the floor?"

"Papers everywhere."

"Ohhh-noo." Helen shook her head. *"Were they doing anything?"*

"Eating lunch. I saw them opening brown bags."

"I should tell Janis."

" 'Better to do nothing than to overdo,' " quoted Ralph. *"Don't make trouble."* He started a new list, What Old Chao's Affair Means.

1. May be preoccupied.
2. May be doing many things other people don't know.
3. May not be chairman forever.

May not be chairman forever. Was it possible? The very idea felt like a revelation of sorts.

"*A Chinese woman,*" mused Helen.

Ralph started another list, What It Would Mean If Old Chao Were To Have To Resign In Shame.

1. Would never have to see Old Chao again.

What a prospect! Ralph felt so exhilarated that he immediately started a third list, What I Would Do If I Never Had To See Old Chao Again.

1.

Miss him, Ralph thought, but he couldn't write that.

"*Someone Chinese!*" Helen shook her head.

By the day of the decision, Ralph had talked himself out of wanting to be a professor anyway. First of all, he was not interested in engineering. Secondly, he was not interested in research. Thirdly, he was not interested in teaching. So why should he be a scholar? Just because Old Chao was? He decided that he would rather be a fireman. A funeral director. Anything that didn't require books, or a slide rule. What he'd give never to have to see a slide rule again for the rest of his life!

"*You got it!*"

Ralph was so surprised to hear Old Chao shout that he almost couldn't understand what his friend was saying.

"*You got it! You got it!*"

"Tenure?" The phone waves seemed to be generating a harmonic in his stomach.

"*Tenure! You got it! Congratulations! With everyone going over to space, we really did need someone in straight mechanics.*"

Helen invited Old Chao and Janis over to celebrate.

"*You know what I'm going to buy?*" she told Ralph. "*Champagne!*"

"What fun!" he enthused. *"Great idea!"*

The only wet firecracker was that Theresa couldn't come.

"Department dinner," she explained, as she and Helen put away dishes.

"So last-minute," Helen said.

Theresa fussed with a dish. *"Well, you know,"* she said. "Typical American no-consideration-for-other-people."

"Maybe we can move the date. It's rude, but —"

"Oh, nonono. Don't worry about it." Being tall, Theresa was in charge of the high shelves. Now she stretched, trying to make room for a large Pyrex casserole.

"I don't know if that's going to go," Helen warned.

"Well, it has to." Theresa tried to maneuver it in.

"We'll find another place for it."

"No, no. It'll go. It will."

"Don't worry about it."

Theresa set her jaw. *"It'll go."*

Helen peered at her carefully. *"Are you tired?"*

"Tired?"

"You seem a little . . ."

Theresa reorganized some other dishes.

"Just found out today, huh. About the meeting."

"That's right. Today."

"You didn't know until today?" asked Helen again.

"Why do you ask?" Theresa countered — casually, she hoped.

But as she spoke, the casserole tipped out of the cabinet and plummeted to the floor.

ON

THE MILK BOX

AT TEN-FIFTEEN, when Theresa came home, everyone was still talking and toasting. Helen had forgotten about the champagne until after supper, so that just as the party had begun to break up, it had started again. Now volleys of laughter exploded across the lawn. Theresa, keeping out of range, sought refuge on the milk box near the driveway. Every so often she stood up to warm herself; otherwise she waited patiently, the hard metal under her.

Ten-thirty.

It was a miserable night, damp, the air solid with fog. From the driveway came a series of shrieks and scrapes; a squirrel, Theresa discovered, had gotten into one of the garbage cans, and was frantically trying to find its way out. The can jiggled and danced, as though possessed by a ghost. What a racket! Theresa tipped the can over; the squirrel, looking ragged, scooted toward liberation. Its bare patches glimmered in the fuzzy light.

A small event. Still, her milk box sentinel, when she settled back into it, seemed even lonelier for her having yet one more thing to keep to herself. Her hearing sharpened. A neighbor's screen door opened and clacked shut. A police car radio cackled raucously. Crickets. The month had been unusually wet; certain pools of water had reappeared so often on the driveway that Theresa actually recognized them now. Three larger ones, one smaller.

Ten-forty-five. Finally she snuck around to the front of the house, feet sinking in the soft dirt. Trying not to disturb the azaleas, she peeked in the dining room window. There they all were, a little round of people. Two couples, each half of a group. There being only four of them, the china matched. The chandelier glittered, its crystal teardrops like small golden suns. Would she never sit at a table like that? Everyone was leaning forward, toward one another; even Old Chao seemed to be enjoying himself hugely. Listening closely, Theresa could just make out his words as, his face bright with liquor, he repeated a joke she'd told him that afternoon. She waited for the punch line, her shoes growing soggy.

She ate lunch with Old Chao in the lounge. *"They think we're having an affair."*

He stroked her hand with his thumb. Back and forth.

"A rotten egg, my brother called me, to my face. 'Chinese people don't do such things,' he said."

"Did you tell them the truth?"

"I tried." She regarded her feet. *"Anyway. What others think makes no difference to me one way or another. 'True gold does not fear fire,' right?"*

So she said. And yet after three weeks of reprehension — Helen was short, Ralph cool, even the girls seemed wary of her — she began to feel her attitude weakening. Perceptions shaped her; proving her only human, a social being. She was disappointed to be misperceived, and more angered than ever — this time she could not box herself up — and these emotions opened others. Curiosity. Recklessness. For these she would not atone.

The censure of her family was like a hard shell under which she found a certain freedom. One day — after how long? — she finally let Old Chao kiss her. This brought pleasure. And with pleasure, its on-and-off companion, regret. All her years, it seemed to her now, she had stood against life. She had studied it; she had made forays into it; but mostly she had stood by while others braved the field. Did she love Old Chao? She didn't know how to love anyone — though she did believe he loved her, that he found her a doctor for his many ailments, both those he could name and those he could not. She believed he would go on as they had, indefinitely. Yet now, in repayment for his love, in hope of finding a return love for him, she allowed him more. Then more still, surprised at how soft his lips were as he pressed them up and down her neck. She was surprised that the wet point of his tongue at her ear could make her whole body shiver, as though with fever. The firmness of his touch surprised her too, and how many parts of her body could be cupped, and what bursting tenderness was this in her nipples? She found she liked roughness and gentleness both, and that kissing back made her tingle more; and that when the time to stop came, she ached. One day he eased her back until she was leaning on the arm of the sofa, and then he scooped her ankles up. She stiffened, afraid he was going to rape her. But he didn't rape her. He simply lay down, clothed, on top of her. She could feel his legs along the length of hers, how his continued on. He was heavy; she had to push her lungs to breathe. She filled her lungs, filled her lungs, and in her concentration, almost didn't notice that Old Chao had begun moving according to the rhythm she'd set. She would not part her legs; still he thrust, a throb against her, but pushing into bone. Was this desire? She felt his, but less of her own than she had sitting up; until, almost as she thought that, he eased his body lower. He wasn't moving against bone any more. Now she could feel him, a bulge like a pear. She relaxed, knowing it wrong to go on, but knowing it wrong, too, to stop him, to stop this rocking, rocking. She relaxed more, separating her legs ever so slightly — allowing him. Now they fit together, now they were moving together, her whole body tightening, arching.

"What are you watching?" he whispered. "Don't watch."

"Am I watching?"

"You don't have to watch," he urged. "Nothing to watch."

She closed her eyes.

PART IV

Structural Weakening

MYSTERY

WHERE in himself had he found it, after everything he'd been through, to try Grover's line once more? What had he been thinking? Who was he? It was years before Ralph even knew to ask himself those questions; and then it was only to find that he didn't know their answers — that his own nature eluded his grasp, like a solid sublimating straightaway, from between his fingers, to gas. What could be more frustrating? Why try? It was a uniquely low return enterprise. And yet he found that in America, in practical, can-do, down-to-earth America, he had much company in this activity — that a lot of people wondered who they were quite seriously, some of them for a living. It was an industry. This astonished him. In China, people had worried more about being recognized; even here, if Helen were snubbed, she might sigh, *"Of course, he did not realize who we are."* *Who we are* being so many hard facts held like candies or coins, just up one's sleeve — one's father, one's mother, all the things that might quaintly be termed one's station. This was useful information in a terraced society. How should people treat each other? How expect to be treated? In close quarters, relationships count so heavily that to say something *has no relationship* in Chinese — *mei guanxi* — is to mean, often as not, *it doesn't matter*. In spread-out America, though, this loose-knit country, where one could do as one pleased, a person had need of a different understanding. Ralph needed to know what his limits were, and his impulses, what evil and what good he had it in his soul and hands to fashion.

Instead, he got mystery for his pains, more and more mystery. It wasn't fair. It wasn't right. How could his own motoring heart, with its valves and pressure systems, turn out an unknowable thing? He had always understood the world to be only part engineering; he'd always understood there to be another, murkier sphere. But he had always pictured them as somehow adjoining. Organized. Earth and heaven. Down below, verities; up above, mist. How could it be that bright fact and cloudy mystery were actually all mixed up, helter-skelter, together? And in him! Even in his own breast, his own brain, just as in the chaotic world outside. Some days he saw mystery everywhere, in earthworms and holly trees and basset hounds, and the inexplicability of even the simplest life so angered and stupefied him that he almost resented any balancing elucidation. He did not care to know how many female holly trees a single male could bring to berry. He did not care to know the odds of a basset hound developing swayback, or by what process part of an earthworm could make itself whole.

Still, of their own accord — mysteriously! — certain realizations emerged, as if they too had a life, a schedule urging them into the realm of conscious knowledge. For instance, Ralph realized that if he had not called Grover, if he had not remembered the number, if no one had answered, he probably would not have landed up a pondering sort of person. If Helen or Theresa had walked into the room as he was talking, so that he had had to hang up, he probably would sit around less. His daughters would never have presented him with a copy of *Calorie Counters, the* 1-2-3 *Way to an All-New You*. If the telephone had not yet been invented, his sister would still be knocking at the door when she heard him sneeze. Why did he call? Before he made that call, he would have said he was a man who aspired to peace, and rest. Before he made it, he would have said that he yearned for a larger tenure than any department could grant; to go with his professional tenure, a sort of life tenure. He wanted simply to stay put. No more scrambling! He wanted to laze away the afternoon at a dumpling house, sip plum juice by a green pond flickering with orange-and-white carp. Or, well, he would have settled for iced tea, anyway, by a crabgrass-free lawn with a sprinkler leaning one direction, then the other, charmingly indecisive. Hadn't he once wished, achingly, ardently, only that no revolution should ever take his wife from him?

But then he took his own wife, his own family, his job, his house, and gambled as though they were nothing to him, as though his whole life were nothing to him — as though, indeed, his whole life weren't his. What sort of thing was that for his father's son to do? So reckless! He hadn't done anything so completely wrong since he fell in love with Cammy; didn't that seem like a lifetime ago now. And yet, that lifetime was a kind of scale model for what followed. He saw that. He saw how then, as later, he strode away from his family, only to discover that he could not return. He saw how he had hated his father and sister both. If only he had known how to at once hate and love them! If only he had been capable of more than nostalgia!

A chastened man, an older man, he remembered:

All summer, to begin with, he felt elated. The department had approved his tenure, the College of Engineering had approved it, the university had approved it. He took the family to a picnic of the Society of Chinese Engineers — something he'd always avoided before — and ate tea eggs. He played horseshoes. He laughed at the jokes and swore at the mosquitoes and liked everyone. Everyone! Some people talked of nothing but China; others of nothing but America. Some had houses, some didn't. Some spoke Shanghainese. Ralph listened to them all whether he understood their dialect or not.

Then he went on vacation. It was the first vacation he had

taken since coming to America, and he felt as though he had discovered the whole idea of an earth that from time to time nestled closer to the sun, as though the pleasures of a cottage, a seafood shack, a bluff high above the water, of children flapping their ball-and-stick arms at curtain-winged gulls, all began in him, all grew out of his tremendous accomplishment. He felt a secret kinship with the ocean. Mornings, he would stand midthigh in the surf and feel he understood its power, that he understood greatness — that he was neither fooled by its easy majesty nor afraid of its violence. He still did not know how to swim, but that summer he taught himself how to float on his back; he spent so much time rocking in the water, feeling the swells pass under him like wheels in endless travel, rolling and rolling, that he turned brown as a peasant. On just one side — Helen and Theresa, huddled in long-sleeved shirts and polka-dot sun hats under the additional shade of a beach umbrella, laughed at him. They called him half-cooked, half-black, half-and-half. A mixup. An open-faced sandwich. He didn't mind. He taught Mona and Callie to float too; all three of them bobbed out there like rafts, together. Also he taught the girls how to make their sand castles more realistic (down along the moats they put in windows for a boiler room), and when he got home he announced he was going to teach Helen and Theresa to drive.

"To drive?" At first they didn't know what to think. Then they were excited and anxious to prove fast learners.

"Don't watch the houses," Ralph told Helen. *"Pay attention to where you're headed."*

"Stay in your lane," he lectured Theresa. *"Watch you don't get yourself killed."*

He taught proudly, like a great professor, a professor everyone agreed deserved his tenure. When they did well, he praised them. When they did poorly, he encouraged them to do better. That summer he taught a neighbor how to change the stresses on his garage frame so the door wouldn't stick. He taught the newspaper boy a way of folding the paper so that it wouldn't unroll when he threw it. He taught Callie that when she added, she should stack the numbers one on top of the other. He taught Mona that she should always hold books right side up.

Then September, time to teach some more. His very first class with tenure, due to a shortage of space, was in a tower. A tiny room, with exposed pipes. How could it be? So high up, and yet the room was like a basement. Halfway through his opening remarks, he found himself figuring from the way the pipes ran that there was a bathroom upstairs. A bathroom in a tower? An odd design, a bad design. And at the end of class, more bad design — he discovered that it was hard to get out of the tower. The stairs were so narrow, that with more students coming up, his had to file down one at a time. They waited patiently in the doorway, like a pool of backed-up water. It seemed to Ralph that there was no air in the room. And wasn't it hot? He wanted to ask one of the students, a pallid twitch of a boy, if it was hot. But instead he asked, "Are you on so-called engineering track?" If you are, get off! he wanted to say. Of course, he didn't. He mopped his brow as he signed the boy's slip. Another slip. Humid too, he thought. Wasn't it? As the professor, he was the last one down the stairs. How glad to escape! How relieved to see the open (if stony) sky! And how chagrined to discover, squinting at his schedule in the breezeway, that for his next class he had that same room again. What a semester it was going to be! All he could think of, as he headed back in, was what his father used to say about people lost in narrow, dead-end specialties — that *they had crawled into the tip of a bull's horn*.

Now he stared once again at the pale green pipes. He stared at the students; this fresh batch looked suspiciously like the one that had just left. Doubts thronged him. Should he have gone into space research after all? Maybe he should have gone to work for a firm. He heard himself droning. The first day of a new school year, and already everything seemed old.

The pipes, he noticed, shaded to powdery gray on top — dust.

"Excuse me, Professor Chang, could you repeat your office hours?"

Professor Chang. That still gave him a lift. He, Ralph Chang, a professor! And now, with tenure. He obligingly repeated his office hours, throwing in his office address for good measure, as a way of reminding himself that he had a nice new half office, with a window. Tenure. What a pulse-quickening idea to the nontenured! Too bad, though, that he was going to have to live down the hall from Old Chao for the rest of his life. Clear from China they'd come, a whole country to settle in; who could believe they'd find themselves sharing a soda machine? Every time Ralph saw Old Chao, he seemed to be orbiting the halls over his ever more significant findings. Maybe he was just trying to steer the conversation away from Theresa. Still — while Old Chao worked on turbulence, Ralph lectured on about all that had been exciting and important and new in the nineteenth century. Gears. Stresses. Torques.

"Excuse me, Professor Chang? Could you repeat . . ."

Could he. A good question. And how many times?

Dust on the pipes!

On the way home, although the sky had sobered to a duty-stiff gray, Ralph decided to put the top of his car down. As he hadn't done this in a long while (the mechanism had grown cranky with age), it excited him. The street bustle excited him too, as he drove, and though he could feel the damp grit of the city lodging in his skin and clothes — mister, it was great to be out and around! If his job was the dead-end tip of a bull's horn, the city was the bull. So giant! So clangorous — such screeching, rumbling, blaring, banging! Such hiss! Everything buzzed, in a blink things changed, the mind boggled at the striving that went on in a single block. So much ambition! No equation could begin to describe it all. So many people, aiming to do so many things besides lecture about crack stress to blinking undergraduates, that after five minutes he found himself gratefully focusing on the red light in front of him, a headache coming on. He helmeted himself in abstractions. The greatness of America! he thought. Freedom and justice for all! The light changed. It began to drizzle. Now he noticed how bedraggled some of the men looked up close. Some of the women too, but mostly he noticed the men, how they hunched their shoulders, how they stood their short collars against the fine lines of rain. One tattered fellow collapsed in a doorway. He had a brown knit cap pulled all the way down over his eyes and nose; his jaws chattered uncontrollably.

Ralph drove on, feeling his good fortune. Freedom and justice for all, the greatness of America, but a man living in a country sending satellites into space could still land up a heap in a doorway. How was that? He genuinely wondered, even as he estimated himself to fall in the top twenty percent of the general population, careerwise. He felt himself to know things that other people didn't, that he could tell just by looking who was going up, who was going down, who was suffering through. At each stoplight, his gaze would light on someone — a brooding beatnik, a determined shopper — and he would have to fight down an urge to shout that he saw them. He saw them! The fine lines of rain had thickened, but he didn't want to stop to put the roof up; and so he didn't, even when his car hood began to drum loudly. Afraid of a little water? Not him.

A downpour. Still he drove. People on the sidewalks were holding newspapers over their heads, like little roofs. He turned onto the highway, speeding away from the city. Though his clothes were soaking through, though water whipped the back of his neck, though his face dripped, he continued his escape from the classroom out to the suburbs, land of greater promise.

Only to discover, as he approached, that the towns seemed box-like, and overtidy. He disliked their small-change sense of order. When he slowed, he saw that people took notice of him driving in the rain with the top down. This made him uncomfortable enough that finally, before he came to the many-eyed cluster of shops closest to his house, he stopped by the reservoir to put the top back up. How wet everything was! The seats were soggy; his leather briefcase had dulled and darkened; there was a pool in each of the four footwells of the floor. He yanked at the roof. Water piped out from the accordion folds. The mechanism was stiff; between the wet vinyl and his raw hands, he could only get it to straighten halfway before it stuck. Struggling, he pinched a finger, which bled pink in the rain. He gave up. But then he couldn't get the roof to fold back down, either. Pull as he might, it remained a luminous rising in the twilit air, like a stairway to nowhere, or the headless incarnation of a jack-in-the-box.

Could he drive the car like that? Would the wind snap the roof off? What Ralph needed was an oil can — which, of course, if he did things the right way, he would have. Anyway, he decided to walk home and get one; it wasn't far, if he cut through the woods. He was wearing his good shoes, it was true, but he didn't care. So he reported to class in ruined shoes, so what? What would Old Chao do if he saw them, hit the roof on his way into outer space?

Though it was almost dark, he could see pretty well by the light reflected off the reservoir. When he turned away from the water, though, he was surprised how much darker it got.

Creaking.

He'd taken the girls on this path before. Buddied up to the other side of the reservoir was a small hill, where children went sledding in the winter. But how different the path was without snow! With snow, it was level. Now it was treacherous with tree roots. His feet turned capricious, slipping off at odd angles. Sometimes a heel would touch ground first, other times it would be a toe, or an arch. His weight was always in the wrong place, every step such a jolt that after a while he found himself feeling his way forward, not picking his feet up at all. He told himself, They're opportunities, those trees, every one of them. Opportunities for what, though? Paper. Houses. It was such hard work to imagine houses here that the idea of them became itself a kind of roof, with walls. How dangerous could these woods be, anyway? He was no more than a quarter of a mile from the road, he figured; it only seemed more. How had it gotten so black out? His own two hands at arm's length looked menacing. He tried to remember what he'd heard, once, about attacks in these woods.

Attacks of what?

Heart attacks, he joked to himself.

Was that a rustle?

He stopped. In the distance he could hear the *whhuz-whhuz* of cars; nearer in, the *pt-pt-pt* of the rain. The rain was abating. Good, he'd had enough of being undaunted by water. He started moving again.

That *was* a rustle.

He froze.

He never did find out what it was, that black swaying in the all-but-black path. It might have been a dog, or a raccoon, or an opossum, or a skunk, or a porcupine, or it might have been something more dangerous. Whatever it was, it stopped dead silent in front of him. Ralph pictured teeth. His heart kicked. What now? A breeze picked up; burdened leaves poured their watery hearts out to him as he tried to *xiang banfa* — to think of a way out of his predicament.

Another rustle.

He considered climbing a tree.

Above him, the sky seemed to lighten.

Then, as the animal lumbered away, a sudden white glare switched on full in his face, shocking as a blow; the moon loomed so low and large that it almost seemed to have abandoned the sky for a roll on the field just ahead of him. He dazedly blinked. Before him now lay the path, illumined; and when he turned, he saw that the world that had been darkness was returned to him, magnificent in deep blues and grays and black, streaked gold. Enormous clouds were blowing by, a spectral procession.

What had he done, to be delivered out of every trouble? No matter. In the elegant way of innocent men, he accepted his gift graciously. He felt how his suit hung on him, sodden and heavy; still, he was happy. Stars were coming out — now one, now two, now three — for him. He remembered: If you don't get out for a spin every now and then, you forget all about them. Anything is possible. A man is what he makes up his mind to be.

He felt his mind open, open, open.

RALPH

IS ANSWERED

"THE CAR BROKE DOWN," Ralph announced when he came in the door.

"You're kidding." Hand outstretched, Helen tried to direct him to the kitchen, so that he would drip on the linoleum rather than the living room carpet, but he ignored her. His shoes, as he worked them off, slurped loudly.

"You must be freezing," said Helen. *"How did it happen?"*

He mentally commanded her not to ask more, and sure enough, though she started to — he could almost see the questions pressed to the front of her mind — she stopped when he placed his shoes, one at a time, in her hands.

"They're ruined. Throw them out," ordered Ralph.

Mysteriously drawn out of sleep, the children appeared, slack-mouthed, on the stairs. Callie higher, Mona lower, they clung with all four of their hands to the railing.

"Something wrong?" said Ralph. "Go back sleep."

"You're *wet,*" Mona objected. "You're *dripping.* If you don't —"

Callie nudged her in the back with her big toe.

"Right now," said Helen. "If you don't want spank."

The girls crabbed their way up, using their hands and feet in combination.

Ralph lay his sopping jacket in Helen's arms, across the shoes. *"Bring me my bathrobe."*

"Girls, be quiet," called Helen, even though they were already quiet. The jacket dripped. "Girls, close that door."

Dry and fed, Ralph settled himself in front of the telephone. He never did find Grover's card that day Theresa stumbled upon him sneezing amid his papers. But now he picked up the receiver, and experimentally let his fingers dial; and sure enough, he found that they recollected easily what his mind had strained uselessly to remember.

Ringing. Ringing. No answer. What surprise was that? This his ear, his neck, his elbow seemed to recollect. How many times, after all, had he tried Grover's line in the days after their drive? A hundred times, without luck.

"Ding residence."

Ralph started. "Grover?"

Everyone knows this much about faith: that it is preceded by doubt the way day is preceded by night. Ralph recalled the priest at church once saying this. "Risk faith. Doubt doubt." Ralph tried. He recited from Norman Vincent Peale, " 'I believe I am always divinely guided. I believe I will always take the right turn of the road.' "

Meanwhile, in the darkest booth of a deli, over double cheeseburgers with everything, Grover was chummily confiding how he'd been wrongly charged with buying barrels of stolen grease. "How could I know those barrels were hot?" he was saying. "You tell me now."

Ralph shook his head, obligingly outraged. He noticed how Grover, though still handsome, had grayed since he saw him last. His voice, correspondingly, had lowered and become gravelly, so that his jaw, which had always jutted, now seemed to reinforce an impression of firmness and purpose. How long had it been since they last talked? Six years? Seven? Many years, they'd agreed. Grover hadn't seemed much interested in figuring out the exact number, its significance eclipsed by this story, which Ralph wasn't quite sure he believed. He wanted to believe it, though, if only because smart, prosperous Grover had remembered him almost right away, and demanded to know why he hadn't called before, and immediately invited him to supper, where he'd asked Ralph all about his job, just like a long-lost friend.

"The restaurants put their grease in these barrels, which they then leave out in back of their stores. Collectors haul it over to me. Okay? But sometimes these crooks — don't ask me where they come from — they go sneaking up there and rustle the barrels away. So then what? Does the grease look any different? I implore you to answer."

Ralph shook his head.

"And would you do business with crooks? Knowingly?"

Ralph shook his head again.

"Of course not, right? How can you trust a crook?"

"Impossible."

"You're right on the money. And that's what I'm going to tell the judge, you wait and see."

Ralph ordered another double cheeseburger. Grover lit a cigarette.

"Now." Grover restarted the conversation. "Do you trust me?"

"Of course. Old friends."

Grover leaned across the table and lowered his voice. "I've been giving your work situation some consideration. Maybe I can be of some . . . help."

"What do you mean, help?"

"Let's just say some kind of help." Grover smiled mysteriously, his gold tooth gleaming. His breath smelled of smoke.

"Like your fats and oils boss help you?"

"Something like that. But first I must request that you write me a check."

"A check?" Ralph drew back. Now was the time to have faith, of course, but it was hard. Doubt doubt, he told himself. Still he could not help asking, "Why?"

Grover waved one hand, stubbing out his cigarette with the other. "Listen, forget it. If you've got to know why why why, we're not walking on the same side of town."

Grover got up to go to the bathroom. Ralph played with his food, reflective; and when Grover returned, asked, "How much would that check be for? If I write."

Grover looked as though he would not reopen the discussion, but then said, "Listen. You can have it right back if you want it, you just have to ask. What do you think I am, some two-bit crook? I've got no designs on your nickel. I just have to know who I'm dealing with. You ask why why why, now that alerts me to certain possibilities."

"Like what?"

"Like the possibility there's no deal here."

"How much would that check be for?"

"Oh, I don't know. Say a grand."

Ralph gulped. "I can have it back?"

"I do believe I just said that, verbatim."

Ralph wrote.

"To get somewhere," said Grover, "a man has to understand his assets and his liabilities. You, for instance, prefer not to lose this money."

"Yes."

"For reasons having to do with your family."

"Yes."

"Family can be an asset. Or it can be a liability, depending."

"My wife — Helen, you remember — is asset. Also I have two little girls."

Grover lit another cigarette.

"But my sister —"

"I remember that sister of yours." Grover shook his head. "Skinny one."

"How could I forget." Grover shook his head again. "That sister of yours, that Old Chao —"

"How did you know!"

Grover watched his cigarette ash grow. "Come on, now. Everybody knows."

"Everyone?"

A faint smile.

Ralph felt suddenly overcome with exhaustion. "I should not ask this . . ." he started to say; and though he thought he *should not continue,* he did. "Maybe even you do not know . . ." Grover's head was disappearing in a cloud of smoke. "But so many months, I wonder."

"What about?"

"Wonder." Ralph hesitated; it seemed to him that his head was ensconced in smoke too. "Do they talk about me?" His voice, small and scratchy, seemed to originate from the back of his head, up behind his ears.

"Do they talk about you!" Grover laughed. "No, no, they've got better things to, ah, discuss."

"And do they laugh?"

"At you? No, no." Grover reassured him again, but was so close to guffawing that he had to stub out his cigarette and drink some water. "Listen. Enough of this," he went on. "You keep your wad for now. If you get the itch to do a little business, mail me something next couple of days. Okay?"

Ralph nodded as though in his sleep.

"No obligation. Sleep on it. And listen, in the meantime — I notice you don't have a watch."

"I have one. But I don't wear it."

"Allow me to present you with this one." Grover took off his watch and presented it to him with a flourish. "In consideration of your joining me this evening."

"But I already have watch. Solid gold."

"No wonder you don't wear it. This watch is practical. Look here." Grover turned it over. "Stainless steel. Please accept it. A small consideration for your time."

Could he keep the check and the watch both? It seemed vaguely wrong to Ralph, in violation of some code; he felt confronted with a language close to one he knew, yet strange. What to do? The next day, even as he pondered the question, he ran into Old Chao, who raised an eyebrow at his shoes — or so Ralph was convinced. If only Helen had thrown them out, as ordered! But she had refused to, until he had replacements; and so he'd been caught in shoes that swooped up gaily at the toes, like a clown's. The unstitched soles flapped so loudly that people turned to look at him as he passed in the hall.

During lunch he slipped the check into the mail.

Then, nothing. Until Helen discovered what appeared to be a mistake in their bank balance, that is. She called the bank. She called him at his office.

"*My* love seat," she wailed.

He checked the time by his stainless steel watch. The watch, he'd discovered, ran slow. He called Grover feeling foolish.

"I've been trying to get hold of you!" Grover said.

It had been his error of judgment, Grover explained (over a quadruple-decker club sandwich deluxe), to have once done business with the lunatic owner of a fried chicken take-out counter, who now claimed to have had his grease stolen several times. That Grover would not have knowingly bought stolen grease went without saying. ("How can you trust a crook?") Still, this lunatic chicken king was planning to testify against Grover. "So I figured, why not do the guy a favor?" Grover flicked his lighter. "It pays to be nice."

"It pays be nice," repeated Ralph.

"For instance, how about if I did this guy a favor and bought that business of his? He's been wanting to get out for some time. A real cash cow, this operation, but he's got the Florida itch. You know — retirement beckons. We Americans, our brains turn to golf balls when we're sixty-five. So my idea is, maybe I try and locate this guy a buyer. I think, that business of his could be the start of a real success story. This could be the start of a self-made man." He blew a smoke ring.

Spellbound, Ralph watched the ring rise. "I know what your meaning is," he said finally. "You mean me."

"I can take care of everything, don't worry."

Ralph thought. "Does he make money?"

"An insightful question. The answer: he rakes it in."

"So how come he have trouble sell?"

"He's asking the moon for a price, that's why," Grover explained. "But this business of his is a cash cow, I'm telling you. Listen. This is how I got it figured . . ."

What luck! Ralph spent the better part of his drive home congratulating himself on his good fortune. At every traffic light, he regarded the other people around him, stopped in their cars; how many of their stories were of hardship following hardship, orderly as boats in a canal. And how extraordinary his life was already. Was it really possible that it was only just beginning? He thought about what Grover had said, that this could be the start of a real success story. This could be the start of a self-made man. Of course, it was a modest start. He'd been almost disappointed to see the store, the smallest shingle building he'd ever seen stand up by itself. But who knew where it would lead? He saw past the present moment as though with a magic scope; through this special lens he saw an empire rise, grander and mightier than anything his father had commanded, even in his heyday. Ralph tingled with anticipation. Small doubts rained on him from time to time, but mostly he floated in hope, fabulous hope, a private ocean, gentle and green.

At home, he stood once more on hard ground. It was the

talking that did it; how could he make words convey what had happened, what could happen? *Shuo bu chu le.* The conversation ground along, an exchange of facts.

"*So why doesn't Grover buy it himself?*" Helen wanted to know.

"*Even an innocent man has to watch what he does,*" Ralph explained. "*If he bought it himself, it might look as though he were trying to bribe the owner into not testifying against him.*"

"*Isn't that what he's doing?*" said Theresa.

Ralph ignored her. "*We do Grover a favor and he does us a favor. For us, it's a sure deal.* No money down! Do you know what that means? We buy the business in our name, then sell it quietly to Grover. Then we buy it back from him, gradually, out of our profits, until it's one hundred percent ours. If we don't make money, or if we change our minds, I go back to teaching. It's that simple. We have nothing to lose.*"

"*Is the store dirty?*" asked Helen. "*Greasy?*"

Ralph promised she wouldn't have to work there.

"*Sounds — what is that English expression? —* too good to be true," she said.

"*But it is true. And who knows what might happen after that —*"

"*That man,*" said Theresa, slowly, "*is a liar and a cheat.*"

"*Like you?*" Ralph answered, offhand. "*You have nothing to say.*"

Helen knotted her knuckles.

"*It's a chance for a new life,*" Ralph continued.

"*But you already have a new life,*" said Helen. "*What about teaching? You just got tenure.*"

"*I'll take a leave of absence. If I ask Old Chao to arrange it*" — he looked hard at Theresa — "*I believe he may say yes.*"

A BRAND
OF ALCHEMY, INDEED

BUT HE just got tenure! In fact, Ralph did have misgivings about switching careers. Teaching might be the tip of a bull's horn, his father's idea, and nothing he was good at, but he sporadically recalled what it was like not to have any degree, and that gave him pause. Sometimes he saw himself hunched over his rooming house desk, working on his master's thesis; he remembered the lonely desperation with which he'd worried the equations. And with what had might he had striven for tenure! For how many years he had oriented his very being toward it, like a Muslim toward Mecca! Now, finally, he was truly Professor Chang; he wasn't sure he was ready to return to plain Ralph, or, worse yet, Yifeng.

Still, this was only a leave of absence he was taking; and in winning over Helen (which took a few days), he also won over himself. He became the most fervent sort of convert. There was nothing he didn't know; his former life, that dark age, could not recede fast enough. Handshakes, phone calls. Negotiations. What passed in between was nothing. A president came in, an invasion failed — both in meaningless suspension. It was as if the Changs had run flat life through a fancy new sewing machine, and seen it emerge smocked. Papers were signed; the art of seasoning was revealed to Ralph, the key to crispiness.

And the next thing anyone knew, Grover was dropping in to say hello all the time. It was because of the woods behind their house. Ralph had tipped Grover off about the developer being in over his head; Grover was thinking to buy him out. This necessitated visits to the property. And wouldn't it be rude of him not to stop by while he was in the neighborhood? *"Coming!"* Helen would warn, if Theresa was home, so that she would know to shut herself up in her room. Sometimes Theresa plugged her ears so she wouldn't have to hear Grover's booming voice. *"These walls are like paper,"* she began to complain. *"These walls are no walls."*

Variations: *"Anyone who wanted to could kick this door in."* *"We should get stronger locks."*

But what door, what lock, could keep out of a house what someone inside hankered for? Just as Theresa had found a way to an affair, and Helen a way to her split-level, Ralph had found his way to Grover; and as Theresa and Helen had been changed for the finding, so had Ralph, in inalienable ways. The sorts of things Ralph talked about had begun to change; his voice had taken on a new boldness; and with other small changes of manner, it became suddenly striking that he and Grover were both five four, more or less, with haircuts they sometimes slicked down, sometimes let reach for the sky like wiry versions of the Kennedys' lawn. Their faces remained very different. But from the back it was noticeable that they moved more and more alike. Both strode rather than walked; both stood very straight when they stopped; and when they ate, both tended to stick their elbows in the air as though they were sitting at an unusually high table, that came to their chins.

"Who knows? Maybe we're long-lost cousins," Grover joked once — to which Theresa exclaimed when she heard, "Impossible!" And of course, as she said, she ought to know. But one day, Ralph told Mona and Callie a long story that began with their great-grandmother's father, who was, he said, a rich guy.

"That guy has lotta, lotta money."

Mona and Callie nodded; they'd heard this before.

"And because he has so much money, that guy is not have one wife, like here. That guy is have five, ten wives."

"Ten wives!" Mona and Callie were amazed.

"Sure." Ralph shrugged. "Chinese guys, those rich guys, they have as many wives they like. I'm talking about those guys, really rich.

"So my grandmother's father, he has ten, twenty wives. And so he has lotta children. Mister! Lotta children. Some boys, some girls. And most of those children, they are good ones. But so happen, one little boy not so good. This boy is something the matter with his head." Ralph pointed to his own head. "I don't know what's happen. Maybe one day he fall down, hit his head on one piece rock. Anyhow, this boy does all kind of crazy thing. One day he is play with knife, you know? Big cutting knife. Another day he is throw everything into the lake. And nighttime, he is not sleep in regular bed. Everyone else sleeps regular bed, he sleeps in some kind of strange bed. You know what that bed is? That bed is a big box he is built by himself, make out of one piece wood. And inside the box is not the regular blanket. Inside is all those paper money."

"Money!"

"That's right. Inside is all those paper money, big pile, and when nighttime comes, that's where he's sleeping. Instead of use the regular blanket, he's hide himself inside there.

"Of course, his father, mother, everybody, thinks he is crazy. But what can they do? Father blames mother, mother blames grandmother. Everybody crazy now. Then one day, the boy say he's like to leave the family. So father talks to grandmother, mother talks to grandmother, and finally grandmother says okay."

"So then what?"

"So then the boy leaving."

"And then?"

"And then nobody knows what's happen to him." Ralph nodded thoughtfully. "But I think maybe that boy go somewhere, have children. And then those children maybe come to United States, and then maybe one of them has a son who come to New York, become manager of grease factory and so forth." He winked.

"How could it be! That's not true. He's making it up!" Theresa's voice pulsed when she heard. "Your father is talking nonsense. I've never heard such a story!"

Still Ralph laughed and insisted, "Sure is true," until finally she confronted him. *"You're just joking,"* she said, *"but the girls believe you."*

Ralph gave her a look. *"You have nothing to say,"* he said — what he always said now. There was uncertainty in his voice, though, and later Theresa hearkened to this. Grover might be rubbing off on Ralph, but Ralph was still Ralph. Or was he? One day she happened into his office, only to discover an entire wall of it papered with inspirational quotes.

ALL RICHES BEGIN IN AN IDEA.

WHAT YOU CAN CONCEIVE, YOU CAN ACHIEVE.

DON'T WAIT FOR YOUR SHIP TO COME IN, SWIM OUT TO IT.

FOLLOW THE HERD, YOU END UP A COW.

She sank into the desk chair, thinking *cheng yu* — idiomatic sayings, the Chinese had a lot of them too. But no, these were different. She stood back up; the quotes fluttered with her motion, a flock of starlings.

YOU CAN NEVER HAVE RICHES IN GREAT QUANTITY UNLESS
YOU WORK YOURSELF INTO A WHITE HEAT OF DESIRE FOR
MONEY.

There were books everywhere. *Making Money. Be Your Own
Boss! Ninety Days to Power and Success.* Theresa pictured her
brother, feet up on the desk like Pete the super, thumbing
through these. Where was the Ph.D. he'd worked so hard for?
Helen had taken it to a special place to have it framed, Theresa
recalled. Now it languished on a high shelf, under a box full of
cash register tapes.

Ralph was teaching the girls again. "There are five, six people,
look for some treasure. One man tell them, the treasure buried
under a special sign, look like a W. He say, you see the W, then
dig there. So the people look, look, look. All over. Finally, give
up. Nobody can find the W. Impossible. They ask the man, where
is that W we cannot find it? And he point up, in the sky. And
then they see that the shape of the trees make a big W. 'You
people,' he say, 'you all look for a small w. The big W, you
don't see it.' You girls understand what I'm talking?"

The girls nodded.

"Got to keep eye on the big picture," Ralph told them. "The
important thing. Don't crawl up in the end of the bull's horn."
He paused. "And you know what's the important thing in this
country?"

The girls shook their heads.

"Money. In this country, you have money, you can do anything. You have no money, you are nobody. You are Chinaman!
Is that simple."

If only Theresa hadn't compromised herself! If only she could
do more than bow her head and listen, listen, listen. But Ralph
was right. Theresa *had nothing to say,* not anymore; her authority had evanesced. And so she listened on, listening for so
long that some of what Ralph had to say almost made sense.

She'd seen how poor people were treated in the hospital; they died waiting. And to be nonwhite in this society was indeed to need education, accomplishment — some source of dignity. A white person was by definition somebody. Other people needed, across their hearts, one steel rib.

But what was Ralph teaching? Money worship! On her own, when she could hear herself, she was outraged. She could not approve, she thought; surprised at the same time to realize that silenced, she was another person. A more seduceable person, like Helen. How roundly Ralph's little store was succeeding! With just that simple sign, FRIED CHICKEN. She could not begrudge him his industrious amazement. Sometimes, watching the customers file in, the sales ring up, she began to see commerce as part of the stream of life. Wasn't it? And when Helen sighed happily and said, *Now I've got my* love seat *back,* or *That's enough for a* bridge table, it did seem a brand of alchemy that turned those metal trays of mottled chicken, with their loose flaps of pimply skin, into a happy household.

Ralph showed off his product. *"Ni kan,"* he said — look at this. "Outside, special blend of spices. Inside, tender and juicy. What could be better?" He still wore a pair of mechanical pencils clipped to his shirt pocket, just as he had in his professor days, but now he wore a white apron too, and a brown pot holder. "This one, perfect. This" — he used his tongs as a pointer — "is so-called undercooked. And this" — he pointed again — "is o-ver-done."

The girls jumped down from their seats on the big windowsill to taste. "They all taste good." Callie smacked her lips. Mona started on a second drumstick, eating just the skin.

"Forget how taste. Listen. Some are right and some are wrong," Ralph lectured.

The girls nodded, kicking the wood panelling below the take-out window.

"Will you try one?" Ralph asked Theresa.

She hesitated. Really she wanted very much to taste it and tell him how good it was. But she couldn't.

"Just one bite. Special spices."

"Delicious!" Helen told her, a wing in hand.

"Delicious!" chorused the girls, their noses greasy.

"Another time," Theresa promised.

When would that be? Talking to herself in the hospital, Theresa knew the answer — when she found out what Ralph was doing these days in his office. For following the proliferation of quotes had come something secret. First he and Grover put a lock on the door; then Ralph began to spend an hour or so in there alone, every night. What was that noise? A certain *wha-ingg!* over and over and over.

"*A cash register,*" said Helen.

"*But why would he be ringing a cash register?*"

It was very mysterious. Every night he rang, rang, rang, making a new register tape to replace the tape for the day.

MUSIC
TO THEIR EARS

UNDERREPORTING made all the difference. They weren't rich, but by paying less tax they became respectable. Besides making the payments on the store and (with Theresa's help) the house, they added new appliances to their home, all push-button, like the register. They bought a barbecue, and a secondhand piano for the girls. Helen bought her love seat, a sky blue velveteen fold-out, and also her bridge table. At this she played cards with a bridge-a-matic, that she might do better in the neighborhood club. Whereas they used to wrap food in waxed paper, now they used Tupperware. They bought a big picture book, *Scenic Wonders of America,* and talked about making a trip to the Grand Canyon. They talked about how long it would be before the chicken store was theirs. At the rate they were going, only six years, they figured. What a deal it was! (*"How can we not invite Grover to supper every now and then?"* Helen pleaded with Theresa. *"Look at all he's done for us."*) They planned for the future. Should they buy another store, make a chain? Or should they branch out to other things? Grover advised them. They had him over to eat yet again. Again.

Now Theresa curled up in her room by herself, trying to read. Was Grover sitting in her chair? In fact, the dining room table sat six; he wasn't necessarily in her seat, he could easily be in the seat next to hers. All the same, she wondered; and wondering, heard the noise from downstairs even more clearly. She applied herself to her book but still heard laughing, laughing. She *felt* the laughing. The noise seemed to emanate in rays from the page; she felt these on her face, a warm mask of embarrassment. Once a patient had come in to the hospital, her face burnt from a beauty treatment. The girl's cheek was blistered and raw and scabrous; a plain girl this was, young. She had asked, Would it scar? with the simple blinking fear of a fourteen-year-old. But when Theresa answered, "Probably," the girl had shrugged like a tough and said she didn't care.

Wasn't that the oldest tide in the world, Theresa thought now — one cared, then didn't care, cared, then didn't care.

Downstairs, a lull. Grover was telling a joke. The punch line. More laughter. Theresa tried to ignore it, scrunching down her pillow to support her back. Though she had not read the page in front of her, she turned it anyway, vaguely hoping the next page would prove more involving — that the action, maybe even the sound of paper being flipped, would sharpen her concentration. It had worked before. But then, singing! She couldn't believe it. Grover was singing: "Some en-chanted eve-ning, you may see a strang-er . . ."

She sat forward. Her pillow inched up the wall. Applause.

Another song: "Make of our hands one hand. Make of our hearts one heart."

More applause. So he liked love songs. What did that mean? He had a surprisingly resonant voice, which had literally moved her, quite against her will, to the door. Grover sang more. Another plaintive love song, she didn't recognize this one; though as she listened, she began to hear, beyond his voice, the delight of her family. And that pierced her, even as she endeavored to doubt she was hearing that at all — Grover's voice taking on that special keenness of beauty that is half a matter of the exquisitely rippling air, and half a matter of pain.

Here he had her, ear to wood, an eavesdropper in her own house. The light from the setting sun glinted on the brass-tone doorknob. Grover seemed to be singing his sad song forever, but she thought she could hear now that he wasn't really sad. He could be sad, then smile and nod to the clapping; whereas she had sunk with genuine weakness to the floor. No one had come to bring her supper. Of course not; they were waiting for Grover to finish singing. Before, it had been different. The first time Grover came, Helen, feeling bad, had sent up a giant bowl of shrimp and peas with Virginia ham. How festive it was! Those sweet pink shrimp especially, a luxury. Helen had included a good paper napkin too, the expensive kind they used for company, and one of their only two pairs of real ivory chopsticks, which Helen had brought with her from China.

But now they'd all gotten used to the idea that Theresa would do this — hide herself away, for her brother, for her family — and as they'd gotten used to it, it began to seem silly to treat the invisible Theresa as company. Theresa had said so herself. She preferred wooden chopsticks, she'd said, the ivory ones were too slippery.

So that was what she got. Once. Twice. She wondered if they were going to remember her at all tonight. Grover had stopped singing. Now he was talking. Was Helen looking for a chance to stand up and go? It seemed to Theresa that Helen could leave if she wanted to, that it was Ralph to whom Grover needed to speak, about business. Even as she thought that, though, she could hear everyone laughing again, the girls too. She heard their piping voices — "Uncle Grover! Uncle Grover!" — and knew he was speaking to them all, the whole family; and that they, in turn, were all listening.

"So then what? Did you get to eat?" Old Chao's voice on the telephone was raspy with concern.

"Finally, I did," Theresa told him. *"Callie brought it up."* She

blessed her niece in her heart. *"And do you know what he does now?"*

"What?"

"He brings beer."

"Beer?"

"Beer! They drink it with dinner. Sometimes my brother even lets the children have a sip."

Old Chao fell silent. *"I don't know why you call me,"* he said finally. *"I thought you wanted to end this. Clean. Snap like a twig. Good-by."*

Had she said that? She had. But had she meant it? Would it bring back her place in the family? She couldn't think for the noise downstairs. Such riotous laughter. What could be so funny? Theresa couldn't imagine, until Callie knocked.

Fried chicken.

"Your mother didn't cook tonight?"

Callie shook her head no. "Uncle Grover brought supper." She shuffled her feet.

The next morning, Theresa found a special breakfast laid out on the kitchen table. All Chinese food — a bowl of sweet, hot soybean milk, and two long, twisting oil sticks to dip in it; also two onion cakes. A dream meal. Sitting down, she touched everything before she ate, shaking her head; she felt like crying. She took a long, greedy draw of the scallion smell. Where had Helen gotten hold of it all? She'd thought you had to go to Chinatown. And where was Helen so she could thank her? Helen had to be up, around somewhere. But she didn't seem to be. So Theresa ate, waiting. In the thin light, even the whirling boomerang print of the vinyl tablecloth seemed tranquil; it was easy to imagine Helen sitting across from her, head bowed, asking forgiveness. *Of course, I forgive you,* Theresa answered, tipping the bowl to her mouth. She lowered the bowl, only to behold — rising above its rim like the morning sun — Grover.

"Good morning."

Theresa swallowed again, so hard her heart thudded, or that's how it seemed, everything oddly linked. "Good morning."

"That's some spread you've got there."

"What are you doing here?"

"We were so late calling it a night that I had to camp out on that new Hide-A-Bed of yours. Very comfortable."

"This?" She pointed to the bowl.

"My, ah, assistant, Chuck, made a run out for it. I understand Helen likes this sort of thing."

He leaned across the table, so close she could smell his after-shave. He wore something spicy, thick, a cloak of scent. Or maybe it wasn't an after-shave, for he hadn't shaved. From her plate he picked up the oil stick she hadn't eaten yet, dipped it in the soybean milk. "Delicious," he said, taking a bite. He dipped the oil stick in again. It dripped onto the boomerang tablecloth. Then he kissed her on the mouth. Or was it a kiss? Theresa almost did not know; only later did she recollect that what he had actually done was run his tongue over her lips — he'd licked her. True enough. Why hadn't she screamed? She ought to have screamed! Instead, she had kept hold of herself, saving face. She'd even felt a certain satisfaction when he nodded, mock-impressed. He took another leisurely bite of the oil stick before proffering it to her.

Mornings, Theresa had trouble getting out of bed. She bought an extra alarm clock, which she set to go off two minutes after her original one; then a third clock, to go off after the second. She placed the trio on her nightstand, on her dresser, on the windowsill. In this way she was able to get herself out of bed every day. She was not always able to make herself do other things — to brush her teeth, for example, or to put cream on her face. These were tasks that, more and more, she did at the clinic where she'd recently, finally, started her practice. Young female doctor, just out of training. How could she afford to appear anything but composed? She stood at a large shallow sink with a swan neck faucet and steel-edged mirror and, by the shadowless light, rinsed her eyes with cool water. She tidied her hair.

She tried to talk to Helen. *"These days,"* she said, *"we seem to be far, far away from each other."*

"Are we?"

Was this the Helen she knew? Helen's glance was evasive, her face expressionless; she could have been holding still for a department store cosmetician.

"Things have changed."

"I don't know what you mean."

Theresa tried to participate more at supper. One evening, Ralph was talking about hiring an employee. He had interviewed three people, two of whom seemed possibilities.

"Hmmm," Theresa began. *"Is the boy with the red hair —"*

Ralph loudly sucked the cheek out of a steamed fish head.

"I wonder, have you considered that maybe —"

"Is this a meeting?" said Ralph.

Theresa looked at Helen, who looked down. *"Isn't it?"*

Ralph flipped the fish head over. *"Ahh."* He set about sucking the other cheek out. *"Umm."* He set the fish skull on a plate. *"Meeting adjourned."* He winked at Mona and Callie, who started to smile.

"Eat your supper," Helen snapped.

At least Helen still had that much feeling for her. Theresa ate with the children. *"Little Brother,"* she said, after a while.

Ralph winked at the girls again.

"Eat your supper," Helen repeated.

Ralph grinned.

"Is something funny?" Theresa said.

"Funny?"

"Is there some joke?" Theresa felt like a schoolteacher. *"Are you drunk?"*

Ralph positioned the fish skull so that it faced his sister, opening and shutting its jaw as he mimicked her. *"Are you drunk?"* Theresa stared.

"He *is* drunk," whispered Helen in English.

"This is a meeting," he continued, switching to English too. "A meeting with a rotten egg."

"She's not a rotten egg," said Helen.

"What does that mean, rotten egg?" Callie wanted to know.

"Just eat," said Helen.

"Chinese expression," said Theresa evenly. "Meaning a woman of no virtue."

"What's a woman of —?"

"Eat," ordered Helen. Then to Ralph, "Enough."

"Roll away, egg," squawked Ralph. "Roll away."

"This," said Theresa, her voice tight, *"is what I knew would happen. This is Grover's influence."*

"It's terrible," agreed Ralph, still working the fish jaw. He clucked. "Grover's influence. Just terrible."

" *'Near ink, one gets stained black.' You have completely forgotten how to behave."*

"Oh really," said Ralph, in a normal voice now. "And how about you? Two boyfriends now, one wasn't enough, huh?" He made smacking noises in the air.

Later he would regret his cruelty; it wasn't even true that she had two boyfriends, he knew that. But he said it anyway, a small man making fun.

"Eat your supper," said Helen. And to Ralph, warningly: *"Your Older Sister, don't forget."*

"Older Sister!" Ralph laughed. "My *Jiejie* with two boyfriends! Kisses everybody! Everybody!" More smacks in the air. The girls looked up. Ralph cradled the fish head with his two hands, stroking it with his thumbs. "O love, love." He kissed it. "Love! O love!"

Callie looked to her mother. Mona tittered. "Love!" she echoed. "Love, love!" Ralph gave her the fish head to kiss also.

"Stop," said Helen.

"She kisses everyone," Ralph told Mona. "You know who she kissed?"

"Who?"

"She kissed Uncle Henry, and Uncle Grover too."

"Uncle Henry?" said Mona.

"*Stop,*" said Helen.

Callie's eyes widened. "And Uncle Grover?"

"*Stop.*"

"Like this." Ralph put the fish head to Mona's cheek. "Like a fish."

"To me too, to me too!" cried Callie.

"*Stop.*"

"Smack!" said Ralph.

"Smack!" shouted Mona. "Smack, smack!"

ONCE
A CHANG-KEE

HELEN watched Theresa pack. *"He went too far."*

"He did."

"I understand."

"Good."

Theresa emptied out her sweater drawer. Determined to leave nothing behind, she had bought three large, brown-plaid suitcases, only to find that her clothes would not even fill one. Her sweaters, which she had imagined quite bulky, proved in fact to be flat and few. She wished Helen weren't there to see how few. How wrinkled all the clothes were going to get! There was nothing worse than a half-packed suitcase; even if tied in, the clothes all shifted around. Should she leave the other suitcases behind? She wished she could pack Mona in one, Callie in the other. Instead, she calculated. She could fill the second suitcase with her winter coat. The third she could pack with books.

"Give us another chance," pleaded Helen. She began to cry, her bottom lip curled out so that Theresa could see where her lipstick ended and her inner mouth began. *"I know we were wrong. Give us another chance."*

"What's the matter, are you worried about the mortgage?"
"Please forgive us."
Theresa zipped the clothes suitcase shut.
The children, when they saw Theresa by the front door, looked concerned. "Suitcases!" said Mona.
"Moving to another house?" asked Callie.
"An apartment."
"Going on vacation?" asked Mona.
Theresa nodded gently, smoothing Mona's cowlick. "Going on vacation."
"On vacation in an apartment?" puzzled Callie.
Theresa gave her a kiss. "Sounds funny, doesn't it."
The taxi honked.

As Theresa appraised her new apartment from the doorway — four bare walls, two filmy windows — she could not help but imagine what Helen would think of the decor. This metal bed in the corner, for instance, with what Helen would have called its burnt sienna spread; she thought about how Helen had learned that name, they all had, from Callie's big box of Crayola crayons. Sixty-four of them. Such a rich array, compared to this small dresser — what brown was that? And what color was this linoleum floor? Mist gray. A radiator. A kitchenette. Always she had faulted Helen for caring so about looks. But of course it was easy to be indifferent about them herself when she could count on Helen to spruce things up. Now she longed for a set of white frilly curtains. What had Helen called them? Café curtains. The kind with eyelets, she wanted, and to go with them, a scatter rug. And maybe a love seat too, that folded out to a bed, in case anyone wanted to stay.
Is to leave a family to embrace it? She perched on her suitcases. She ought to unpack them, but was too tired. Which meant she ought to sleep. But how could she lie down on that bed? Upstairs, the plumbing ran. She heard a whooshing, like the sound of a defective heart — someone flushing the toilet. Then, a dying

groan — the sink. A stranger, washing his hands. Cradling her head the way Ralph had cradled the fish skull, she cried. Why was she shutting herself up in her room forever? Because she could not endure that one strange sound that was Grover, she had put herself in a place where all the noises were strange. Because she could not stand to be sometimes fed, sometimes not, she had put herself in a place where she would never hear that ladylike knock, low on the door, that was Callie's. Callie always knocked; Mona could never remember. Yet what would Theresa do to have Mona bang open her door right now! Look, Auntie, look, her niece would cry, and when she opened her hand there would be a shiny flake of mica to see, or maybe a bisected worm, all squiggly confusion. This apartment could use a few worms, Theresa thought. Instead, she was the squiggly confusion. Surely she would rather be taunted than subject herself to the smells of this place — smoke, she made out, and other odors. She had decided on this. She had chosen it. Yet her choice seemed someone else's choice. The suitcase under her slipped; she adjusted her weight. She watched herself wipe her eyes in the mirror over the dresser. Once a Chang-kee, always a Chang-kee. What an ugly woman she was! The room lost light, slowly. And then there was nothing to do but stand up, and feel for a switch, and unpack.

HELEN,
BREATHING

THAT WAS mostly what Helen heard: breathing, and breathing, and breathing. All hers — Grover hardly seemed to breathe at all, a surprise. Or maybe she simply could not hear him past her own breathing, so loud in her ears the house seemed to resound with it; she thought the neighbors must be able to hear. She begged him to please close the windows. How could anyone hear, he argued, gentle, innocent. He started, his hands advancing in the thick orange dusk like the hands of a blindfolded child, finding her. If anything, he said, what they heard was that cash register. *Wha-ingg! Wha-ingg!* — Ralph noisily secreted in his study downstairs. "True." Helen had to admit it. So long as Ralph played at his register, who could hear Grover? Grover here, and here. "This tab," he joked, pressing. "This tab, this. That's a hundred bills, miss." In the end he did close the windows — with mock groans — to please her. A simple gesture, but charming. "Anything else, my dearest?" How he talked! *You have to know how to talk,* her mother used to say; Helen understood now what she meant. "I've got all I want right here," Grover told her. It pained him to see how her hands had roughened. One day he brought a pumice stone out of his suit jacket pocket, and cream; he brandished a nail file, cuticle scissors, a bottle of nail polish. "One manicure, coming up," he announced, and would not be deterred even when she pointed out that he had forgotten to bring cotton balls. "Ah, cotton balls," he murmured. "That female essential." "And polish remover," she said. She asked him, "Did you ever put on polish before?" as if she did it all the time. He insisted that he didn't have to know what he was doing, then went on to get cream and polish all over the love seat. "I never saw such a job," Helen laughed. She did not even mind that he'd spotted the sky blue velveteen upholstery. He'd done it so endearingly! — trying afterward to clean it off with a fine white handkerchief.

"Don't," she said.

"Damn! Am I making it worse?"

She laughed and let him paint her toenails too, something that would not have occurred to her. She asked, "What did you tell Ralph?" "He thinks I'm waiting on him. 'Make yourself at home,' he told me." Helen winced. But when Grover blew on her toenails and proclaimed, "Now I've got you," she let him kiss her. "I thank you humbly," he whispered, as he slid a finger between the buttons of her blouse. "Just your belly," he assured her. "That's it." She let him nest his fingertip in her belly button. "Ahh, you've got me now," he murmured. "I'm satisfied."

Sometimes while he touched her, she thought how much she'd enjoy him once he'd left. Odd as it sounded, the considering of him was almost her deepest pleasure. A man with monogrammed shirts, a maid, a mansion, and all he wanted was to finger her belly button. She felt herself to be someone else, someone much prettier. A commanding presence. What power in pliancy! If only there weren't her husband to think of, right underfoot, at most six feet away. What kept him from knowing what was up? Some linoleum tile, maybe some plywood, maybe the buzz of the fluorescent tube light. Mostly his own absorption. She could not contemplate it. And yet she did. Whenever the ringing stopped, she held her breath, believing, Now he is going to come storming upstairs. Or would he be too hurt to storm? She could see him, white-faced, stunned; but preferred to see him red-faced, red-necked, cleaver in hand, bellowing so loud the neighbors would call the police. Such a scene! While Grover tried to sweet-talk him, he would hack a chair to pieces. He would lunge forward, enraged, dangerous; nothing would placate him, except for her to beg his forgiveness, hugging his knees — finally sharing a place with him, at the center of things.

One day after supper, she'd found her apron pockets full of sugar. That was how it all started. Grover had been singing; the windows were open. Just that week the lilacs had thrown their first flowers. The family was eating by candlelight — Grover's idea, naturally. Earlier, he'd brought the candles out of his pockets and sleeves like a magician. How the girls had squealed! And how reluctant she'd been to leave the flicker and glow of the dining room for the hard-lit kitchen. Grover had sensed it. "Forget the cooking next time," he told her. "How about next time I bring the vittles?"

"Fried chicken!" Ralph joked. "Take-out!" Helen laughed, a little drunk too. The idea of a guest bringing his own supper! Inconceivable. As was a guest filling her apron pockets with sugar. She suspected Grover at once. Before leaving, he had nestled his face into his shoulder like a bird, so that only one eye showed, giving her a cartoon wink. Of course, she checked with the girls anyway. Casually. Sugar? Solemn denials. No guilty laughter. This was before she found, on the sole of her shoe, a heart drawn in pencil. There were words in the middle. She held the shoe up. It read, Don't tell R.

What if Ralph had found it? Chagrined, she looked first for an eraser, then for other signs — as Grover no doubt intended. All day, she searched. In the beginning, properly shocked. Then, secretly delighted — the search becoming a game. Sugar in her pocketbook. She swore she detected sugar in the milk. Everything made her think of him. Things out of place, especially — a canister swivelled out from the wall, an umbrella come partly open in the closet. The house tantalized. At lunch, in the twinkling noon light, she found what looked to be a faint heart traced into the grime of the kitchen window. Was it really there? She examined it from several angles before washing the pane, thoroughly. While she was at it, she washed the rest of the window too. She wore rubber gloves.

When she went to bring in the mail, though, and found the mailbox full of lilacs, her heart flooded. If only, right after that, she hadn't found one of her small bushes stripped! She trimmed the broken twig ends, so that the cuts would be cleaner, less apt to harbor disease.

Why hadn't she told Ralph right away? She could hear him accusing her, *You hide things*. But it was the difference between having something and having nothing. Plus she had hardly expected that anything would come of it. This man had stripped her lilac bush! And hadn't she shaken her head for hours when she heard about Theresa and Old Chao? People did things like that, of course, but not people like Theresa. Not people like her. She had thought she'd never take it in.

That finally she had, though, was probably no more amazing than, say, a snake's being able to swallow a rat. One day Callie had explained to her all about how the snake unhinged its jaw for the job. "Is this what your teacher teach you?" Helen couldn't believe that at first either. "Waste of time!" But then *xi guan le* — she'd adjusted. The strange became familiar. The utterly inconceivable lost its massive inconceivableness.

As Theresa would probably be horrified to hear. Another woman might have looked on that first moment Grover touched Helen — bumping a thumb up her spine — and felt comradery. Theresa would have been pained. She would have told Helen to move away; Helen should have moved away. Instead, she had held still, shivering, heady with the scent of the lilacs, which she'd brought in from the mailbox and arranged in a large vase.

*   *   *

Grover was always satisfied; she was the one who, with time, wanted. What stopped her was an image — naughty Mona, nosy Callie, padding sleepily to the doorway, only to be jarred wide awake. "What are you doing?" Maybe understanding, maybe not. It was easy to forget many things in Grover's arms, but not the children, so impressionable. They remembered all kinds of things — the jars she kept in the cupboard, the jars she kept in the icebox. The exact spot on the bridge table the gold vase belonged. Who knew what they would learn if they caught her with Grover? *Bu yao fa feng,* she used to tell them all the time — stop acting crazy. Now she grew more specific. "Don't make faces," she told them. "Don't shake." "Take your hands off your hips." She grew stricter by the day. "No need to shout." "Talk something nice." "Don't stand in front of the icebox."

RALPH
HAS AN IDEA

RALPH, meanwhile, all blind focus, saw nothing but the register. In one way, he found making the phony tapes tedious; in another, he liked the simple sensation of it — pushing the tabs, feeling them latch. He liked the shape of them, the way they fit his fingertips. Then, *inggg!* Press. *Ingg!* There was a rhythm to it. He had removed the cash drawer so that it wouldn't be endlessly launching itself into his midsection; the simplicity of his solution pleased him too.

If only the rest of the business were so simply mastered! The mortgage payments were no small trouble, what with his sister gone; he needed to improve his profits, dramatically. Yet how could he? He felt in control but not in control, the business being his but not his. Until recently, there had been no difficulties. He had hired two employees. He had replaced the refrigerator. He was testing the chicken of a new vendor; so far it tasted the same and cost ten percent less. He and Grover had talked easily, their exchanges rat-a-tat-quick as a tap dance. "Got to spend money to make money." "The customer comes first." "The whole trick is good help." "The whole trick is price." "The whole trick is good taste." They had nodded, nodded, nodded. "It's all accounting." "It's all location." "Above all, watch the overhead." Everything was, as Grover said, hunky-dory, until Ralph had his idea.

"There should be some place for people sit down."

Grover, listening, snitched two packets of sugar from behind the counter. It was late. Rain dribbled down the storefront window, the watery lines pink with the light from Sam's Pizza across the street. Half of Grover's face glowed pink too; half swum in shadow.

"When nice, sunshine, people come to buy because they eat in the park. But when rain comes, they go to pizza. You should see them this afternoon, packed inside like sardine can. What's going happen to our business when snow's coming?"

"Good thinking," said Grover absently, lighting a cigarette.

"Customers need some place for sit."

"Hmm." Grover slipped another two sugar packets into his back right pocket. "Good thinking."

"You supposed to ask, Sit where? No room, right?"

"Sit where."

"My idea is, build one addition."

"One, not two?" joked Grover. He flicked his cigarette ashes onto the floor. "*An* addition, you mean."

Ralph nodded earnestly. "On top of roof."

"On top of *the* roof."

"*The* roof."

"Anyway, forget it, pal. You can't."

"Fools say impossible. Wise men think, how?" Ralph drew pictures on a napkin. "Raise roof. Look here."

Grover gazed fixedly at the wall. "Forget it."

"Why forget it? Is good idea. 'Think like the customer.' 'Sky's the limit.' 'A man afraid for take risk is no man.' " Ralph took the drawing back and added a large sign above the door: RALPH'S HOUSE OF CHICKEN. "A new name."

"Chicken house. Not house of chicken."

"But chicken house is . . . you know. Dirty place."

"Look —"

" 'The whole trick is advertise.' "

"Listen —"

" 'A man is only so big as his dream.' "

"I'm telling you. You can't do it. Believe me."

"Believe *me!* I'm engineer. All you need is one big beam. Those steel beams are something, mister!"

"Listen —"

"We can double business. I'm sure." The more Ralph thought about it, the stronger his hunch became. "Can do, can do, can do!"

All the next week Ralph went to bed thinking of his idea. He woke up thinking of his idea. He drew pictures of it. A man besotted, he calculated what it would weigh, calculating again and again that the building could support the load easily. He drafted plans, elegant plans, in eighth-, quarter-, and half-inch scale. He contacted six contractors about estimates. How much more profitable the store would be! Enough to make the mortgage payments and more. "And the next thing I know, I'm millionaire." Ralph could hear himself telling this story to some lost soul in a diner. He straightened the lapels of his bathrobe, a big shot.

The store began to feel too small. When business was good, he yelled at the employees as usual. "Mike, are you blind? That chicken's not brown, inside is probably raw." Or, "Otis, open your ears up. Buzzer going off!" But when business was slow, he paced back and forth in front of the store window, monitoring Sam's Pizza. He admired their blue canvas awning, taped together on one side though it was; also he thought the soda machine a good idea, and the ceiling fan for summer. He calculated some more. Profit, loss, payback. How long for his addition to pay for itself? If business doubled, say. Or what if business tripled? Quadrupled? The numbers began to take on a life of their own, which was at the same time the life he gave them. More and more, as he paced, he found he could make them come out however he wanted. He could predict business to go way up. He could predict business to go through the roof. If only he had room for a parking lot! Or what if he cut down on the income he reported? He figured out how much money would be saved if they reported half of their intake. A third. A quarter. A tenth.

He had to build the addition. He told Helen, *"I'm right."* He scrawled out a page of numbers and showed them to her. *"What do you think?"*

Helen frowned, her delicate features rucked together.

"It's a good idea." He tapped his mechanical pencil. *"I don't understand why Grover keeps saying no. He's willing to discuss it. He'll even make special trips here to talk it over. But in the end, no results. What do you think?"*

Helen bit her lip.

"Maybe he doesn't want to put any more money out. But why doesn't he just tell me?" Now Ralph frowned too, concentrating. *"Will you say something?"*

"Maybe he doesn't tell you everything."

"Maybe." Ralph pocketed his pencil with the lead unretracted. *"Tell me more. What are you thinking? You must be thinking something. Tell me."*

"Not here," Helen told Grover. "Please."

"Not here?" With mock surprise, he settled into the love seat, draping his arms along its top. He reached easily from one end of the sofa to the other.

"Ralph suspects something wrong. I don't like him right downstairs. Too dangerous. Please."

Grover crossed his legs.

"I'm afraid."

"Time to find a better place?"

"No better place."

"No?" He circled her waist, pulling her toward his lap.

"Please no."

He laughed, releasing her. "Okay. But I brought you some flowers." And he had — five June peonies, all pink petticoats, just like the ones the Kennedys were growing across the street.

" 'Borrowing flowers to offer the Buddha,' " said Helen. "You know that expression?"

"What?"

Downstairs, she could hear the cash register. *Wha-ingg! Wha-ingg!*

He uncrossed his legs, edged forward on the couch, and clamped her knees between his. "You've got me. I'll do whatever you say." He stroked the backs of her knees with his hands, then inched upward, under her skirt. "I'm your slave."

She softened. "Be careful my stockings. I don't want to get runs."

"I'll do anything."

"Okay. Just tell me one thing. Where did you get these flowers?"

He laughed, releasing her again. "Why, gosh darn. I plum forgot. Better put them in water, though." He sank back into the pillows, hooked his thumbs in his belt. His shirt rippled over his torso in smooth, expensive rolls. "Something the matter today? Ralph bothering you?"

"Of course he bothers me. He's my husband."

"Ah, yes. Your husband."

"What do you mean?"

"I mean, you deserve better." He sat up and grabbed her roughly, as if knowing that he had her this time. *Did* she deserve better? She admired her peonies — they were flecked with crimson — as Grover unbuttoned her blouse. "Just one button. That's all." He unbuttoned two.

"The girls," she protested.

"I understand." He stopped where he was. "You love those little half-pints."

"I do."

"So much that you would continue on with your matrimony just for their sake. If you had to."

She didn't answer.

"Ralph is one lucky guy. How'd he get so lucky?"

"What do you mean?"

"Well, that you agreed to marry him to begin with."

Helen struggled up from Grover's lap, replacing herself with the flowers. "I don't want any more of this."

But a week later, three buttons undone, she was listening.

"I know what transpired," Grover said. "Shall I tell you?"

"What?"

"You married like a good girl. I know." He nuzzled her stomach and, through her bra, her breasts. "You married because he was your friend's brother. A friend of your family's. You figured your parents would want you to. It was the right thing to do."

"I'm proud I did the right thing."

Grover pushed her gently backward, opening her blouse more, easing it back over her shoulders so that her arms were pinned. "You did the right thing. You did not think, This is America, I can marry who I want." He laughed. "You did not think" — he mimicked an American girl — "I'll choose. I'll pick."

"Stop."

"You were a nice Chinese girl."

"Stop."

"It was the right thing to do."

"Stop."

"You did not moon about love. You kept your eyes on duty." He chuckled. "Duty. Very important."

She tried to sit up, but his hands were on her shoulders, and all his weight. She strained with her neck.

"What's the matter?"

"The girls."

"The girls are asleep. The day is over. You can relax now." He lay on top of her, reaching under her skirt.

"Stop!"

"Shh. Do you want to wake up the girls?"

"Ralph," she called then, softly. Then, loudly, "Ralph!" But all that came from downstairs was *wha-ingg! wha-ingg!*

"What's the matter? You uncomfortable? Here, come on. Sit up."

She began to cry.

He produced a fresh-pressed handkerchief. "Relax. You got this all wrong. Listen, I just wanted to inquire of you one thing."

She shook her head, but he kept talking.

"I just wanted to inquire of you, do you realize you could leave that Ralph?"

She did not answer.

"Listen," he said. "You and me, maybe we've got a future. I mean, I have this big house, but not much in the way of inhabitants."

"What do you mean?"

"We'll talk about it," he said, and then he had eased her backward again.

"I've got to get going," Grover said.

"Oh, no, no!" Ralph protested. "Stay here! Fold out the sofa." His face was flushed with drink and with talking about the addition, to which Grover appeared about to agree. All night he had been warming — except for the times he seemed to have forgotten ever having discussed the subject before. "So you think it's a good idea?" Grover asked at one point.

Are you kidding? Ralph almost said, but instead answered, "I do."

Grover turned to Helen. "What do you think?"

"Getting late now. Time for you go home."

Grover and Ralph exchanged glances; and later, in the kitchen, Ralph reprimanded her. *"You don't know what you're saying. You don't know what you're doing."*

She said nothing. In the end Grover not only stayed, he even discussed what color the letters of the new sign should be. "Red,"

Ralph said. "From far away you can see it. Stands out better. Also we should have a light, so at night it will show nice too. And did I tell you I have a new idea for the store name?"

Grover shook his head.

"Chicken Palace! Ralph's Chicken Palace. What do you think?"

Helen lay with Grover in the dark, on the sheets of the folded-out love seat. "No," she said. "No."

He wheedled. "You were intended for better things. A mansion. Servants. Pretty clothes."

"No."

"You weren't meant to live like this. To struggle."

Helen didn't say anything.

"You were made to be loved."

"Ralph loves me."

"Ralph!" Grover snorted.

"And you don't love me either."

"Now how do you figure that, miss? What do you know about love? What you read in magazines? Why do you think I set your husband up in business, eh? Why do you think I got involved?"

A

PINCH IN TIME

SINCE Theresa's moving out, Helen had called her four times. In each case, the conversation had been stilted; they had tiptoed through the talk as though through the bedroom of a fitfully sleeping child. How much worse the separation seemed then! — at least for Helen — how much more real. She had fondly believed that all that was needed were apologies; she'd believed that what had happened could be undone. Why couldn't it? Theresa's empty room bothered even Ralph. He could not stand her door open, could not stand it shut. The situation was nothing they had chosen. If someone had laid out the consequences of their behavior, they would have unquestionably behaved otherwise. Who would have dreamed, though, that the easily willed minutiae of their daily actions could amass so — solidifying, mountainous, beyond their control?

No one had visited Theresa. Neither had she visited them. Ralph asked Helen how Theresa was doing, once; Theresa asked after the girls. Nothing more was possible. In China, families lived in compounds; a splintering in the family was called *dividing the kitchen,* and often meant that, literally. A brick wall would be put up — a labor. Yet how much harder to take it back down! There was too much face to be lost.

Still Helen stood now, desperate, prideless, before Theresa's blank apartment door. She rang.

"Are you busy?"

Theresa stared at Helen as if she'd never seen her before, though she was the one who'd cut her hair. Gone her neat bun; her hair hung loose, tucked behind her ears. And who was this behind her?

"You have a cat."

"Two." Theresa pointed. *"Callie, this is, and that's Mona."* They were twin Siamese, one too comfortably settled on the bed to do more than twitch an ear. The other pedalled its narrow shoulders up and down, stalking the open door. *"For company."*

Helen noticed a red rug, piles of books on the floor, white eyelet café curtains on the windows. On the walls, reproduction Chinese paintings, mostly landscapes. *"I brought you a present. Actually, two presents."*

Theresa cleared her throat. *"Not, ah, chicken, I hope?"*

Helen handed her a brown and green tile ashtray. *"Callie made it, but look who signed it."*

Theresa turned it over and saw in large, wobbly letters: LOVE, MONA. COME BACK! *"It's beautiful."* She laughed sadly.

"Also, this."

Theresa unwrapped a stem of lavender moth orchids. *"Symbol of unappreciated virtue."* She laughed sadly again. *"Have you eaten?"*

Helen hesitated.

"Don't be polite," said Theresa, scooping Callie up before she escaped to the hall. *"Come in."*

Monday morning, thinking of Theresa (*There must be something you can do,* she'd said, *you're so resourceful. Remember how you fixed the furnace?*), Helen called the Salvation Army. "Do you pick up furniture? What, three-week wait? Yes, well, this is brand-new, beautiful, let me describe to you. No? Then let me describe to your boss, okay?"

By evening it was gone.

"*What's going on?*" Ralph wanted to know.

"*The color was wrong. Too light.*"

"*Are you crazy? That sofa was expensive.*"

"*Also it had fleas.*"

"*Fleas?*"

Grover coughed. "To the Salvation Army?"

"That's right."

Helen was eating melon seeds, Chinese style. This involved shelling the seeds in her mouth with skillful discretion. She raised her hand to her lips, delicately emitted the empty hulls.

"I get your drift," said Grover.

"Do you?" She lowered her gaze girlishly, depositing the seed hulls into a dish. "But I don't get it myself."

"Is that right." He hesitated, then with a straight arm reached and undid her top button.

She waited.

He undid another. He ran his fingertip from her collarbone to her bra.

"The girls," she protested.

"You love those half-pints." He eased her to him.

"There's no place to lie down."

He grunted.

"Did you see my nails?" She fluttered her red fingertips against his palm. "Special for you. Watch I don't pinch, though," she sang. She nipped his thumb.

Grover smiled indulgently. "I'll tell you what this hand is for."

"For better things?"

"The best."

"No more kitchen floors?"

"Not a one."

"You promise? You give me a maid?"

"Two maids."

"Three?"

"As many as you want. Four maids."

"Five?"

"A staff. That's what you want, right? A staff?"

As she nodded, he unzipped his pants.

"That's what you got," he said.

She peered cautiously at her handful. "All mine?"

"All yours."

She hesitated.

"Relax."

"To do what I like with it?"

"Whatever your sweet heart desires."

"You mean, I say left, it goes left?"

"Sure."

"I say right, it goes right?"

"Sure."

"I say it's good, it gets petted." She stroked him, her nails flashing. "I say it's bad, it gets —"

Grover yowled so loudly the register downstairs stopped ringing.

LIVING
BY THE NUMBERS

"*NOTHING HAPPENED?*" Suspicion mottled Ralph's face; he crossed his arms in front of him, a barricade. "*Nothing?*"

Helen hung her head.

"*Say something!*"

"*I need to . . . to . . .*" To what? "*To think.*"

"*You want to think?*" This in a tone Ralph had learned from Grover; it was as if Helen were still discovering evidence of that man all over. Would he never be gone?

"*He's left,*" Ralph said.

He said, "*Something's happened.*"

"*Say something,*" he said.

She shook her head heavily, fanning her red-tipped fingers.

"*Say something!*" He shook her hard, he slammed her against her chair. Warm frustration had turned cold rage, a snap freeze. She started to sob.

"*Enough.*" Ralph whispered to himself then, stunned. "*Enough.*" He shook out his errant fingers.

He would not ask. It was a species of agreement. It was a matter of discretion that was also a matter of survival, a matter of being unable to live the life they would otherwise have to lead. They settled on this complicity: they would not heal their rift — their mysterious rift — but bridge it, with manners. There would be coolness on both sides, a twin coolness.

Three days later, frosty warming. "Tell Mom we ate too much broccoli this week already." "Tell Mom she can pull down the screen windows herself." "Tell Mom my blue jacket, one button came off." And, "Tell Mom my jacket, blue one, button came off, I'm not going ask second time."

"Dad says to tell you again he really needs that button sewn on," Callie told Helen.

"Yeah!" said Mona. "He says he's" — she mimicked Ralph's voice — "not going to ask second time."

"Tell Dad he can sew it himself." Resolute, Helen rinsed more broccoli.

The girls whizzed from the kitchen to the living room. "Mom says you can do it yourself," reported Callie.

"Myself!" said Ralph.

"She means get lost," explained Mona.

"And guess what's for supper!" shouted Callie.

The girls giggled.

Another day: "Tell Mom Uncle Grover say yes for the addition, we paying five percent interest."

The girls flocked to the kitchen doorway. "Dad says —"

"What you say?" Helen sidled, nonchalant, into the living room. "Don't 'tell Mom,' tell me."

"Five percent interest. He'll write us a second mortgage." Ralph looked thoughtful. *"It's nice of him. Who would accept a house with such a big first mortgage as collateral? Only a friend."*

"Hmm."

Silence. Outside, the newspaper hit the screen door — *thwap!*

"That boy!" exclaimed Helen. *"I told him not to throw the paper like that!"*

"He's going to ruin our screen," agreed Ralph.

More silence.

Finally Helen, shifting her weight, asked, *"Did you put your jacket on the sewing pile?"*

Ralph cleared his throat, a peacemaking response. *"We're going to start construction as soon as we get* so-called building per-mit.*"*

"You're sure it's a good idea?"

"I'm sure."

She hesitated. *"He thinks so too?"*

"Who? Grover?" Ralph was studiously offhand. *"For a long time, as you know, he was lukewarm about it. But now all of a sudden, he's hot on the idea."*

"All of a sudden? Just like that?"

"He wants to give me a chance to show how smart I am."

How could they proceed with business as usual? It was true that anything was possible when men were involved; yet Helen had to wonder if there weren't twists to the story she couldn't discern. Suddenly Grover had changed his mind. What did it mean?

She teased the facts anxiously but, as she told Theresa, without result.

Anyway, so long as the project consisted of talk, it did not seem quite real to her. It was as if, in the close muff of a January dusk, she had been asked to imagine streaming, rose-smattered summer, the children in bug bites and grass stains. Who could believe such a time was coming? It would; yet she was taken aback the day Ralph had indeed gotten together his land title, deed, plot plan, photos, and drawings (that was elevation and side view for the drawings), not to say his floor plans, existing and proposed. He'd written his statements, completed his tables, secured his signatures. He'd appeared at meetings. Before boards. He'd paid fees. And finally now, just when he'd mastered the parking patterns at City Hall — he even knew which meters were jammed, so he could park free — he had his building permit. He came home waving it like a banner. *"Ready to start construction!"*

That's when Helen, tumbling to attention, asked to see the numbers.

"Sure!" Her belated interest so delighted Ralph that as they huddled over the kitchen table, he kissed her several times, ardently. She kissed him back, though for today all she cared was that the calculations laid before her like a nice cooked lunch should turn out digestible.

"Three hundred-sixty-five days a year," Ralph said, *"times three meals —"*

"No holidays?" wondered Helen. *"Three meals a day?"*

He waved her questions aside. *"The thing to watch is the overhead. Say the heating bill runs to this much a month, and in the summer, air conditioning to this amount here. . . . We have to consider that the cost of the chicken may rise, probably it won't double, but let's take that anyway, just to be on the safe side . . ."*

Though Helen had had little trouble understanding the purchase of the house, she found following these numbers harder. She went over each section of each page several times, yet still felt she was not being thorough enough; certain numbers seemed to her to be mysteriously reappearing, like mildew. Three pages in, she wondered if they couldn't start all over.

"That gives us these figures here —" continued Ralph.

"But the after-tax income *depends on the* projected income," she protested.

"You can call it whatever you want," Ralph explained. *"What I'm trying to say is, this number here is what you end up with.* So-called money in the pocket."

"But it's not money in the pocket. *It's a guess."*

"Of course it's a guess." Ralph held patient. *"All the numbers are guesses."*

"They're not real."

"*Sure they're real. They're real guesses.*"

"*What if they're wrong?*" The page shifted and blurred before Helen's eyes.

"*If you didn't have to believe something, you wouldn't be doing business.*" Ralph patted her. "*Relax. Have faith.*"

CONSTRUCTIONS

THE ADDITION was under way. First, the store had to be closed — Ralph hung a sign — then the demolition began. Such dust! It was a wintry hell. Just strolling through, Ralph found his eyelashes coated, his teeth gritty. In the bathroom mirror, he saw that even the rims of his nostrils had whitened; they looked like an oddly placed pair of spectacles. Still he continued his inspection tours, telling Grover (when Grover was there), "You're smart to wait downstairs." To which Grover would answer, with a sideways smile, "I've seen all manner of things come down before." And such a racket! The din could be heard from blocks away, a whole crew of men swinging and banging, bashing, prying; the old attic avalanched to the metal dumpster with a thunder that could have been an airplane taking off. The roof opening quietly grew. More banging, but this was careful banging. Dainty banging.

Then, silence. A clear plastic tarp flapped and ballooned in the breeze. Ralph fretted. The lost income! But nothing could be done. The steel support beam had to be craned in; the crew was waiting for the crane. Another day. Another. Each day bulked, a wrong guess, a thing Ralph had failed to take into account. At night, in his dreams, he saw red X's pencilled down the side of the store. Wrong, wrong, wrong. The building that had fairly convulsed with activity was now deceased. There were no workmen on the site, only Ralph, a lone mourner. Until the crane arrived, that is — a colossal arm reached out of the sky to stage a resurrection.

Life! Hope!

Followed by more delays. Now the crew waited on the building inspector. Ralph reworked the numbers.

"How many days have we lost so far?" Grover thought they should sue.

Ralph complained to Bud, the contractor. "Do you realize we lose twelve days already? Twelve days! And all this time the roof open like that! We going to sue!"

Bud bristled. "Don't you go threatening me, now." They argued, to no conclusion.

Yet all the same, progress resulted. The framing went up, the exterior walls, the siding. The roof was tarred. An indoor ladder grew stilts, turned into stairs. Tilers came, plasterers.

Now Ralph drove by, marvelling at life. At *his* life. Everything was going up, he was going up, up, up! What more could he ask for, but this — the late-day sun gilding the top of his new store gold as the knob of a flagpole. Ralph's Chicken Palace. Though the shingles of the original storefront were smaller than those of the addition, they blended together fine, he thought; plus with the sign as a distraction, who would notice? He admired the two upstairs sliding windows, even as he vaguely supposed he *could* ask one thing more, one small thing — that Helen might be returned to him. He did not want to think of it now, in his contentment; but sometimes he looked at her, and it seemed that his Helen, the real Helen, had moved away. He spoke to her as though on the telephone. *How are you?* He missed her even as he saw her. Particularly when he saw her. The resemblance between the old Helen and the new was so

striking, he could not look too long. It was as if he had spotted
a certain stranger on the street; if he didn't look away he might
grasp the stranger's arm, insisting, *You look so familiar,* only
to have the stranger pull away. You're crazy, she'd tell him,
knocking his love to the sidewalk.

Still, life was improved in ways he'd never dreamed possible;
in one step, he'd reached heaven, just as in the saying. Now
when he saw people for whom America was a disappointment,
for instance — the Petes of the world — he did not look away.
He did not fear he would turn out like them; he only felt sorry
that some people worked hard but proved unlucky. The grocer
family around the corner who had gone out of business, for
example. One day he'd walked by, and there they were — a girl,
her parents, an assistant, looking disoriented and somehow ragged around the edges, as though they'd been torn out of a book.
Their heads were bent, in sorrow or in prayer; Ralph, passing
by, bent his head in sympathy. His fortune was to live in the
other America, the legendary America that was every wish come
true. What did it hurt to allow them a place in his heart? At the
end of the block, he picked a fairly clean paper bag up off the
ground, filled it with all the money in his wallet. Then he turned
and headed back toward the family, his hands sweaty as a suit-
or's.

Though they joked about hiring a *fengshui* expert to determine
a propitious day for the grand reopening, in the end Ralph and
Helen — more practically — simply planned to resume business
as soon as possible. *"Let the contractor pick the day,"* they
quipped. And so it was that the day was a perfect day, so clear
and sunny that they had to squint, even indoors. They positioned
potted plants with red ribbon pompoms in the window. Nervously, they festooned the front serving counter with ribbons —
not believing, quite, that people would come.

But people did come, and did sit and chew and swallow, their
Adam's apples bobbing, as if there were nothing remarkable in

the cheery red-and-white-striped wallpaper, with its matching red booths and bright white Formica tabletops; as if there were nothing even a little breathtaking in Otis the waiter (formerly a cantankerous cook) actually waiting table, exactly as ordered. A few people asked if the upstairs had always been there, wished Ralph and Helen luck, that sort of thing — no one didn't like the new name — but for the most part they ate ensconced in the satisfactions and treacheries of their own lives, wiping their mouths absently. Except, that is, when Ralph shouted, "Otis!" from downstairs. Using a small hole in one corner of the addition, Ralph had rigged a series of mirrors so that he could keep an eye on what was going on up there; Otis called this apparatus the periscope, and sometimes talked down through the opening in the floor. "Aye, aye, scope," he'd answer, "I'll get that table one-two."

This, Ralph noticed, made people look up.

It rained three days that week; and just as he had predicted, they made much more money on those days than they had before. Helen began to relax. How tense she'd been! — clenching her fists at night, digging her nails into her palms. Also she'd been straining her eyes until her sockets throbbed. Trying to see what? Maybe she had overestimated her importance to Grover entirely. Maybe he was mad for a while, then not mad. Who knew? Emotions sometimes lingered, but other times they shattered like thermometer mercury; and wasn't everything on plan, businesswise? She gave up straining to espy, past the apparently real, something denser. Ralph described a customer who apologized to his chicken before eating it; she laughed. He reported that Otis had returned to the stove; she shook her head. The new busboy, Morton, boxed in his spare time; Helen, like Ralph, hoped he wouldn't pick any fights in the chicken palace. Someone ripped one of the new red vinyl seats; she agreed that instead of using tape, they should replace it.

The news, when it came, therefore shocked her. *"Grover gone to jail?"*

Not for the stolen grease, Ralph explained — that charge Grover had beaten, just as he'd boasted he would — but for tax evasion.

"*I didn't even know he was in trouble for that.*"

But that was what Grover's right-hand man, Chuck, had told Ralph. Chuck had exercised as they talked, flexing his arms with nice ferocity, his veins straying over his muscles like snippets of blue yarn. He had narrow, pointy teeth, cowboy boots to match, and a letter "nominating" him to act on Grover's behalf, in all of Grover's "enterprises, interests, affairs, and loans." The letter (clearly in Grover's handwriting, which Ralph recognized) had been notarized.

"*So now we make the checks out to Grover, but give them to Chuck,*" Ralph told Helen. "*We're not supposed to try to call or write until things calm down. Grover doesn't want the government to know who he deals with.*"

"*So sudden!*"

"*No warning at all.*"

"*Another sudden thing.*"

What could be wrong? Business was booming. People were sick of pizza, it seemed. Thinking ahead to the day they'd be sick of chicken too, Ralph considered adding hamburgers to the menu. Maybe barbecued ribs. Or what about egg rolls?

"*We're all right?*" Helen asked.

"*Better than all right.*" Ralph explained just how much so. "*Which is a good thing.*"

"*What do you mean?*"

"*Think. Grover just went to jail for tax evasion.*"

"*No more tapes?*"

It seemed to Ralph, as he and Helen tried to figure out what paying their full taxes would mean, that mistakes were harder to erase than he remembered. Was he using a different kind of pencil? Also, the numbers themselves seemed solid, obdurate, much less fun. Instead of many ways, among which he could pick, they came out one way. And the way they came out, he and Helen listed between barely squeezing by and undeniably short. Maybe, he said, they could still cheat a little; in the restaurant business, everyone did.

"Do they, though?" asked Helen.

"That's what Grover said. Of course, Grover got caught and went to jail."

"Or at least that's what Chuck said."

Ralph began erasing the numbers, slowly.

What a coward he was! Afraid to find out the truth — first from his wife, and now from his partner too. Ralph had never even asked what jail it was that he wasn't supposed to call. How then would he marshal the courage to dial Grover's house? He sat at the telephone, wishing he could forget Grover's number. He remembered how once he could not summon it up. Now he could no more excise it from his brain cells than he could sever his past from his future. Helen. Grover. Chuck.

His black telephone sat captive in a pool of light, ready for interrogation. Ralph switched off the light, put out his hand. He felt the heat radiating up from the receiver, hoping to take heart from this release of stored energy. How unpredictable a thing it was, really, that light should produce heat, and that a telephone should be able to absorb it. Was that a thing anyone would have thought? He never would have figured it out, certainly; it was the sort of thing that occurred to smart guys. As for guys like him — there was much they didn't know, much in which they were mistaken. Thankfully; perhaps then he was wrong in his forbodings. He grasped the receiver, locating his faith.

As a first step toward cutting costs, Helen volunteered to go to work in the chicken palace, as the cashier. Ralph objected, but they both knew there was no choice; and so she found herself sitting at the front register, on a stool, no lady at all. The whole trick is watch the overhead, she told herself.

Once she'd gotten used to the idea of leaving the house, of *going outside to work* — after all these years in America, she still envisioned a wall between her home and the world — she did not particularly mind the work involved. Neither did she mind that the family now ate at the restaurant every night, one fried chicken part after another. She just found it hard to be owned by customers; men especially thought nothing of appraising her through her clothes. Cross-examining her. "You Chinese? Japanese?" They'd squint. "Filipino?" Sometimes adding, "I once had a little, ah, woman like you. In the War." They patted her when they felt like it, grasped her hand. She tried to smile. "How do you like the chicken?" she'd say, pulling away. Or, "Thank you, please come again." It was her penance for having taken those lilacs in from the mailbox. "Please come again." One day a bum grabbed her. "You're my dragon lady," he insisted, in a drunken slur. He thrust his face into hers, forcing her to breathe his rancid breath; his untrimmed nails bit into her arms.

She got herself a larger apron after that, one that covered her whole front, rather than just the waist down, with very large ruffles. For a while, she pretended to barely speak English. "Dank you, prease come again." Then she began to look boldly at people — she stared, even — finding that this brazenness made them look away. She was glad she could not see herself do this; she shuddered to think what her opinion of someone who did this would be, though it did make work more interesting. She felt as though she had come once more to a wholly new country, where certain heavy girls dragged their feet, almost knock-kneed. Where certain sorts of men marched in ahead of their wives. There were fashions to look at too, the new sheath dresses, the bouffant hairdos. But mostly she saw the way the wives felt their hair for flyaways; the way their children flocked to one parent, then the other; the way their babies twisted unhappily, as if finding the world already too tight. She saw the way groups of boys jostled each other with their elbows, keeping their hands carefully in their pockets.

And also she saw, after a while, that the wall of the first floor of the chicken palace had developed several fresh, fine cracks; it looked as though someone had drawn a few pencil lines from the new wood panelling up to the new suspended ceiling.

WATCHING
THE OVERHEAD

"NOTHING," Ralph pronounced. "*A little settling.*" His stomach clutched as he said it.

"*A little settling,*" Helen said. "*I see.*" And from then on, they referred to it just that way. "*The settling seems a bit wider today.*" "*I don't know if the settling's going to get better.*" "*Perhaps we should think about patching the settling.*" What else could they do? They'd been riding a tiger; it was hard to get off. They fixed the cracks themselves, carefully, with dabs of joint compound from a pint-sized container. "*Did you notice? That* pain-in-the-neck *settling's back again.*"

"*Again?*" said Ralph. "*I've never seen a building with such a settling problem.*"

Other walls began to settle too. How long was it before they moved up to buying their joint compound by the quart?

That was the year people starting talking about the economy, and unemployment. And protests — by the time troops had turned their muzzles on the marchers down South, the family was buying its joint compound by the half gallon. Then, in buckets the size of wastebaskets.

"The inspectors inspected every step." Ralph was weary, older. His stomach hurt all the time. *"We put in an extra beam for support. I checked the calculations over and over."*

Every night after the help left they snuck back into the restaurant to doctor the crack-crazed walls. Mona and Callie had grown tall enough to help a little, and old enough to understand that certain things should be kept in the family. "We won't tell," they promised. "Cross our hearts and hope to die."

Still, one day, Morton, the boxing busboy, announced, "I quit."

"Something wrong?" asked Ralph.

"I ain't going to hang around here, you or nobody can't pay me any amount," he declared. "This building be falling down."

Ralph searched through his files. The previous owner was one Jeremy Finch, who at the time of the sale had lived in Larchmont. Of course, he was supposed to have since moved to Florida. Still Ralph dialed information, and sure enough there was a listing; Mr. Finch had not moved. All Ralph had to do, now that he had the number, was try it.

He called Grover's number instead, quickly, before he could reconsider. Three rings, and a familiar voice. "Ding residence."

"Hello, Grover," said Ralph. His voice seemed to reverberate, loud, unnatural; it sounded like his voice come over a loudspeaker. "This is Ralph."

"Ralph."

"I thought you were supposed to be in the jail."

"Oh, ah —" Grover laughed.

What was there to say? Ralph hung up.

He returned from his visit to Jeremy Finch with this to report: that there were logs in the soil. At some point their lot had been a pit, into which someone had dumped trees. These could no longer be removed, having long since started to rot; the land, therefore, was unstable and unbuildable.

"And cheap." Ralph felt as though he had a cardboard tube

down his throat as he described how Grover had bought the land, built anyway, then sold it. Of course, when this Mr. Finch found out the building was sinking, he tried to sue. The judge being Grover's good friend, though, Finch was stuck.

Except that he was losing barrels of grease from the back. This didn't bother him too much actually, but when he heard Grover was being charged again, in a case with a different judge, he threatened to testify unless Grover bought the property back. Grover didn't want to, however; he thought it would look bad.

"*On our side, it wasn't a bad deal. The building would have sunk, but very slowly, and in the meantime, we were able to buy it with no capital at all. So, great. But then Grover let us build. And now — trouble.*" Ralph gazed off into the air like a tourist at a panorama. "*Of course, I wanted to build. That part was my fault. The question is, why did he let us go ahead?*"

Helen held her breath.

"A tree is not a tree, it's an opportunity." Ralph swallowed grimly. "*Ha. Trees are trees.*"

What should they do? At supper they continued to talk while the girls ate quietly.

"What does Daddy mean, *san banfa?*" Callie asked finally.

"*Xiang banfa*. Find a way," Helen explained. "That's what Chinese people like to say. We have to find a way."

"Find a way to what?"

"Typical expression," said Ralph absentmindedly, and went back to talking to Helen in Chinese. They could stop paying Grover for the store itself. But what about the loan for the addition? They discussed this knowing that Grover had claim to their house.

"*Seems like there should be someone we can sue,*" Helen said.

But how could they sue Grover over property they didn't own?

They went on serving chicken, trying to keep operating for as long as they could, figuring and figuring as they went. What if Helen got a job and if, in addition to his usual course load, Ralph taught summer school and night school? "*We should sell the house,"* Helen acknowledged once; but when Ralph *contin-ued the subject,* his common sense seemed a cold box into which he could not ask her to place her heart. So instead he took down all the signs in his study, and in their place put up a new piece of paper that read, *Bai lian cheng gang* — a hundred smeltings, become steel.

They carried on for another month, every night inspecting to see how dangerous things had gotten. They didn't want anyone to get hurt, after all. They put up signs — PLEASE DO NOT JUMP! — both upstairs and down, so as not to arouse suspicion. They hung posters to hide the cracks.

The cracks got so large that one of the letters outside fell off and could not be put back up. Now the sign read, RALPH'S CHICKEN P LACE.

Ralph shrugged when he saw it. *"At least it still spells some-thing."* This was part of his new pragmatism.

They stayed open one last month, then one last month again. For upstairs they hired the smallest, lightest busboy they could find. They tried to discourage fat people from going up.

"Maybe the building's not going to fall down after all," Ralph mused. *"If it didn't have to be inspected every year . . ."* They began to wonder how to get the inspector to pass their building.

Even as they conferred by the register, though, they heard the building creak loudly — a strangely ancient sound, it seemed, a foreign timbre wholly out of keeping with the pop and sizzle of the chicken, the *wha-ingg!* of the register. Ralph spoke through the periscope. "Everyone come down," he ordered. "Everyone. Please. Down to the ground."

PART V

A Man to Sit at Supper and Never Eat

A MAN
OF STEEL

ALL THROUGH the closing of the store, Helen and Ralph agreed on everything. They agreed who should hang the sign, and when, and what the sign should say. They agreed on what to tell the employees, and what to tell the neighbors, and what to tell Chuck. If being married was a matter of becoming one, they had finally achieved what in better times they could not. Even their moods seemed to meld together, so that when one of them was dispirited, the other also drooped; and if Helen grew philosophical, Ralph found himself stretching his neck and clearing his throat, as perspective and clarity irradiated his mind. *"Every river has its own course,"* Helen reflected. *"It is not for people to try to change destiny."*

Ralph shrugged, antiphonal. *"Can't always make money, sometimes have to lose."*

Like bamboo, they bent but did not break, agreeing as they did that, despite their difficulties, they were the luckiest people in the world, having each other, and the children — a family anyone would envy, even if there were no boys. How fast Callie and Mona had grown! It was hard to believe they were both in school already, much less that they could jump rope, and say the rosary, and play the piano. They were taking ballet lessons; Mona wanted to be a ballerina. Callie wanted to be a saint. Ralph and Helen talked again about having more children; two sons would be perfect. Even without the sons, though, how much luckier they were than Grover! How empty his life! They agreed they wouldn't change places with him for the world. *"For a* million dollars," Ralph said. They agreed that there was something the matter with Grover. *"With his head,"* Ralph said. Helen said that she had read articles about people like him in magazines. *"His family probably didn't take very good care of him,"* she said. *"He was like a child, in need of attention."*

"Not like a grown man," Ralph said.

"People like that will do anything," Helen said.

"If I ever see him again, I'll kill him," Ralph said.

That is, until Helen said, *"I feel sorry for Grover."*

Then Ralph's anger was transformed, and he realized that he felt sorry for Grover too. *"That man, he has no family. All he has is his empire, and so much money, he doesn't know how to spend it."* He shook his head.

It was a kind of sympathy he had begun to feel for almost anyone — not only bums, and orphans, and dogs with porcupine quills in their snouts, but also people he might at another time have envied. Presidents of corporations, state governors, movie stars — people he didn't know but nonetheless understood to be lonely, and afraid of failure. How much wiser he was than they! He talked to their pictures in Helen's magazines, explaining the nature of life difficulties — how matters that one day seemed material, and hard with importance, could the next day simply vaporize. *"You'd be surprised,"* he told them, *"I've never had such a peaceful mind as I have now. After a hundred smeltings, I indeed have become steel."*

Sometimes he drove by the building, just to feel how dispassionately he could look upon it. What self-control he'd achieved!

He was Confucius. He was Buddha. He was his idling car motor as he looked, looked, looked — observing with some satisfaction how almost impossible it was to tell from the outside of the building that inside it was collapsing. There was that one letter missing, and the framing bulged slightly out of kilter, but overall, it looked as solid as ever. It was not a building to sag pathetically. It was firm in adversity, especially the well-designed addition, which showed no cracks at all.

If only he could separate his part of the building from the part that came from Grover!

But, of course, he couldn't. He accepted this with an equanimity so complete that he had to get out of the car and go for a walk. He paced. Was it fair, what Grover had done? Was it right?

He thought how sorry he felt for Grover, stuck with his hollow victories. He thought of Grover letting Chuck in on a little scheme he'd come up with: "How about we tell him I've been thrown in the slammer . . ."

Ralph calmly paced faster. Just around the block, swinging his arms with nonchalant vehemence. It was a gray day, the clouds so low and heavy and ready to rain that they begged, Ralph thought, to be punched. How sorry for Grover he felt! How sorry, sorry, sorry! His sympathy was like one of those clouds in the even blue of his calmness — that's how sorry he felt, so sorry, and sorry, and sorry. What was this frenzy of sorriness? He felt so sorry that he gave a dollar to a panhandler, so sorry that, tears leaking from his eyes, he found himself holding a door for a woman with two shopping bags and a stroller. And when he came upon a couple trying to give away a box of snarling puppies, he felt so sorry that, quick, before it rained and the box got soggy, he picked out the noisiest tough of the litter as a present for the girls.

"*A dog?*" said Helen, at home. "*Now we really are* Americanized."

Ears back, the puppy yapped furiously at her, baring his teeth as though he'd been assigned the kitchen cabinets to defend with his life. He was a shorthaired dog, gray with black and brown spots — to call him nondescript would be a kindness. He had a flat, triangular head like a crocodile's, and his legs were strangely spindly; they looked as though they were not his legs at all, but a charitable donation from a relative with a spare set.

"*I felt sorry for him,*" explained Ralph.

Helen frowned. "*Your sister got a cat not long ago. Did I tell you? Two of them, actually.*"

"*This has nothing to do with that,*" he insisted. "*This is a present for the girls.*"

But the girls were terrified of the dog, who, growing more and more excited, barked and lunged at Callie, and nipped Mona's socks.

"Stop!" yelled Ralph, trying to catch him.

"He bites," wailed Mona.

"And goes *xu-xu,*" said Callie, observing the several yellow pools dotting the kitchen floor.

"Can you bring him back?" asked Helen.

The dog, still yelping, was circling the girls, who huddled together in the middle of the room. Ralph chased after him. "Come here, dog! Come here!"

"Go away," yelled Callie. "Shoo!"

"How come he doesn't bite *you?*" Mona cried. "How come he bit *me?*"

"Because you're the smallest," explained Callie.

"How come he doesn't run after Dad?"

"Because I'm not afraid of him." Ralph ordered, sternly, in a deep voice, "Stop."

The dog looked up, cocking his head. His tongue lolled, long and unnatural, out the side of his mouth.

Actually Ralph felt leery of the dog too, but because the girls were watching, he picked him up. The dog yelped some more, then licked Ralph's hand and panted before struggling away.

"Please give him back," Helen begged.

By the next morning, though, the girls had decided the dog was cute. Ralph came down to breakfast to discover that Helen and they had reinstalled some old baby gates; also they had set out newspapers for the dog to go *xu-xu* on, and put out a plate of food. His claws, clattering across the linoleum, sounded like mah-jongg tiles in play.

"He licked me!" said Mona. "We're friends!"

"We're going to call him Daddy," said Callie. "After you."

Mona tittered.

"Girls!" admonished Helen. "We're going to find him a nice name."

"No, Daddy, Daddy," sang the girls. "We want to name him Daddy."

"No," said Ralph firmly; and just as it had worked on the dog, it worked on his daughters.

Momentarily, at least. "How about Uncle Grover?" Callie piped up then. "Can we name him Uncle Grover?"

"He's not your uncle."

"He used to be."

"He's not anymore."

"Anyway," said Helen, "those are people, and this is a dog."

"How about —" The girls thought. "How about —"

"Grover," mused Ralph.

"Grover!" the girls shrieked. "We'll name him Grover!"

Grover wagged his spotted tail, lifted his flat head and, side-stepping the newspaper, went *xu-xu* again.

"He needs," said Ralph sternly, "to be trained."

Ralph had never heard of taking a dog to school, but Helen said that was exactly how dogs got trained in America, so he signed up for a class. It was good to have to be someplace every once in a while, and though he did not like the way the dogs nuzzled each other — such familiarity! it was obscene — he took intense pleasure in the classes themselves. Who would've believed people could reach an understanding with dogs? Ralph burst with pride when Grover was paper-trained; and when he'd shrunk the paper down and moved it successfully outside, he felt such a profound sense of accomplishment that all his organs seemed to relax and settle. He had been having some trouble with his stomach; Helen thought he was swallowing air, but it felt more like fire. Anyway, his appetite now seemed to be returning to him, and eating more put the flames out.

Ralph taught Grover to sit, and to sit and stay longer than any other dog in the class. Teaching him to stop straining maniacally on the leash was harder, but Ralph kept at it like a man who knew what he wanted, and after a while it was sheer joy to take Grover out for a walk. Particularly as Grover never bit anyone, but often looked as though he might; so that Arthur Smith, for one, was much more respectful when Ralph ran into him. A few months before, he'd asked what Ralph was going to do with the restaurant, and when Ralph answered, "We have so many buyers, we have to consider which to choose," he'd more or less snickered. "I had me a business once too," he said. Now he unsquinted his eyes and unbunched his mouth and edged away, and he wasn't the only one. In general, Ralph did not have to talk to people for as long as he used to, unless they had dogs; and then, as the dogs socialized, he could chat dog-owner style. He'd learned all the things he should say in dog training class — What kind of dog is that? How old is he? What's her name? It was easy.

With Grover, he patrolled the neighborhood calmly, like a man of steel. This gave him time to evaluate different people's grass and bushes and cars, and to ponder. *"What are we going to do?"* Helen had asked a hundred times. Meaning, Ralph knew, what was *he* going to do.

"Do?" he joked. Of course, he realized they had to do something. Why else would he spend so much time walking around with the dog?

"We have to do something," she said.

"*Don't worry,*" he told her. "*Relax. You'll see. 'Dying ashes will burn again.' We'll 'rise again from the East Mountain.' Believe me.*" He hadn't been able to tell her about Grover's pretending to be away when he was not; even so, she wasn't sleeping very well, he'd noticed. "*I'm investigating possibilities,*" he said. "*I have a feeling we may be wrong about the taxes. Maybe we can still cheat some.*"

"*How can we still cheat? What do you mean, don't worry?*" She didn't seem any more able to have faith than to sleep. "*Are you doing anything?*"

"*Sure. I have ideas.*"

"*What kind of ideas?*"

Since when did she cross-examine him? He didn't like her tone; he thought he ought to train her the way he had Grover. Step one, remain unfazed. "*Well, for instance, maybe we should take the addition off. Take the beam back out.*"

"*You said before you didn't think that would work.*"

He hesitated, then smiled. Unfazed. Watching the fire from a distant bank. "*I'm joking.*"

She had no faith. To Ralph's mind, that was the main problem. Just when he was thinking, for example, that maybe he should call up Old Chao and find out what was going on at school, Helen spoiled his initiative, saying, "*If you want to sign up to teach some summer courses, you'd better call right away. They're doing assignments now.*"

"*How do you know?*"

Helen blushed violently. "*Janis told me,*" she said, though it was not Janis, actually, to whom she'd spoken, but Theresa.

"*Janis told you? Janis? And what did you tell Janis?*"

"*Nothing.*" True enough.

"*Nothing?*" Ralph glared at her. "*And what is she going to tell Old Chao? Did you think of that?*"

"*I didn't.*"

"*You didn't? But I think you did. You must have.*"

Helen blushed again.

"*I know,*" said Ralph. "*You think I don't know? You think I'm like Grover here, I know nothing? I know.*"

"*You can't just walk around training Grover forever.*"

She showed him the bankbook then, and again the next day, and again a few days after that, trying to provoke a response.

But it didn't work. "*You think I don't know?*" said Ralph. "*I know.*"

HELEN'S
HOUSE

"HE SAYS HE KNOWS," Helen told Theresa. *"He says he knows everything."*

They were visiting each other more and more often. Now they sat together in the gathering dark, their backs to the window. Theresa could touch the floor with her feet; Helen hooked hers around a chair rung. The cats stalked a paper bag.

Helen sandwiched her hands below and above her teacup. *"You know, we got a dog."*

"A dog!"

"We named it Grover."

Theresa chuckled. *"Whose idea was that?"*

Helen laughed too, forgetting to answer. One of the cats leapt fearlessly into her lap; she rescued her teacup, lifting it high and out of reach.

Ralph signed up for Advanced Dog Training. Grover had finally gotten the hang of fetch; now Ralph tried to teach him to play dead. He threw all his energy into this project, even demonstrating to Grover what he should do. "Like this," he said, flat on his back in the study. He gathered his fingers into paws, drew up his arms and legs. Grover eyed him quizzically.

The phone rang.

Ralph answered it, then lay back down.

"Old Chao, asking me to come work," he volunteered when Helen poked her head in the door. He scratched his nose with one of his paws. *"Inviting me."*

"So what did you say?"

"I said no."

Sometimes it seemed to Helen that the real Grover lay between her and Ralph, in the aisle between their beds. It was as if one of the magazines she used to keep under her mattress had escaped, except that this was no magazine; this was a man on the floor, reminding her that she could leave. Since when did she talk so much, Ralph had asked recently; she had shaken her head in answer, wondering at herself, thinking that ever since the addition got going, she'd had to. Or had breaking one enormous rule enabled her to break others? She could leave — she knew that now. Of course she never would. And yet how much more daring she'd become with that idea under her arm!

Daring enough to tell Ralph about Grover?

She debated whether she should, always ending with the same conclusion. Yes. She concluded that she had to. Her secret would come out sooner or later; paper could not wrap up a fire. It was only a matter of finding the right time and place. Ralph seemed to know already anyway.

And yet night after night, she did not tell him. It was a question of the light. She simply could not imagine herself switching off the light and announcing into the dark that she'd had an affair. At the same time, she could not imagine making her announcement with the light on. She lay awake reaching her conclusions, mentally switching the light on and off, until she began to see other things. Once she saw Ralph with the dog. Grover's leash was red — she thought, *the red string*, then she saw herself, being taught to play dead. To heel. Of course. The wife should obey the husband; this, according to the Three Bonds of Confucianism. Still she shuddered.

Another time she saw Ralph swinging something on a rope, around and around his head, like a lasso. She didn't know what it was at first; then she realized it was Grover, strangely shrunken. *Stop!* she tried to tell him. *You could wrap that around someone's neck.*

Ralph turned to her. *Yes, I could strangle someone,* he said simply, continuing to swing. He approached her. *I am that cold.*

How should I tell you anything? How?

I am a man become fury.

I'm going to turn the light on.

I am a man become steel.

I'm going to turn the light off.

He moved closer, unhearing.

She floated far above the forms as she filled them out, recalling (as she crammed her life into the small blanks and narrow lines) how she'd once hoped to go into real estate, like Janis. "It's a cinch," Janis had said. And what had she answered? *Bu hui, bu hui* — I'm not capable enough. Not wanting to offend her friend.

Sheer politeness. Who would have thought anyone would really believe that about her? But now it appeared that many people did. By the end of the afternoon, she hoped at best to be a shopgirl in one of the department stores. Which wouldn't be so bad, as she told herself; at least she'd get a discount on everything.

But though, what with the new war, the unemployment rate was supposed to be dropping, there were still enough women around for the stores to be picky. They could afford to have white women, who spoke English without accents. "You know, I shop this store quite often," Helen told a personnel clerk. Casually — not wanting to seem to be making a point. "I bought a lot of stuff here."

"Fabulous," said the clerk. "Would you like to apply for a charge?"

She tried smaller shops — bookshops, stationery stores, gift boutiques. "Are you a gook?" someone asked her. "Gook?" she answered. She tried the five-and-ten.

And she got Theresa to ask Old Chao to call Ralph again.

"Little Chang! Old friend!" Old Chao said he had a favor to ask. He did not say anything about Ralph's having hung up on him before.

Ralph listened apprehensively.

Two courses for the summer, and what about his slot for the fall? Was he coming back? It was his slot, Old Chao emphasized. *"We need you, we really hope you'll come back."*

"So Janis told you, huh," said Ralph.

"What?" said Old Chao. *"Janis?"*

"He lied to me," Ralph told Helen.

"I've applied everywhere. You don't know how hard it is to find work."

"He lied to me."

"We can't afford not to work."

"You know what we can't afford? I'll tell you what we can't afford."

Helen braced herself.

"What we can't afford," said Ralph, *"is this house of yours."*

"What do you mean, my house?"

"Your house," he insisted. *"You just want to send pictures of it home to your family."*

"What are you talking about? I don't even know where my family is. How can I send them pictures?"

"How lucky we are," he said, *"to have our marriage and our family."* And as casually as he might pick up a steaming hot bowl of rice, he tossed a brass vase out the living room picture window.

A
BLACK HOLE

THAT WAS HOW the fighting started, with a sense of ending. The incident had been punctuated; it could have been recorded in a book, which could have been closed. Mona and Callie retrieved the vase. Happily, it was unscratched. The Kennedys' house shimmered for a few days like a mirage, an oddly distant but pretty vision, framed by jagged points of multicolored light.

Then Ralph covered it over with a square of plywood so large that the outside world could not be seen at all. *"Need to turn some lights on,"* Helen murmured when she came into the living room; but Ralph said she was wasting electricity. And so the room remained dark, a black hole in the center of the household. Of course, they had to fix the broken panes. Ralph, though, said he wouldn't pay for it. *"You can pay for it,"* he told Helen, from the couch where he lay all day. *"Since this is your house."* He stroked Grover, whose spots seemed to expand and shrink as he panted. *"In which you do as you like."* Ralph laughed weirdly. One day he put a FOR SALE sign up on the front lawn.

Helen continued to look for work, and to economize. They drank powdered milk instead of fresh. They stopped subscribing to the newspaper. One night the gutters overflowed; water sheeted over the front of the house. "*Like* Niagara Falls," Ralph observed. "*Our glorious honeymoon.*" Luckily, that problem turned out to be nothing more than a tennis ball lodged in a downspout. Another night, though, several roof shingles blew off. Helen found them the next day, scattered over the lawn like a giant's idea of fertilizer.

"*Why do we have so much trouble with roofs?*" Ralph wanted to know.

"*We should do something soon,*" Helen answered. "*Before it begins to leak.*"

Ralph agreed. At last he realized something had to be done! They debated, concluding that they needed a professional. As they could not afford a professional, though, Ralph applied himself to finding a way of doing the work for less.

"*An old guy, trying to make a new start,*" he announced not too much later. "*He just hopes we'll recommend him to other people if we're satisfied.*"

"*Perfect,*" said Helen, and he would have been, if only he hadn't stepped through a knot in the wood under the shingles and broken his uninsured ankle.

The fight Ralph and Helen had then broke them both. How was it that she went sailing, like a human version of their brass vase, out the bedroom window? Later, they were not quite able to fathom this themselves; they sifted through the facts with grave purpose. What were they yelling about before the burst of glass? And if their lives were their own, why couldn't they repossess this part? They put their minds to it. Yet neither one of them could remember exactly what had been said; the words had dissipated, leaving only charged air. Going up, going down — that had mattered. Her looking for a job. The house, certainly. They had argued in the kitchen a while; upstairs, Helen had turned on the radio to mask the noise. "*The children,*" she'd warned. "*Quiet.*" And when he could not keep quiet, she told him many things — that she thought about leaving him, that she wished she had not married him, that she knew herself wanted by other men. How much talk spilled out of her, a lifetime of talk. Yet did she mean what she said? Never before had she wielded words of such force; she spoke to hurt, but was amazed when she succeeded. She called him a failure, a failure, a failure; Ralph hurled her to the ground. She in turn threw a hairbrush at him, her favorite hairbrush, ivory white, with an embossed back. Having never thrown anything before, she launched it like a child — flung it, really — starting somewhere near her ear, so that it teased a few strands of hair before whirlybirding, surprisingly heavy and dangerous, toward Ralph. As it flew, she remembered he had given it to her; she was relieved when it smashed a picture instead of him. When he lunged forward, she was taken aback. Shouldn't he be relieved too? But he was not relieved. As someone warbled on the radio, Ralph's thumbs hooked themselves around her windpipe. His face looked strangely melancholy and sallow; his hands might have been candles, he might have been about to bless her like a priest on Ash Wednesday. When she should have stood up from the altar rail, though, he squeezed, almost courteously, as if he only meant to be holding her breath for her, and just for a moment. Still the room spun before he came to his senses and shoved her back away from himself, out of his murderous hands. He shouted then, like a parent, *"Xiao xin!"* — Be careful! But it was too late. Glass tinkled; she felt the impact afterward, the firm, cool glass, breaking through.

THE
WHOLE FAMILY,
TOGETHER

MIRACULOUSLY, Helen had not broken anything. Her fall had been softened by a bank of overgrown hemlocks, and she had missed the flagstone patio, tumbling instead onto the thick grass. No one had thought much before about the backyard's downward slope, but that had counted too; she had rolled a bit before coming to a stop, which helped. Probably. Maybe. They tried to make out by what agency she had been saved. And in what incidental details did their future fate lie?

"You sure are a lucky duck-duck," said Mona, in the hospital.

Besides her many cuts and bruises, though — some of them luridly three-dimensional — Helen had a concussion. Headaches, she explained to the girls. She could not go on looking for work. And now the hospital bill hovered overhead too, yet one more steel beam threatening to bring them all down. Should they ask Theresa to move back?

"*Whatever you like,*" Ralph agreed in a whisper. "*I'm sorry, sorry, sorry.*" He offered to give Grover away in penance, but Helen said, How about if he called Old Chao instead? Ralph called. Old Chao promised to do everything he could. "*Thank you."* Ralph said he was *having difficulties.* He removed the FOR SALE sign from the lawn and sprinkled grass seed in the hole it left. He fixed the bedroom and picture windows, glazing the edges of the glass with care. He scrubbed the panes until his reflection shone in them, spotless.

Meanwhile, Theresa packed. It was her duty, she told herself. She was in many ways Americanized, but in this respect she was Chinese still — when family marched, she fell in step. And wasn't this what she'd longed for? Reunification, that Chinese ideal, she could not eat an orange without reciting to herself, as she did at New Year's, *quan jia tuan yuan* — the whole family together. Her exile was over. Helen had called. Theresa wished it had been under different circumstances. Still — she was going home! She went on working. Already her suitcases bulged with items she'd accumulated; she was surprised how many of these there were. Pictures, books, pots, pans, a set of four blue-and-white bowls she hadn't needed but had bought for fun, a window fan, a baseball mitt, scarves. What a spendthrift she'd become! Three new skirts. A geranium. Would it get enough light in her bedroom at home? And how about the cats? Would they like it there?

Enough questions; she taped a box shut. She'd made her decision. Now she should brace herself for a shock. For was there such a thing as a real returning? She knew better than to think so. One left; things shifted in one's absence; one returned to something else. Time frustrated all. There was no sneaking past its rough guard, even to get to one's own yard of intimacies.

All the same, she braved a run at the border.

"Welcome home!"

"Little Brother!" So thoroughly had Theresa prepared herself for alienation, that she was taken aback by the familiarity of Ralph — that bottlebrush hair, those stuck-on ears.

"Older Sister!" Ralph clasped her hand with the sharp-eyed equanimity of a diplomat. *"Come to save us."*

"*That's not the way to talk,*" said Helen.
The tone of this exchange, Theresa knew too.
"Auntie Theresa!" yelled the girls. "Auntie Theresa! Yay!
Auntie's home!"
His tail drawn like a sword, Grover bared his teeth.
"*This is Grover,*" said Ralph.
"*Lucky,*" Theresa said, "*that my cats are in a box.*"
"*Cats?*" said Ralph.
"*I have two cats.*" Theresa smiled. "Mona and Callie."
The girls bubbled. "Mona and Callie!"
Ralph frowned; Theresa, turning, sighed.
Grover growled.

Ralph civilly requested first that the cats be renamed. Everyone
agreed that since Theresa could now see the real Mona and Callie
as much as she liked, the cats should go back to being plain
cats. Named what, though? "You choose," Theresa told the
girls; which was how the cats became Barbie and Ken, even
though they were both girls.

Ralph's second civil request — that the cats be confined to
Theresa's room — was less easily granted. Though Mona and
Callie both swore never to let them out, Barbie and Ken kept
getting loose. One day there was a squabble in which Grover's
nose got clawed; Ken lost a star-shaped patch of fur. Finally
it was settled that the cats would have the run of the house,
while the yard and driveway would be Grover's domain. Ralph
built Grover a doghouse with windows and a hinged door.
He staked the doghouse into the ground with three stakes, all
he had. For the fourth corner he used a nail. Everyone was
satisfied.

Except what to do with the cats' litter box? Ralph wanted it
in Theresa's room. Theresa wanted it in the basement. Ralph
suggested that in the basement it might stink up his office. And
so it was that the litter box landed up in the nook off the kitchen,
where the love seat used to be.

"*I guess it's just as well,*" sighed Helen. "*Who knows when we'll be getting a new one?*"

Everyone agreed. Theresa's salary was barely enough; they were economizing less stringently than before, but still had to watch their expenses. And what were they going to do with a love seat anyway? They had no use for it.

That was until Old Chao started to come around to visit Theresa. "*We're back together,*" Theresa told Helen. "*Now he wants to marry me. But what about Janis? What about their children? I told him I can't. He says it would be more honest. But the honest thing would be to break it off. I even made him tell Janis. I was sure something would happen then. But no. Nothing.*"

Helen hesitated. "*She told me she's getting used to the situation.*"

"*Really?*" Theresa considered, then said, "*I tell you, I don't know what the point would be anyway. I'm getting old, you know, too old to have children.*"

All the same, Old Chao would come, he couldn't help it; and she could not refuse him. Their visits were awkward at first. Old Chao and Theresa were stiff with each other, embarrassed in front of Helen. With time, though, everyone adjusted.

"*Old Chao's changed,*" Helen observed. It wasn't just that his ailments had all cleared up; or that he went to movies now, and baseball games. Out in the backyard, he planted strawberries with Theresa, it was true; also he grilled fish with her, and argued. Sometimes they ignored each other, sometimes played catch. Certainly he had never been so playful. But what Helen noticed most of all was something else, a small thing — that Old Chao did not monitor Theresa. Janis had kept an eye on him, of course — she seemed to take it for granted that husbands bore watching. Less obviously, though, he had watched her too, with a certain impersonal alertness; she might have been an experiment in progress. Never had meditative looks come over either of them, the way they came over Old Chao, sometimes, now. His face, which had always appeared smooth, seemed smoother still, in this new state; he almost reminded Helen of a monk — a man at some profound leisure. Was this what trust brought? Old Chao had turned into a languorous man. He rested more. He lazed.

IN
THE CAT HOUSE

WHEN Old Chao came, Ralph shut himself up in the bedroom. *"Because of the racket,"* he told Helen.

"They're not that loud."

But Old Chao and Theresa seemed to him to be making an outrageous clamor even when they were quiet. Maybe especially when they were quiet. For what were they whispering about? Sometimes Ralph put his hands over his ears the way he had as a child. Still he heard them, laughing. It was worst when they wandered through the house. How he wished then that they could sit in the kitchen nook, where they would at least be confined! Instead they roamed all over the first floor, from kitchen to dining room to living room, owning the place. He couldn't even use the study, because it had a window out onto the driveway, through which Old Chao might see him.

"So what if he does," Helen said.

"Then I'd have to say hello. How could I not say hello? He's my boss."

"So come down, say hello."

"Where are their morals?"

He sprawled across his bed in his T-shirt and undershorts. He worried the footboard of the bed with his toes, wishing he had a beer. He pictured himself downing a six-pack. He needed a TV in the bedroom too, then he would be like Arthur Smith. He understood Arthur now, he thought; he'd like to have a gun himself. Arthur was like Pete the super, more pride than dignity. Which was better at least than no pride and no dignity — his own situation come fall semester. He pictured Old Chao, endlessly removing the last soda from the soda machine. How was it that he, Ralph, had turned out the sort of person who would find the machine empty?

Ribbons of laughter rose like cooking smells from downstairs. So Old Chao had scored one. Then, worse — actual cooking smells. What was Helen making? Placing his hands on the shag carpet, Ralph walked himself off the bed some, closer to the door. He lowered his nose and sniffed. Something with ham in it. What? He sniffed again but could not make it out; there was a cat odor in the rug, he realized, past which it was impossible to discern anything.

More laughter. Helen and Theresa's voices seemed to perch like sandpipers on the stalwart breakwater that was Old Chao's. Was this his house? Legs still on the bed, Ralph sank to his elbows. Why was his wife cooking for another man? When he was teaching, Helen had sometimes helped him dress — how he loved to have her straighten his tie, tuck in his shirt so that it ballooned evenly all around! Sometimes she brushed his jacket free of hair and dandruff; he adjusted her worn quilt robe in return, tugging at the shoulders, buttoning the rhinestone buttons. The inside of her button flap was warm when he slid his hand in, her flannel pajamas warmer. And yet even at those moments, moments like these remained a possibility. These moments sprang from the others like frogs from children's pockets.

He sniffed some more, an abandoned man. He put his ear to the door, down near the scuff marks. Now Theresa was talking, something about the hospital. Helen congratulated her. Old

Chao whooped. Ralph wrapped his head in his arms, and hugged it, and wept.

Eventually he took to walking Grover when Old Chao came. He walked and walked and walked, every now and then circling back to the house, to see if they could go in yet. He inspected Old Chao's newest car a thousand times. A Ford Mustang this was, maroon, with cream-colored bucket seats and air conditioning. It hurt Ralph to look at it. Better the car, though, than the house, which he now understood to be Theresa's house, full of cat odors and cat hairs.

Sometimes Old Chao visited at night when the girls were asleep. Or supposed to be asleep — once they woke up, as Ralph knew by peering through the dining room window. The light was on; he saw as though on a TV show how Mona and Callie clustered around Old Chao, hanging onto the arms of his chair. He turned from one to the other, paternal, delighting them. With what? Ralph took in the thumbnail moon, the young trees like tracery, edging the indigo sky. The neighborhood lawns spilled into each other, a continuous carpet; the bushes bristled, bushy. All bespoke bounty, and peace, a world never ending. If only he could imbibe some of that night rest! But he might as well have been circling Pinkus's house again — the scenery seemed protected from him, shellacked. His daughters, his daughters. Would Callie and Mona someday come to wish he were like Old Chao? Would they respect him? He recognized his old desperation coming around, a personal comet. His daughters! Did lives have laws, could he have described his with an equation? It would have comforted him to think so; to have been able to plot his out, to know there would be a bottom to his curve, that he would not simply fall and fall and fall. But there were no guarantees. Even China, enormous China, had fallen, fallen, fallen, until it became a thing recalled. An experiment it seemed now, whose premise did not hold. A quaint idea. A misguided idea. How should he prove more durable?

He continued to circle. The streets hollowed out, corridors; the trees blackened. A plane passing overhead set his bone marrow to quiver. He gripped the leash tightly, holding on, let Grover lead him to all his favorite spots. He tried to understand the attraction of certain hedges. Grover was fascinated by dead animals and, tail low, would growl at them as long as allowed to. Ralph found this calming. "Louder!" he told Grover. "Louder!" He began to teach Grover to growl on a certain tug of the leash, a rewarding enterprise. Darker moods lurked around the corner, prowlers in shadow, but fierce Grover forced them to think twice.

Grover, Grover, Grover.

Another small consolation — Grover's house, right out in the backyard. Why did that matter to him? It wasn't a real house. Even for a doghouse, it was flimsy. It wasn't staked properly to the ground. Still he told Theresa, *"I don't ever want to see the cats outside."*

"They don't ever go outside."

Just to be sure, Ralph began to train Grover to recognize the cats' scent. He rubbed an old washcloth on the cats, then presented it to Grover, yanking on the leash, so that Grover growled. After a while Grover would growl whenever given the washcloth, even without the leash. One day Grover grabbed the washcloth in his teeth and shook his head wildly, grinding his jaws.

"Good," said Ralph. *"Good. If those cats ever come out of the house, you do just that."*

He said this almost hoping they would.

But Helen and Theresa and Mona and Callie all knew the rules; and so he waited, as he waited for everything, in vain. It was like waiting for the world to turn. What a ridiculous idea!

Until it's turned: one day he found out through Arthur Smith that the woods behind their house had been bought by a Chinese developer.

"Not a man, I hope," said Ralph, "by last name of Ding?"

*   *   *

No place in the house; and now, with Grover Ding returning, no place outside of it either. Ralph circled. Leaving him what? The doghouse? Construction wasn't starting for another six weeks. That gave him some time. To do what? Ralph walked the dog through the woods, pondering. He wondered what his old partner had planned. Where would the road be? And why had Grover, who had been helping him, suddenly turned against him? His stomach burned. How he'd like to be working with Grover again! Except how could he work for a man who had sold him a store that was sinking? He considered what he should say if he ran into Grover. Should he say, Grover, I'd like you to meet Grover? He laughed out loud at the idea. Grover, meet Grover! He resolved to laugh in Grover's face.

Then, even as he rehearsed, he spotted his old partner. The scene was perfectly ordinary. Grover was hiking, with Chuck behind him, to the top of a small hill. He stopped and gestured grandly. Chuck nodded and gestured too, in seeming imitation; they could have been playing a children's game. Both were wearing suits. Grover's was light tan, Chuck's was blue. Grover's jacket was open. Chuck's was shut, and rode up over his hips. As always, Chuck was wearing cowboy boots, but these were a pair Ralph hadn't seen before, blood red. Ralph was surprised how small Grover looked next to the woods and Chuck. And yet clearly Grover was the big shot. He strode on; he surveyed his surroundings. He felt his breast pocket for a cigarette. The late afternoon sun was behind his back, so that he glowed at the edges — shadow, penumbra.

Ralph scrambled partway up the slope. "Grover?"

Grover squinted down at him.

"It's Ralph. Ralph Chang." The dog leash tangled around his shins.

"Ralph Chang," said Grover. "My favorite phone caller."

Chuck laughed. "How can you talk to him? He's in jail."

"Of course I remember you," said Grover.

"The one with the wife," said Chuck.

Grover turned away, lit his cigarette, and puffed.

"Good with her hands," pressed Chuck. "Isn't that right? Had a nice love seat?"

Grover grinned broadly. "I did enjoy your . . . upholstery." His gold tooth gleamed out from his dark face.

THINGS
FALL OUT

"*I'M TAKING YOU for a drive,*" Ralph told Helen. He gripped her upper arm in his hand, hard, and jerked her toward the car.

"*Is something the matter?*" she said. "*Has something happened?*"

"*Has something happened.*" He smiled grimly as he opened the car door.

She climbed in, massaging her arm. "*It's red,*" she told him.

Ralph backed violently out of the driveway, foot to the floor, without looking. A car that had been wending its way up their block stopped short, so as not to be hit; even so, bumpers kissed before Ralph changed directions. "*You hit that car. You can't just drive off.*" Helen waved at the couple in the other car. They were gray-haired and wore matching green-tinted sunglasses above their matching dropped chins. "*I think you've dented something.*"

"*I'll tell you what's been dented,*" he said. "*I'll tell you.*" But then he didn't tell her; he was too intent on speeding through the neighborhood streets. "*Are you crazy?*" she said. "*You must be crazy. You've gone crazy.*" Still he drove and drove, through stop signs, through red lights. Screeching. *"The police are going to come after you,"* she said. But their town had become a town without police. They bounded over a bump, landing with such a jolt that the glove compartment door popped open; Helen screamed with fright, then began to cry. *"The maps,"* she said. *"Stop. Please. Everything's falling out."* They were in an older part of town now, a part of town they would have moved to if they could have afforded it, with "mature landscaping"; it was what Helen had hoped their neighborhood would look like in twenty years. Bucolic. Now the same rambling streets and stone walls and enormous trees that had signified peace, though, turned ominous. Gunning his way up a long hill, Ralph sideswiped a metal garbage can; empty, it fell racketing down the incline. A child shrieked. Helen tried to turn and see what had happened, but her neck locked with fear. The climb grew steeper. *"What's the matter?"* she whispered. *"What's the matter?"*

They had reached the top of the hill. Ralph slowed for the first time. He stopped. The motor idled. *"You tell me,"* he said. *"You tell me what's the matter."* His eyes glittered; if he were a child, Helen thought, she would put him to bed for fever. She would soak a washcloth with cold water for his forehead; she could almost feel his cheek under her hand, moist and hot.

The car started down. *"You breathe,"* he told her. *"You take a deep breath and tell me what happened between you and Grover, or I will steer this car right into this tree."*

He headed for an oak the width of a small cabin, swerving away at the last second. Helen was thrown so hard against the door that her head bumped the window glass. Ralph careened toward another one. *"No brakes!"* he shouted. *"Do you hear me! No brakes! You tell me! You tell me!"*

Terrified, Helen opened her mouth, but *shuo bu chu lai,* she could not speak.

He swerved again, laughing. They were picking up more speed. *"Grover! Grover! Grover!"* he shouted. *"Talk!"* He ricocheted off a curb. *"Talk!"*

Helen grabbed the door handle. The door flew open. *"I can't hear you!"* Ralph yelled, steering straight down the hill now. Helen's door swung back and forth like a broken wing; Helen clung to the dashboard. *"I can't hear you! I can't hear you! What's that you say?"* Helen slid off her seat, down into the footwell. *"Louder!"* yelled Ralph. *"Louder!"*

FEEDING
THE DOG

WAS THERE something wrong? It wasn't like Ralph and Helen to leave Mona and Callie alone — Theresa found the girls tossing tin foil balls to the cats. "Where're Mom and Dad?" they asked. They said they had come home from school to an empty house with an open door. "Gone someplace?"

"I don't know," said Theresa.

Supper — egg rice and leftovers. They huddled in front of the TV set. "Should we call somebody?" Callie asked finally.

"In a while."

"In how long?"

"In an hour. We'll call the police."

Someone ought to have turned the TV on, but instead they set themselves to waiting out the hour in front of the blank screen, snuggling with the cats until they were all zigzagged with cat hair.

A half hour passed. Callie said, "It's been an hour, I think."

"*Over* an hour," said Mona.

"Okay," said Theresa.

But the police had no information. "Time to go to bed," Theresa announced then. "When you wake up, you'll know everything."

"Where are they," Callie complained.

"Maybe they've been murdered," Mona said. "Shot with machine guns."

"Time for bed right this minute."

What was the matter? Theresa tried not to worry as she ushered the girls upstairs. After she finished the dishes, she would call the police again, she decided. She prepared to feed the dog, who probably should have been fed hours before. Canned food instead of dry, a special treat.

Outside, it was not an evening in which a person could imagine catastrophe elbowing its determined way toward her. She relaxed a notch, smelling barbecue and cut grass in the air. The sky shimmered an even tiger yellow she had not known to fall in the range of atmospheric effects; she beheld it with a wonder much like that with which, recently, she considered her life. How had she come to where she was? She hardly knew. And what did that mean, that Janis was getting used to the situation? Impossible. Yet in the weeks since Helen first mentioned it, the idea had put on girth in Theresa's imagination, until now she could almost begin to envision a future in which she and Old Chao were reconciled with Janis. It was too much to hope for. Still, as she pulled Grover's empty bowl away from him, she did. No more closeting; she could have one part of Old Chao, Janis and the children another. The arrangement would be open. Accepted. Why not? In China, there were concubines — not what she wanted to be at all, but which proved human nature capable of different sorts of marriage. Maybe there could be a ceremony whereby someone like her was taken into the family; just thinking of it made her prickle with happiness. A string of fireflies flashed on the lawn, as though with kindred enthusiasm. Why not, they blinked, why not, why not? Theresa smiled on the lush world. Was she finally in love? She pictured the way Old Chao's ears rose when he grinned — they literally perked up, she'd never seen anything like it on a human; Old Chao hadn't believed it when she told him. *But it's true,* she'd insisted. They'd had to go to a department store with a three-way mirror so that he could see for himself.

Grover snarled at her. *"What's the matter, don't you think it's funny?"* she asked him. *"Or do you just want to know how I'm going to get the food out of the can?"* She realized that she ought to have brought a spoon or something.

Grover growled again, more deeply, then lunged. The doghouse creaked and leaned.

"Easy. Just one more minute."

She eased the food into the dish with a stick. What *had* happened to Ralph and Theresa? A ladybug landed on her right wrist; she held still. In the late-day light, its maroon shell shone iridescent as mother-of-pearl.

Grover lunged again. His nose was wrinkled; he almost seemed to be smiling. Theresa nudged the half-full dish toward him with her free hand. *"Calm down. Here it is, you don't have to wait anymore, okay?"*

But Grover did not calm down. Ears pricked forward, gray teeth bared, he lunged a third time, at her. Was there something he didn't like? Her looks? Her smell? The ladybug's shell split, turning into wings as the house came unmoored; neck straining, Grover was dragging it behind him. The hinged door swung open. *"Is this what you want?"* Running, Theresa pitched the can at him, grazing his snarling snout. Lucky that he's dragging the house, she thought, just as the back and side walls tore away from the front. His spindly legs broke into a gallop. How much darker the evening had turned — an unnatural, swampy brown — and so quickly. Unable to make it to the front door, Theresa raced for the open garage; there she could at least arm herself with a shovel or rake. But then — the car! Everything was all right! As it wheeled quickly into the driveway, too fast, clipping the corner, Theresa saw that Ralph and Helen were both in it — thank heaven — if she kept on running, Ralph would be just able to cut Grover off. *"The dog!"* she yelled, waving. She dashed out in front of the headlights.

DOWN
THE WHITE HALL

THERESA is the only person not screaming. The girls are screaming, Helen is screaming, he might be screaming too, for all he knows. Grover, in confusion, wags his tail and lifts his head to be petted. Where are the police, where is the ambulance? I've killed her, I've killed her, Ralph thinks. Wondering, in the simple way of the profoundly shocked, What happened to the doghouse? And why is there so much blood?

He is surprised that she is warm as they bundle her into the car, though that of course is why they are hurrying, because she is alive and not dead, even if blood trickles out of her mouth and nose; and now he is driving like a crazy man again, slamming, hurtling. The roads confound him; they've knotted up, dark, antagonistic; he pits himself against them, valiant, a man doing battle for love. Then he remembers that once she looked in on him when he sneezed, and doubts himself. Maybe there's a better method of help. Maybe he need only sneeze again, and she will rise, solicitous; even now, he can imagine her doing that. Still he drives, drives, until finally the emergency room smiles, that blinding white into which he must give his sister up. A deliverance. The nurses know him from last time, with Helen, they know all about him, everyone knows; he's the last to approach the electric glass doors.

Bloody, Theresa lies on the gurney like a corpse. Her hair has turned wild; her face is slack. Doctors flock around her. As Ralph steps into the light, blinking, they are already breaking into a run. Shouting. Theresa's out ahead as they round a far corner. To where? Should he follow? He hurries down the hall, rounds the turn. Nothing. Helen too has disappeared on him again. Only he is lost. He tries another hall, another, another, thinks he recognizes a certain sink; he triggers an automatic door; ends up among linens. Finally he wends his way back, alone, to the lounge. He sits in a black chair. His lounge mates stare. How bloody he is! He hadn't realized how bloody. He should wash himself off, but at any time someone may come to tell him what's happening. Where is his sister? He waits, suspended, planning how to apologize. How to apologize? He hopes to find a way, to *xiang banfa*. He studies his heart. He tries to have faith. He prays for Theresa. He stands. He sits. He recalls the sight of Theresa in his headlights. Recalls the chill that descended upon him. How he felt humanity squeeze his hand, and how he let that hand go — shook himself free of it, even, like a young boy confronted with an overardent admirer. It was true that he had just heard, from his wife's soft mouth, words that set his mind to riot; she might as well have twisted knives in his ears. But what does that matter now? He saw his sister. And behind her, a second self, her stark shadow against the back wall of the garage — he saw that too. He saw its blackness growing, running, a creature waving monstrous, tentacled arms. It reached the ceiling. It had no face.

He tried to stop the car. He can remember the sweet, solid feel of the brake. But how instantly did his foot move? And even if it flashed, without hesitation, what of the cold heart above it? He's no philosopher, but he understands action without goodwill to equal as much as half an equation. He sees himself at the wheel. He pictures Arthur Smith and his gun, and knows what it means to be armed — that one's house is one's own. In China, one lived in one's family's house. In America, one could always name whose house one was in; and to live in a house not one's own was to be less than a man. In America, a man had need of a weapon. He ought to have killed Grover Ding, that other intruder. Instead, a shadow slid from the wall. Sudden glare. Theresa's body thumped the bumper, gently. Then he saw her — his sister, no shadow; her arms reached up the trembling car hood, the rough motor endowing her fine fingers, her knobby wrists, with strangely nervous life. They twitched like a beggar's, he recalls — her fingertips drummed — weakly imploring, though her eyes had already closed. Had he seen those eyes widen and shine red? They must have; he must have seen it happen. But he had not witnessed it. Fear had tracked her face, and he had not witnessed that either.

She buckled, falling back onto the ground. He shut the engine.

Now Theresa hung in a coma. Ralph asked the doctors to spell the word for him. "C-O-M-A, coma," he repeated carefully. "Understand," he said, as though anyone could understand. How could sleep be so serious? It was like something out of Mona and Callie's fairy-tale book. And what would happen next? In the book, she would be kissed by a wandering prince; and then the happy ending would sprawl across the pages, in scroll-wreathed letters, with purple and yellow banners. In this story, though, there was no prince-at-large; what wandered was her mind. Still they hoped it might stumble on her bruised and bandaged body. They hoped that, in an instant quick as a kiss, she might be brought back to life. What banners they would fly then!

Yet still she lay, still she lay, a mannequin of herself, amid tubes and machines. Tape crisscrossed her face. On a screen they could watch the routine efforts of her heart. So many times they had wished she would hold her tongue; now all they wanted was for it to loosen. From time to time, after her breathing tube was removed, someone would see her shape her lips, as if to sigh or speak. But there was no steady progress; they understood from the doctors that this was only waxing and waning. They understood that she could wax and wane for a long time. They watched for the pattern that meant progress.

No pattern. No progress.

The doctors had taped Theresa's eyes closed, lightly; also they had taped her arms to splints, wrapped her hands around balls of gauze. Still her fingers clamped together, clawlike. Her body curled too; as the weeks turned to months, she shrank into herself like the stiffest of fetuses, shrivelling, her skin sallow and waxy. The doctors grew graver yet. Her chances, they'd say, and shake their heads. Not after this long.

The vigil unfolded, brutal, seasonless. Mona and Callie and Helen sat together. Ralph sat alone. And Old Chao sat too, with his head in his hands, occasionally with Janis, even though they were getting divorced. Everyone marvelled at this. Wasn't she a saint! But Janis shook her head and said No, she was not. As the ordeal stretched on, there was more canonization. Several nurses thought Helen a saint; one nurse even called Ralph a saint too.

But no, Ralph said sadly, he was not.

He sat alone that he might pray. A priest had supplied a rosary, with instructions; day after day, Ralph fingered the beads, moving his lips. Afraid that he might lose it, he had bought a second one to keep in his shirt pocket, and then a third one, with ivory beads, to hang on Theresa's headboard. Our Father, he prayed. Hail Mary. Sometimes he appealed to the spirits of his ancestors too, and to his parents, even as he hoped they were not dead, or dying; neither did he neglect to call on the Buddha, and such boddhisatvas as he could remember, especially Guanyin, goddess of mercy. Mercy — he hoped someone, someone, would have mercy. Please, he prayed. He begged, hands fisted — please, please, please. A miracle. A deliverance. But this time there was no miracle and no deliverance. He was a rank-and-file, evil-hearted human, nothing more, with a sister all but dead. Shock had become sorrow had become grief — a gradual thickening. A change of blood. That brought with it a change of thought — imagineering giving way to nostalgia. Sometimes he watched unmoving Theresa, and saw her move again. He saw her walk and talk and read. He saw her recite her lessons, he saw her tease the servants; he remembered how she was not above putting fish in people's beds. How his heart broke to think of that sister! But even more, it broke for the sister he hadn't known. He had never seen her play baseball, but he saw it now — how she swung, all tilt and pivot, how she stretched up with her mitt and plucked balls from the air like a fruit picker. Was she really that good? He had to think so; he tinted his pictures with sentiment, for lack of other colors. He watched her examine a patient, her authority impeccable. He watched her kiss Old Chao. He was like a nation in crisis, looking back, and back, and back — its history might be ugly, but its past shone perfect.

Rendering the future all the more impossible. How could he begin to atone? He could give the dog away, to a boy in the next town. He could install a pet door in the kitchen, so Ken and Barbie could go in and out as they liked. He could be kind to them, endlessly kind. But what use were these things?

Still he did the useless things. He combed Theresa's lusterless hair, every day. The nurses had said that he could, had shown him how. Sometimes he washed it too, and twice he cut it, with Helen's help. They wet her hair with a bottle of water and a basin, and then they parted it into sections. How white her scalp! Her hair seemed to be turning gray, a cruelty upon cruelty; there were too many clocks running. They began the cutting, with barber's shears. Afterward he watched Helen trim Theresa's nails; that was her job. Theresa's fingers could not be straightened, but Helen did her best to cut smoothly. Unable, as she worked, to look at him — such an intimate estrangement, theirs. He watched her clip Theresa's toenails too. He picked the clippings off the floor. They listened to Theresa breathe. In, out. She breathed the way anyone would, but her breath smelled so heavy and foul, like curdled milk, that they could not associate it with life. Instead, finally, they began to wonder — they had to wonder: Was death possible in this bright country? It was, they knew. Of course. And yet they began to realize that in the fiber of their beings they had almost believed it a thing they had left behind, like rickshaws; so that the very idea of death now seemed twice death for them, doubly absurd — death in some ways resembling a first crocus. There was a dewiness to it. No one in the world had ever died before. They ran their hands over the blue relief of Theresa's veins, and shuddered — then shuddered more as understanding took slow hold. It seemed she had disappeared, as if into a revolving door; and around now to take her place had swung a man to sit at supper and never eat — a man with his eye on everyone, even Helen, even Callie, even Mona.

THE ORDER,
LOST

IT WAS basest betrayal to think of anything but Theresa, but they had no choice. Hospital bills arrived daily; the uninsured roofer had sent a lawyer after them, as had Grover, who stood ready to foreclose. Though Ralph had gone back to teaching, they had to do more. And so the FOR SALE sign was cleaned up and repaired and hammered into the lawn in front of the house. As the ground had compacted, this required some force.

Now strangers toured around, inspecting. They opened closets. Arms folded, they considered the shag carpeting while their brokers talked about "potential." "Visualize," they said. "Imagine." Meaning, Helen knew, that the house "didn't show well." Another owner "could do so much with it." She should have felt insulted. But she didn't care what another owner could or couldn't do. She didn't care what the buyers thought of her, dragging about in her bathrobe, her hair unset. What did it matter? It seemed to her that the meaning had worn off of things like so much gilt.

The offer they accepted was from a couple with no children. This bothered Helen. Would they take the swing set down? The rest of the house seemed so much real estate. Sometimes she remembered how precious it had once been to her, and the memory girdled itself around her chest, squeezing. Theresa was here then. Now, now, Helen realized: Theresa had made that world possible. She must have, for her absence made it impossible. In one thing, Grover had been right — Helen had understood nothing about love. She had understood nothing about how people could come to mark off her life. For example, she had considered the great divide of her self's time to be coming to America. Before she came to America, after she came to America. But she was mistaken. That was not the divide, at all.

She began to think about looking for an apartment. This, she knew, would entail getting dressed, and making phone calls, and examining maps. She tried to force herself to imagine it. But in the end Janis found a place for them, a garden apartment nearby. The girls wouldn't have to change schools. Helen was glad. Sadness, though, streaked every happiness like plaster dust. She recalled a Chinese expression: *Chi de ku zhong ku, fang wei ren shang ren* — eat the bitterest of the bitter, become the highest of the high. Small consolation. She continued to drift. Anticipating nothing; nothing sped up, nothing slowed down. Her moments drove past, one after another. Droning.

And what could change that? Except maybe those sons she and Ralph had always talked about. There was nothing like a baby to put a face on time. But how to conceive? She and Ralph were *keqi* with each other, endlessly polite — keeping their proper distance. Love floated above their marriage, unachievable, divine. Even when Ralph's stomach began to hurt so much that he had to check into the hospital, and came home only able to eat certain foods, she found herself lined with stiff indifference. Not that she blamed him for what had happened, or not simply — she blamed herself too. But when he stirred his food listlessly, she held Theresa's hand; when he lost weight, she felt it lose its grip.

*   *   *

Before they could move, Theresa's room had to be cleaned out; as these days Helen was often too tired to move, though, the job fell to the girls. They had already taken over many household tasks. Besides never leaving their things lying around, and always making their beds, they put rice on for supper and chopped vegetables. They vacuumed, they mopped, they kept after the hair on the bathroom floor. They bought a new shower curtain. How changed they were! They were proud of themselves. Mona had even grown tactful. Callie did not have to kick her, or nudge her, or pinch her; Mona once began to tell someone that her father had hit her aunt with a car so that now her aunt was in a coma, but she did not finish that sentence; and never again did she even begin it. "There's been an accident in our family," she would say instead, correctly. Or else, like Callie (drawing her head up to convey august victimhood), "We've had a family tragedy."

And so it seemed natural enough, after a while, that the girls would help more. One sunny Saturday morning, Callie put on a gray sweatshirt; Mona covered a pink-flowered shirt with a darker shirt of Helen's. They were careful about their work, protecting Theresa's shoes with lunch bags, folding her clothes so as to fill their father's old black trunk with precision. They buttoned all the buttons, zipped the zippers. They packed outfits together, taking sad satisfaction in the ease with which they matched the tops and bottoms. Only once did they argue. Though Theresa had bought an ivory blouse to go with a certain green skirt, in practice she'd worn it with a beige skirt. That left the green skirt without a blouse, which bothered Callie. And what to do with the mauve sweater she hadn't worn once? Mona thought they could put the two orphans together, why not. But Callie couldn't see doing that — mauve and green? In the end the green skirt and beige skirt were sandwiched around the ivory blouse; the mauve sweater was layered in with a gray skirt Callie thought Theresa would have worn with it. If only she could ask her aunt, if only she could be sure! They sprinkled in moth flakes and latched the trunk closed.

That was not the end of the work; there were still Theresa's books to do. These they packed in boxes, preserving the order in which she had shelved them. Which was what? They could see that the medical texts were together, but many books were in Chinese, a mystery. And some of them bore jottings, also in Chinese, in their margins. What did they mean? Callie, leafing through one particularly marked-up volume, began to cry. The clothes had been easy, familiar; *this* belonged to a stranger. She threw it across the room. Then another, another, another. "Stop it!" Mona yelled. "Whaddya*do*ing? You're messing them all up!" And she was right. Callie cried more to see that a page of one book had ripped on account of her, and that several other pages had gotten creased. "Don't cry," Mona said then. "It's okay. She might not ever read them again anyway." Callie cried more still. Mona pretended to remember which volume Callie threw right after the first one, and so on; but they both knew she was just trying to make her big sister feel better; actually the order was lost. Later they taped the boxes up, in silence. "There," Mona said. "All done," agreed Callie. Theresa's geranium they moved outside, with vows to water it every single day.

It was Janis who called the movers, Janis who checked the boxes off as they were unloaded, calling to the men, "Be careful! That's breakable." Hands on her hips, she made sure that what belonged in the living room ended up in the living room, what belonged in the kitchen, in the kitchen. She pointed. It was all part of her trying to stay busy. Helen tried to thank her for coming. After all that had happened. Who wouldn't understand if she hadn't?

Janis answered slowly. Daintily. Hands limp. "*I've never had much pride,*" she said. "*I've never been able to afford it.*" And then: "*Henry just wanted to leave me. I said, if you want to mourn, I'll mourn with you. But he said he had to mourn by himself.*" She stopped.

Helen didn't know what to say; until Janis squinted at a chair, wondering, *"Is that a scratch?"* And then, though she didn't think it was, Helen squinted too, and said, *"Is it?"* to keep her friend company.

Devotion replaced hope. No one knew how or when the change had come, but they did know they went to the hospital mostly to pay their sad respects. And so they were stunned when one day, the hospital called with News! Progress! Helen cried to hear how Theresa had begun to groan with a certain intermittent regularity; and how, if she were rubbed hard just below her collarbone, she would groan louder. "It's good news, good news," Helen sobbed. "I'm so happy."

The rest of the family was as shocked as if Theresa had died. They coalesced, quiet, at the foot of her bed. Waiting.

Nothing.

"She's been groaning a lot," the nurse claimed.

Nothing.

"Come on now, what's the matter with you. Groan for your family like a good girl." The nurse rubbed Theresa's chest again.

And obediently, like a good girl, Theresa groaned.

"She did it!" Mona yelled. "She did it! She did it!"

Theresa groaned again, as if having a bad dream.

"She's doing it! She's doing it!" The girls jumped up and down, rattling the footboard, Helen clapped. Now it was Ralph who cried for happiness. Progress! Theresa gave an encore; the family leaned over the rail like operagoers, glorying in the sound.

But when would she open her eyes? When would she talk? The doctors were straightforward — Progress was only progress, they said. Ralph and Helen nodded. They explained about the progress to the girls. But *ting bu jian* — none of them understood. Mona moved into Callie's room of the new apartment, sharing so that Theresa could have a room. They cleaned it up.

They unpacked the trunk. According to the man at the garden center, Theresa's geranium had died of drowning; they got a new one, the same color, and vowed not to water it more than once a month.

Theresa stopped groaning again. Preparing to break the news, the nurses stocked up on candy bars for the girls. A setback, they said, pulling the sweets from their pockets.

Progress, setback, progress, setback. The bouts of progress began to seem like no progress at all; the family braced for them just the same as for the setbacks. The days of no news had almost been easier. At least then they had suffered peacefully! This suffering allowed them no rest; it was simple but relentless as a geologic cycle. Freezing, thawing. This suffering could split boulders, and did.

Sometimes after work Ralph watched TV now, like Arthur Smith, never bothering to turn the channel, simply letting the words and images wash over him. The stories were nothing like his story; for this he felt a gratitude bordering on love. When the time came for him to turn the TV off, he watched the images waver and disappear as though it were a real world, all his world ought to have been, that was being sucked back into the set. The empty green screen stared back at him; he saw himself in its curved glass, a story as still as the others had been antic. A story with one character, doing nothing. A story no one would schedule for prime time. He swayed, watching his nose enlarge, his mouth, his ears. All was distortion.

Still he sat; and so he was sitting when, one evening, Helen called with news. How he wished he had been there! Theresa had blinked a bit; the tape over her eyes had fluttered up like false eyelashes. Callie saw it and screamed. Mona and Helen hurried over. Theresa opened her eyes a little wider, with a look so like her own that the tape across her cheeks, the tube up her nose — all the hospital artifice they'd come to accept as natural — looked once again, horribly applied. Her pupils dilated;

her eyes drifted right, away from her family, then stopped like an elevator between floors. Was this eye movement, or sight? They followed her liquid gaze to the window — it was snowing madly out. A day to stay home. Did she think so too? Apparently. When they looked back down, her eyes had closed again. Helen began to cry. *"Come back,"* she pleaded, *"come back, come back, come back, come back."*

"Han," rasped Theresa then, eyes wide.

Helen froze.

The moment distended. Had Theresa really taken up residence in herself? They prepared to welcome her, even as they waited for her to be carried back out to the hungry sea, a distant head dipping out of sight once more.

"Callie," Theresa went on. She moved her arm weakly. "Mona."

FAITH

RALPH'S HEART launched up like a rocket. *"I'm coming! I'm coming!"* he exclaimed as Helen wound up her account. Helen said Theresa had asked for him. *"I'll be right there!"*

But how could he face his sister? No sooner had he banged the phone down than his limbs turned so heavy he could hardly stand up. Still he set himself to it, answering gravity, a man. Such happy news, after all. He reminded himself of this. Such amazing news! It was hard to take in. Someone might as well have told him that he had died. Until he pictured Theresa alive; then a sense of unutterable good fortune settled over him. Hidden pleats of his spirit expanded. She was alive. Alive, alive, alive! Now this was a miracle, this was a gift.

Once, as a child, he had slid too quickly off his end of a seesaw. He remembered now how his sister hurtled to the ground; how she lay on her side like an upturned vase. Then she righted herself. They trod back to the house silently, along the path they knew better than anything anyone had ever taught them. He remembered how the gravel crunched underfoot, how they hopped the first step onto the bridge. Their footsteps beat then, on the wood, as though on the skin of an old, deep drum; they stamped to augment the effect, and swung their arms, and on the other side gave a two-footed jump back onto the gravel, running the rest of the way. Through the giant peonies, elaborately staked; racing. His sister won, of course; and at the end they dug up some stones they'd buried the day before. These were just to hold — cool to the touch, though the day was hot. He remembered holding the stones to his cheek, murmuring with pleasure; his sister did it too.

Such was the simplicity of childhood, he thought now — events vanished, wordless. He draped a scarf around his neck, his elation fading. This time, an adult, he would have to say something. He would have to find words. But what words? As he left the apartment, he felt as if he were wearing a great animal of a winter coat. In fact, he did have on a coat — outside it was snowing wildly — and the coat was quite heavy. But his bones seemed to bend under the load, and that was odd; he could imagine a photoelastic image of them, all stress lines. If only he could take the coat off! He searched for his hat in slow motion. His keys. He patted his pants, feeling for his wallet. His stomach clenched. Such happy news!

As Helen had driven to the hospital, Ralph had to take a cab. Outside, he realized that he should have called one from the apartment, but he was reluctant to go back in; to go back in would seem somehow to be making no progress. Instead, then, he raised his weighty arm. Earlier in the day, the snow had been delicate as dandelion puffs; the flakes had perched on top of each other with abandon and ease. But since that time, the storm had turned so sodden that it did not seem like snow at all that was showering, so much as something industrial — some unnatural tonnage dumped without permit out of the sky. Cars skidded. Behind the iced windows, drivers gripped their wheels, swearing. Ralph's hat molded itself to his head. Cold masked his face.

No one stopped.

t stiffened around him, a prison.

cape was possible? It seemed to him at that moment,
ne stood waiting and waiting, trapped in his coat, that a man
was as doomed here as he was in China. *Kan bu jian. Ting bu
jian.* He could not always see, could not always hear. He was
not what he made up his mind to be. A man was the sum of his
limits; freedom only made him see how much so. America was
no America. Ralph swallowed.

And yet even as he embraced that bleak understanding, on
this, the worst day of the winter, he recalled something he'd
seen on the worst day of the worst heat wave of the summer.
This memory was one of watching — of peeking out his bedroom window to see what Theresa and Old Chao were up to.
How hot it was that afternoon! He had wanted to know when
he could come out. So he'd snuck a look: and there they were,
floating on twin inflatable rafts, in twin blue wading pools of
water. Spinning around and around, like airplane propellers.
Theresa lay on her stomach, Old Chao on his back. Both sipped
at lemonade, through straws. *"Join us! Join us!"* they cried,
giddy, to his wife.

On the patio, Helen laughed. *"Whose idea was this?"*

"His idea."

"No, hers! It was hers."

"His!"

"Hers!"

"Not true!" Theresa splashed Old Chao.

Old Chao sat up, bobbing, preparing for retribution. "Watch
out," he warned teasingly, his hand cupped.

Were these people he knew? Ralph had watched the water
fight with sadness in his heart, never guessing the scene would
one day hearten him, as it did now. *Shuo bu chu lai.* Who could
begin to say what he meant, what had happened, what he'd
done? And yet Ralph held his arm up in the snow all the same,
thinking how he hadn't even known Theresa owned a bathing
suit. An orange one! Old Chao's was gray, a more predictable
choice.